LOVE IS NOT ENOUGH

*The first in a new series
from this well-loved author*

1913. Beautiful Marianne Trenwith has
everything her younger sister, Sarah, wants,
including the dashing Troy Pelham. But in
a fit of petulance Marianne breaks off her
engagement. As Sarah and Troys friendship
blossoms, Marianne warns her sister that a
match will never be permitted and their
parents will do anything to avoid a scandal.
But with the war clouds gathering, Sarah
senses time is precious...

LOVE IS NOT ENOUGH

Anne Herries

Severn House Large Print
London & New York

This first large print edition published 2010
in Great Britain and the USA by
SEVERN HOUSE PUBLISHERS LTD of
9-15 High Street, Sutton, Surrey, SM1 1DF.
First world regular print edition published 2008 by
Severn House Publishers Ltd., London and New York.

British Library Cataloguing in Publication Data

Herries, Anne.
  Love is not enough.
  1. Sisters--Fiction. 2. Soldiers--Great Britain--
  Fiction. 3. Great Britain--Social conditions--Fiction.
  4. Great Britain--History--George V, 1910-1936--Fiction.
  5. Love stories. 6. Large type books.
  I. Title
  823.9'14-dc22

ISBN-13: 978-0-7278-7872-4

Severn House Publishers support The Forest Stewardship Council
[FSC], the leading international forest certification organisation. All
our titles that are printed on Greenpeace-approved FSC-certified paper
carry the FSC logo.

Mixed Sources

Product group from well-managed
forests and other controlled sources
www.fsc.org Cert no. SA-COC-1565
© 1996 Forest Stewardship Council

Printed and bound in Great Britain by the
MPG Books Group, Bodmin, Cornwall.

One

'What on earth possessed you to do it?' Troy lifted his fine dark brows, an expression of disbelief in his eyes. 'That woman is rapacious, Barney. She is also beautiful and the kind of woman that might make a man forget caution, I'll give you that much – but to put something of such sensitivity in writing! It was senseless.'

'I've been all kinds of a fool, I know it,' Barney Hale said and made a wry face at his friend. Troy was all the things he wanted to be and knew he wasn't: handsome, courageous and strong, sure of himself and his place in the world. 'I think I must have been a bit under the weather when I wrote that damned letter.'

'Three sheets to the wind I imagine!' Troy laughed but in another moment he was serious, his dark eyes intent on his friend. 'Surely you don't really expect me to steal it for you? Why don't you challenge her? Tell her to give it to your father if that's what she has threatened. If you give into Lady Hastings's blackmail she will bleed you dry. Margaret Hastings is always in debt. I think her husband despairs of her.'

'That is exactly what I dare *not* do,' Barney said, looking woeful. He was a head shorter than Troy, slightly heavier in build, with sandy-red hair and greenish eyes. He envied Troy the extra height and muscle and wished he had his friend's thick black locks instead of his own. More than anything else, he envied Troy his engagement to Marianne Trenwith. 'My father would cut me off without a penny if he read that letter. God knows what he will do if Hastings divorces her!'

Troy Pelham studied his companion for a moment in silence. Barnabus Hale had been in a similar situation once before. On that occasion the outraged husband *had* threatened to divorce his wife, but Lord Hale had managed to buy him off. He had quarrelled violently with his son, threatening all manner of dire punishments if Barney disgraced him in the future. Knowing that, how could he have been so careless, and with Margaret Hastings of all people? He deserved to be taught a sharp lesson, and yet Troy had always felt protective of his friend. When they were lads, he had rescued Barney from the consequences of his folly more than once.

'How do you propose we make sure that she isn't in her bedchamber?' Troy asked thoughtfully. 'And I shall need to know which room is hers. I don't want to go blundering in and find the lovely lady dishabille.'

There was a reckless glint in Troy's eyes, which brought a smile to Barney's face. 'I didn't think you would do it. I would be really grateful, Troy.'

'I might risk it, but I need a plan.'

'You know how she loves to play cards. I thought you could disappear for a while after dinner, and I'll engage to keep her busy at the card table. She is staying in what the Trenwiths call the Blue Room – it's in the west wing, very near the family rooms.

Troy nodded. He knew where the Blue Room was situated, because it was next door to Sarah Trenwith's own bedchamber. It was Christmas now and he and his father were staying at Trenwith Hall to celebrate both the season and his recent engagement to Marianne. However, he had visited alone earlier in the year, and it was during that time that Sarah, Marianne's younger sister, had twisted her ankle badly. Troy had carried her to her room, handing her over to the care of her maid and Lady Trenwith at the door. However, the door to the neighbouring bedchamber had stood open. It was furnished in varying shades of blue and used, he had since learned, for ladies staying alone rather than with their husbands.

Troy knew that he ought to refuse Barney's request. The letter belonged by right to Lady Hastings, but she was planning to use it for blackmail, and he didn't want to see his friend ruined. He was a guest in this house, and what he was about to do was the height of bad manners, but also a challenge. For some reason he had been feeling restless for the past couple of days, and he knew that the very foolhardiness of it was the reason he was about to agree to his friend's request. Ordinarily, he would have refused to do something that he thought of as dishonourable, but the lady in question was behaving badly herself.

'All right,' he said to Barney. 'If you do your part and keep her busy, I'll try to get the letter back for you – but it's the last time. Don't be such a damned fool again!'

'I can't thank you enough,' Barney began. 'You're the best friend a man ever had...'

'Don't thank me too soon,' Troy said dryly. 'I haven't managed to steal the damned thing yet. I've promised I shall try, but that doesn't mean I shall succeed.'

Sarah Trenwith crept out from behind the heavy screen at the far end of the library as she heard the door close. They had gone at last! She had been tucked away in her favourite corner with a book when the two men came in and once they had started to talk she had not dared to come out from her hiding place. The men had spoken in hushed tones so she hadn't heard every word they said, but she had managed to catch the gist of their conversation. Lord Hale's son was afraid his father would disown him if he didn't recover something and he had begged Troy to do it for him.

She could hardly believe that Troy – her sister's fiancé – had agreed to steal something from another guest's room. She understood why he was doing it, of course, but it was such a reckless thing to do. If he were caught he would be disgraced in the eyes of all the people here – the people who mattered, to Marianne if not to Troy himself.

Sarah knew that her beautiful sister was very conscious of her place in society. She had chosen Troy because he was the son of Lord Pelham, wealthy in his own right, through a legacy from his maternal grandfather, and much sought after by others. There had been a queue of disappointed ladies when their engagement had been announced on Marianne's birthday – the fifteenth of December 1913, and just eleven days ago. Sarah herself was amongst them, though she had been expecting it. She had known that it was Marianne Troy was interested in from the start, and that she was being foolish to hope for anything else. Sarah was attractive enough in her way. She had dark, honey-blonde hair and green eyes, but Marianne's hair was like moon silver and her eyes were blue. Slender and delicate, Marianne was the unchallenged beauty of her family.

Knowing that he was courting Marianne hadn't stopped Sarah from falling in love with Troy. She knew it was foolish, but when he had carried her to her room that time, her heart had beat like a timpani drum. The nearness of him, the warmth and smell of his body had made her feel faint so that she had nestled her head against his chest, wishing that he would kiss her ... would notice her. Of course he hadn't. He already had eyes only for Marianne, who was one of the most sought after girls of the season. She was the one who had kept Troy waiting, because, as she had told Sarah, she wanted to be sure that it was the best offer she could get.

How could Marianne doubt that Troy Pelham was the best any woman could get? Sarah wouldn't have hesitated a second if he had asked her, but of course he had hardly noticed her, except for the few minutes that he had gallantly carried her up to her room.

Sarah brought her thoughts back to the present. What ought she to do about the conversation she had just overheard? Having turned it over in her mind several times, she realized that there was nothing she actually could do about it. Troy wasn't the kind to go back on his word, especially when he had given it to his best friend. It would be useless to beg him to be careful. He would do what he thought right, because that was the kind of man he was; he certainly wouldn't listen to a warning from her!

She returned the book she had been reading to the shelves. It was a copy of Wordsworth's poems, entitled *Lyrical Ballads*, and beautifully bound in green leather, like most of the other volumes on her father's shelves. Sarah had been seeking solace here in the library more and more this Christmas. She had thought it the one place she was unlikely to find her sister and Troy. Marianne never read a book unless she was forced, and she liked to show off her prowess at the pianoforte so the music gallery was her more usual haunt.

It was time she joined the other guests, Sarah realized. Her mother would wonder what had happened to her if she lingered any longer and Sarah did not wish to incur Lady Trenwith's displeasure. However, she had decided she would not tell anyone of the conversation she had overheard. It was private and she had had no right to listen.

Troy made an excuse to the other gentlemen when they had finished their port and rose to follow the ladies into the drawing room that evening, where he knew the card tables would already have been set up. He had managed to knock some wine over himself earlier and intended to change before he returned to the others. If he was quick, he could enter Lady Hastings's room and make a search for Barney's letter and then return to the drawing room without anyone really noticing that he was missing.

He turned swiftly into the west wing, counting the doors and stopping outside the third. He glanced over his shoulder but no one was about so he turned the small porcelain handle, found the door gave easily, and slipped inside. Immediately, he was aware of the strong smell of perfume and he wrinkled his nose in disgust. He disliked heavy perfumes and the sooner he could get out of here the better!

Troy made straight for the small, inlaid satinwood writing table by the window, opening the leather folder lying on top. There was evidence that Margaret Hastings had been writing a letter, but no sign of Barney's missive to her. That would have been too easy, Troy thought, and smiled grimly. He had agreed to do this in a fit of recklessness, but he didn't much like the

feeling. He opened all the drawers and searched the contents but had no luck. The next thing
was the leather case on the matching dressing
table. Inside the larger case was a small oval
one, obviously for jewellery. Troy put that to
one side without looking inside and saw the
letter lying beneath it. A brief inspection told
him that it was Barney's – he had stupidly written on quality vellum with his father's London
address printed boldly in black at the top.

Troy replaced the jewellery box unopened,
slipped the letter into his breast pocket and left
the room hurriedly. As he began to walk along
the corridor, he saw Marianne coming towards
him. She looked surprised to see him there, as
well she might, for he was lodged in the east
wing. It was unusual for male guests to come
here unless invited, and then, in the case of a
clandestine arrangement, it was often either in
the afternoon when everyone was taking a nap
or late at night. Marianne was far from naïve
and she was well aware of the illicit meetings
that sometimes went on amongst her parents'
guests, but that did not explain why Troy was
here. Ladies, and gentlemen, often accepted an
invitation to stay for a few days without their
husbands or wives, simply for the opportunity
to conduct an affair. It was the way of things
and obliging hosts turned a blind eye, as long
as everyone was discreet.

'Were you looking for me?' she asked, eyes
narrowing in suspicion.

'Yes, of course,' Troy said. 'I was going to
change and I suddenly thought you might have

come up too…'

Marianne noticed the wine stain on his white shirt and frowned. 'I came to freshen up,' she said. 'Did you want something in particular?'

'I just thought we might go for a walk later – get away from the company for a while.'

'Oh, I don't think we should do that,' Marianne said. 'People would think it rude – besides, it is cold out.'

'We could walk in the orangery.'

'Yes, I suppose we could,' she said, and smiled. 'There are an awful lot of guests, aren't there?'

'Too many,' Troy said ruefully. 'I want to be alone with you, Marianne – just for a little.' At least that part of it wasn't a lie. She looked especially lovely that night in a gown of peach silk that swathed her slender body like an extra skin, leaving little to the imagination. His boredom had gone now, and he was aware of his desire to make love to her. It wasn't likely that she would allow more than a few kisses. Marianne had made it clear without actually saying anything that she was determined to keep herself pure for marriage. He supposed he ought to be glad of that, but sometimes he was impatient for more. 'I'll meet you in fifteen minutes – yes?'

'Yes, if you wish,' she said. He sensed reluctance in her, but he knew that she was very correct in her manners, and she would think it rude to leave her guests for too long. She was also very careful that they should do nothing that might damage her reputation.

Troy walked on, aware of the faint doubt at the back of his mind. Did Marianne actually want to be his wife? He knew that she was excited about the wedding, and marrying the son of Lord Pelham – her father was only a baronet, of course – but did she actually think about what came after the ceremony and all the presents?

Now he was being disloyal to her in his mind. He had chosen Marianne carefully, because he wanted a girl of good family, young enough not to be tainted by illicit affairs or scandal. She was beautiful, a little petulant at times, but pleased easily with presents and compliments. Troy wasn't sure whether or not he was in love with her. He knew he desired her. He was eager to go to bed with her – but was that all there was to marriage?

The poets talked and wrote of romantic love, but he wasn't sure it existed outside of their imaginations. Most of his friends had married either for money or land; it was taken for granted that some benefit should come through marriage, even if it was only the begetting of an heir. Troy was twenty-two and it wasn't desperate for him to be thinking of such matters, because he had a younger brother, Andrew, who would be there if he were to be suddenly struck down. Not that he ever gave such an eventuality a thought. Troy was lucky. He always had been. Everyone said it and he took his luck for granted. It was like that letter ... it might have been impossible to find but it had been easy for him. He would return it to

Barney in the morning, unless he simply burned it in the fire in his own room.

Entering his bedchamber, Troy decided that it was best to be rid of the letter for good. He threw it on to the flames, poking at it until it had crumbled into ash, and then he changed his shirt quickly. It wouldn't do to keep Marianne waiting!

Troy was completely unaware that he had been noticed going into the room by one of the servants, for Rose had drawn back as soon as she saw him. He wasn't supposed to be here, and the only reason she could think of as to why he had chosen to visit a lady's room was that he was having an affair with her. It wasn't unusual for the gentlemen to visit ladies in their rooms on these visits – but not when they had only just got engaged to the daughter of the house. Rose frowned in disappointment, but she had been well trained and she would keep her mouth shut and stay out of the way. However, she mentioned it to her brother later that evening. Jack told her that it was none of her business and she ought to forget what she'd seen.

'Well, I think it was wrong,' Rose said when they were alone in the servants' parlour. Jack Barlow worked in the stables at Trenwith. He wasn't the head groom yet but he would be when old Jethro retired. He didn't sleep in the house as Rose did, in a tiny room up in the attics, but shared a cottage in the grounds with some of the other outdoor men. 'Why would a

15

gentleman go to a lady's room? You tell me that if you can.'

'You shouldn't be in such a hurry to jump to conclusions,' Jack chided. 'Anyway, it's no business of ours why he was there – and you'll say nothing to anyone else, my girl. We've got decent jobs here and you don't want to lose your place, do you?'

'No ... I just felt disappointed in him, Jack. He's only just got himself engaged and...' Rose shook her head. Her hair glinted red in the light from the lamps, because she had taken off the cap she normally wore, allowing it to fall freely on her shoulders. She was an attractive young woman, even dressed in her plain black uniform and white apron. 'I thought he was such a lovely feller.'

'Mr Troy is all right,' Jack said looking thoughtful. ''Sides, I can't see him going for a woman like that – more particular I'd say. And he could have gone there for any number of reasons, none of which are your business, Rose.'

'No, of course not,' Rose agreed. 'And you're right, he could have been there for lots of reasons...' She was glad that she had told her brother but no one else, because she liked Mr Troy. He was always polite and thanked everyone for what they did for him, which was more than you could say for some of the gentry. Some of them were right beggars, especially the women, who complained in shrill voices over the smallest thing. 'I don't like that Lady Hastings and I should be sorry if I thought he was carrying on with her – but it's nothing to do with me.'

'As long as you remember that, you'll do well enough,' Jack said and grinned at her. He was five years older than his sister, who was just eighteen; a big, strong man with good features and hair a much darker shade of chestnut brown than his sister's. 'You get off to bed, Rose, and don't think about it again.'

'No, I shan't,' Rose told him. But in the morning she learned something that ensured she would think about it a great deal.

If Rose had put the incident from her mind, Sarah had not been able to forget what she had heard in the library earlier. She lay thinking about it for some time after she had turned out her lamp, wondering if Troy had found what he had been looking for –if he had actually gone through with his plan. She thought that he must have, because he was not a man to break a promise to a friend.

Troy had disappeared for quite a long time that evening, but then so had Marianne, and they had reappeared together – so that probably meant they had sneaked off somewhere to be alone. They would have been kissing, holding each other intimately. Sarah tossed restlessly on her pillow. It was silly of her to let herself think about things like that, because it just set up a reckless longing inside her. She must not think about such things, because it was highly improper in a young lady.

Sarah had to accept that Troy was not for her.

She would be going to London in the spring and she would meet lots of gentlemen there, and perhaps she would fall in love with someone. A sigh escaped her, because she knew that no one would be like Troy. She had not meant to fall for him, but she had and there was little she could do about it.

She hoped that Troy wouldn't get into trouble over the letter – if, indeed, that was what he had been looking for. She thought so but she wasn't sure. Whatever it was, she hoped that its disappearance, if Troy had taken it, would not cause any bother.

'This is most unfortunate, Lady Hastings,' Sir James Trenwith said when she requested an interview with him in his study the following morning. 'You are quite sure that the necklace was in your jewel case last evening when you came down to dinner?'

'Yes, of course,' Margaret Hastings said. 'I couldn't make a mistake like that. The case was left lying on the dressing table. The maid should have taken it away to the butler's room for safekeeping but she was careless – unless it was intentional so that she might return later and take the necklace.'

'I cannot believe that any of my servants would steal a valuable diamond necklace,' Sir James said stiffly. 'We've never had such a thing happen before, and I find it extremely distressing.'

'*You* find it distressing?' Margaret Hastings said with a lift of her fine brows. She was in her thirtieth year, strikingly lovely with her creamy complexion and dark hair. Her eyes were a greenish-blue, and her mouth had a sensuous softness that most men found very attractive. 'I cannot imagine what my husband will say when I tell him.'

Sir James was no less susceptible than most, and he felt at a loss to know what to say to her. She was, of course, ultimately responsible for her own property. She ought to have made sure the maid took the jewel case back to the butler for safekeeping in the strong room, but it put him in an awkward position, because he could not allow something like this to go unchecked. If he discovered that one of the servants had stolen the diamonds he would see that they received the appropriate punishment.

'I can only apologize that such a thing should have happened,' he said. 'I shall inform Harding and Mrs Harding. An investigation must be made and hopefully we may discover that the necklace has been mislaid. Do you know if your husband had the necklace insured?'

'I have no idea,' she replied. 'I leave all that kind of thing to Hastings. As you know, he is due to arrive later today to take me home, and I dread to think what he will say.'

'We shall make our own investigation first,' Sir James said. 'But eventually we may have to call in the police.'

'Well, that is up to you. Now, if you will excuse me, I must supervise the packing of my trunk. I do not wish anything else to go astray.'

Sir James watched as she walked from the

room. He was angry as he reached for the bell to summon a servant. This was embarrassing and awkward, but something would have to be done about it.

'Would you like me to take this for washing, Miss Sarah?' Rose asked as she moved about the room collecting pieces of clothing that had been discarded. 'And perhaps you shouldn't leave those pearl earrings lying on the dressing chest, miss.'

Sarah turned her head to look at her. Rose had been behaving oddly ever since she had come to tidy Sarah's room that morning. Usually, they talked about all kinds of things, but today Rose was obviously disturbed about something.

'Have I done anything to upset you, Rose?'

'No, miss, of course not.' Rose gathered up several pieces of clothing. 'Is there anything else you require, Miss Sarah?'

'Yes. Put those things down for a moment and tell me what is wrong,' Sarah said. 'I know you, Rose – and I know that you are upset. So what have I done?'

'It's nothing you've done, miss,' Rose said, and frowned. 'That Lady Hastings is saying that a diamond necklace has gone missing from her room – and Sir James has ordered that the servants be questioned, and that our rooms are searched.'

'Oh no! No wonder you are upset,' Sarah said, feeling shocked. 'Father cannot think that you took it – any of you, but especially you,

Rose. You would never do anything like that!'

Rose stared at her for a moment longer and then relaxed, giving her a rueful smile. 'It has proper given me the creeps, Miss Sarah, and that's the truth of it. Everyone is upset about having their room searched. It isn't that we've anything to hide but it makes us seem guilty when we haven't done anything.'

'Yes, I understand how you must feel,' Sarah said. 'Do you think that Father will have my room searched too?'

Rose looked horrified. 'No, miss, of course not! No one could think that you had taken it.'

'Why not? If you can be suspected then so can I – and our guests. Why shouldn't they have taken it as easily as you or the others?'

'You're a proper lady, miss,' Rose said, dropping her air of reserve. 'And I'm sorry if I've been strange with you, but I've been that bothered ... and I don't know what to do.'

Sarah saw the worried expression on Rose's face and frowned. 'What do you know that you aren't telling me, Rose?'

'I can't say, miss ... it wouldn't be right.'

'You can tell me, Rose. I thought we were friends?'

'Well, sort of,' Rose said. 'I like you, miss, and you're always good to me – but your mother would have something to say if she heard you call me a friend.'

'Oh, Mama...' Sarah said and pulled a face. 'Well, perhaps I wouldn't say it to her or Papa, but it is true just the same. Please tell me what is troubling you, Rose. I might be able to help.'

'Well, I saw something last night,' Rose said. 'I don't think it has anything to do with the necklace, but it was odd. Jack said as I was to keep my mouth shut and I wouldn't tell anyone but you, Miss Sarah...'

'Well, go on then,' Sarah urged. 'What is on your mind?'

'I saw Mr Troy going into Lady Hastings's room,' Rose said. 'It was after dinner and everyone had gone into the drawing room to play cards. I came up to turn back some of the beds and I saw him go in.'

'Oh, Rose,' Sarah said, feeling shocked, 'you cannot think that Troy Pelham would steal a valuable necklace? No, it is impossible. He wouldn't do such a thing, besides...' She stopped and shook her head. She had overheard Troy arranging to steal something for Barney Hale, but she had thought it was something that belonged to him, probably a letter. 'You must forget you saw him. Please, Rose. I know for certain that he wouldn't take something like that – he wouldn't!'

'That's what I thought, miss. My brother says Mr Troy is all right, and he is a good judge as a rule. I shan't say anything to anyone else – but it was a bit odd, don't you think?'

'Yes, it is odd,' Sarah agreed, 'and I am very sorry that you've all been subjected to this unpleasantness, but I know you didn't take that necklace – just as I know Troy didn't do anything like that. He is an honourable gentleman, Rose. He just wouldn't behave so badly.'

'No, miss, I'm sure you are right,' Rose

agreed. 'And I shan't say anything. I promise you.'

'Good.' Sarah smiled at her. 'I'm glad you work for us, Rose – and thank you for telling me. No one else tells me anything.'

'I'm glad we've spoken, miss. It was playing on my mind, but I think you are right. Mr Troy has no need to steal anything because he is rich.'

Sarah stared after her as Rose went out and shut the door. She looked at her reflection in the mirror, twiddling a piece of hair around her finger. Troy had gone to Lady Hastings's room to steal something – might it be that he had seen the necklace and taken it on impulse?

She dismissed the unworthy thought at once. Her instincts told her that Troy would never do anything like that. Whatever he had taken was something that belonged to Barney and had nothing whatsoever to do with the missing necklace.

She heard the long-case clock in the hall downstairs chiming and recalled that her cousin Lucy was arriving that morning. It was time she went down so that she would be there to greet her.

'This is awful, Mama,' Marianne said when her mother told her about the theft of the necklace. 'Whatever will people think of us? If we have a thief in our midst—'

'Your father ordered a search of the servants' rooms, which has caused some grumbling, but of course nothing was found. If he had consulted me I would have told him that it was a waste of time. Something like that must be the work of a professional thief. None of our people would have the least idea of its value. Someone must have broken in when we were at dinner or during the night.'

Marianne gave a little shiver. 'But no one else has reported anything missing...' She frowned as she remembered that she had seen Troy leaving the room in question. At least, she thought he had come from one of the rooms, though he had made an excuse that he was looking for her. 'I wonder...' She shook her head as her mother questioned with a lift of her brows. 'I suppose it couldn't have been any of the guests?'

'Marianne!' her mother cried, shocked at the very idea. 'Please be careful what you say. If you were overheard suggesting something like that we could be ostracized by our friends. You simply do not suspect people of quality of doing such a thing – and if you should have reason to think it, you ignore it. One does not accuse one's friends of being a thief.'

'No, Mama, of course not.' Marianne frowned. It was impossible to tell her mother what was on her mind. Lady Trenwith would be shocked and upset, and Marianne was not certain of what she had actually seen.

'Run away now, my dear,' her mother said. 'I daresay Troy will be looking for you, and you must make the most of this visit for you may not get another chance like this until the wedding.'

'Yes, Mama,' Marianne said. She was thoughtful as she left her mother's bedchamber to go downstairs. It was unthinkable that Troy should have taken the necklace, but someone had – and he had had the opportunity. Yet why would he do such a thing? She had heard nothing that led her to believe he was short of money. No, no, of course he would not steal. He had gone to the west wing to find her as he'd said ... or was there another reason? Could he be having an affair with Margaret Hastings? Lady Trenwith had told Marianne that gentlemen often took mistresses, and that a sensible wife simply ignored it, but Marianne felt piqued that he should want to do something like that when he was promised to her.

She saw that her cousin Lucy Trenwith had just arrived and was being greeted by Sarah, and her brother Luke had just come into the hall, dressed in riding clothes. She turned away towards the music gallery to avoid their company. She would play a little music to soothe her fretted nerves. Troy Pelham could not be a thief – but he might just be having an affair with the lady in question.

'This is a damned coil,' Barney said to Troy as they stood together in the library, where they had sought some privacy. 'Did you happen to see it while you were there?'

'I didn't open the jewel case,' Troy said and glared at him. 'What do you take me for – a damned thief?'

'No, of course not,' Barney said, looking

horrified. 'But if it was there when you rescued my letter someone else must have gone there afterwards and taken it.'

'If she had it in the first place,' Troy said, his face like thunder. 'My father has mislaid things a score of times – but at least he never had the servants' rooms searched. Some of them are muttering about leaving, and it isn't easy to get decent help these days. Not that I blame them, the way some people behave. It hurts no one to be polite...'

'Know what you mean,' Barney said uncomfortably. 'I'm sorry about this, Troy. Perhaps I shouldn't have asked...' He quailed under the look Troy gave him. 'But you might be right about the necklace – I know she is always short of money. She could have sold it, and this might be her revenge on me because the letter has disappeared. She probably thinks I took it.'

'Trouble is, there is no way of knowing,' Troy said. 'I wouldn't put it past her to lie – but Sir James would never question her word. It makes things very awkward for him ... the whole family. I suppose he may have to call in the police.'

'Yes, perhaps,' Barney said, looking green. 'It is dashed awkward, Troy. I'm glad you burned that letter.'

'It's gone as if it never was,' Troy said. 'That is the one good thing about this mess. Anyway, we shall just have to ride it through. If you are asked about this just look outraged, that is my advice to you. I had better go and find Marianne. She will think I have deserted her.'

'Yes, of course,' Barney said. 'Best to keep my head low. I hope the police don't want to question me.'

'I very much doubt they will,' Troy said. 'Sir James is saying now that someone must have broken in during the night. He is going to speak to Lord Hastings when he arrives later today. They may try to hush it up somehow.'

Troy was frowning as he left Barney and made his way towards the music room. He could hear Marianne playing. She would expect him to join her, but would she have put two and two together and made five? She had seen him seconds after he'd left Margaret Hastings's room, and she might have begun to wonder why he had been there.

Marianne glanced up as Troy entered the room. For once the music had done nothing to soothe her irritation and she could not put her mind at rest. Why had Troy been coming from the direction of Lady Hastings's room the previous evening? She had thought it over and she was certain that that was where he had been, for her own room was much further down the hall. Could he have taken the necklace? It seemed improbable and yet he had had the opportunity.

She stopped playing as he came over to her. She sensed that he was tense and the question came out of her mouth without her really meaning it to.

'Did you go to Lady Hastings's room last night?'

27

Troy hesitated. It would be sensible to lie to her, but something in him – pride or anger – wouldn't allow him to dissemble.

'Yes, I did,' he said, his eyes cold as he looked at her and registered the shock and condemnation in her face. She clearly thought him guilty of something. 'And the answer to your next question is no – I did not take the necklace.'

'Why did you go there?'

'I am not at liberty to tell you. It is a matter of honour.'

'You mean you do not wish to tell me.' Marianne got to her feet. She felt distressed, close to hysteria. His refusal to answer her question could mean only one of two things. Either he was a thief, which seemed unlikely given his wealth, or he was having an affair with Margaret Hastings.

'Is she your mistress?'

'No, she is not,' Troy said. 'The disappearance of the necklace has nothing to do with me, and I have no personal interest in the lady.'

'I do not believe you,' Marianne said, her voice shrill as she put a hand to her slender throat. 'If you had a good reason to be there you would tell me.'

'I cannot tell you more than I have, Marianne. Yes, I did visit the room briefly, but I am not a thief, neither am I involved with the lady.'

'And you expect me to believe you – with no explanation?'

'Yes, I think I am entitled to expect that,' Troy said in a deadly calm tone. 'You promised to marry me and I presumed you felt some tenderness towards me – but it seems that you do not trust me. I find that insulting, Marianne.'

'And I find it unbearable,' Marianne said a little wildly as she tugged the beautiful emerald and diamond ring from her finger and held it out to him. 'I can no longer continue with this engagement, sir.'

Troy stared at the ring for a moment, then inclined his head and accepted it from her. 'Very well, Miss Trenwith. Our engagement is at an end.' He turned and walked from the room, leaving Marianne to gaze after him in annoyance and frustration.

What a disobliging man he was! Why could he not have explained to her what he had been doing – or at the very least told her an acceptable lie? She would have liked to weep in his arms and be comforted, but he had made her angry and she had acted impulsively. She realized she had done something that would reflect badly on her character, but she had expected Troy to plead with her, never believing that he would accept her dismissal.

Suddenly, her distress boiled over into tears and she fled from the room and dashed straight up the stairs to her bedchamber, before flinging herself down on the bed to weep.

Sarah had just come from Lucy's room when her sister rushed past her. Realizing Marianne was in distress, Sarah hesitated and then knocked at the door.

'Go away!' Marianne's voice was muffled. 'I don't want to see anyone.'

'It's me, Marianne,' Sarah said. 'Are you upset? Is there anything I can do for you?'

'No ... thank you. Please leave me alone.'

Sarah lingered a moment longer and then walked away. If Marianne would not allow her to help, there was nothing she could do. She went downstairs, heading towards the library, her favourite place when there were visitors in the house. Lucy was changing her gown and she would know where to find Sarah when she was ready, for they both enjoyed reading and often sat quietly together for hours without speaking – unless it was to read something from a book that they found interesting or amusing.

She went into the library and then halted as she saw Troy was already there. He had his back towards her, but he swung around as she entered, his expression as black as thunder. His gaze narrowed as he saw her, as if he would say something cutting, but he thought better of it and held back the words.

'Good morning, Sarah.'

'I am sorry if I intrude,' she said. 'I can go away and return later.'

'I am the one who is intruding,' he replied, his manner a little stiff. 'This is your home. I shall be leaving Trenwith Hall shortly, Sarah. If you hear ill of me, I beg you not to think too harshly of me.'

'Why should I think harshly of you?'

'Your sister has just jilted me,' he said. 'She

will no doubt give you her reasons when she is ready, but I am innocent of any wrongdoing – except perhaps a reckless pride.'

A little gasp escaped her. 'Marianne has jilted you but surely...' She shook her head. 'I am very sorry, Troy, but perhaps it is just one of her tantrums and she will change her mind. She often does, you know.'

'Fortunately, I am not of the same mettle,' Troy said, a rueful smile on his mouth. 'I daresay we shall not meet often in the future, Sarah, so I shall say goodbye to you now.'

'You are leaving at once?' Sarah stared at him in dismay. 'But I am sure Marianne will regret her hasty words ... whatever they were...' Her voice tailed off as she saw the stormy expression in his eyes. 'I do hope that we shall meet again, Troy.'

'Perhaps we shall when you come to London for the season, who knows?' He smiled oddly at her. 'And now I must seek out my father and tell him the news. I daresay he will wish to leave immediately. I must also speak to your father, Sarah – and then I shall go.'

'I am sorry you are leaving,' she said. 'I think Marianne foolish to throw you over ... but then she is sometimes rather silly. Oh dear, perhaps I should not have said that...' A faint blush stained her cheeks.

'I daresay you ought not to say it, but I shall not tell anyone,' he said and winked at her, suddenly seeming amused. 'As it happens, I agree, but of course I would not say that to anyone else.'

31

Sarah turned to watch him as he walked from the room. The smile he had given her had made her heart race, and she knew that she liked him more than ever. Others might say or think what they pleased, but she would not listen to a word against him.

Two

'What did you do that made the girl break off your engagement?' Lord Pelham looked at his son in anger and disbelief. 'I cannot imagine why she would do so only a few days after it was announced. This is deuced awkward, Troy. People will imagine the worst, of course. Marianne is well thought of by everyone and your name will be blackened.'

'I did nothing that should have caused her to jilt me,' Troy said. 'She saw me leaving Lady Hastings's room last night and put two and two together, but came up with five. She thinks I am either a jewel thief or having an affair with the lady.'

'And are you?' his father asked. 'Having an affair, I mean? I believe I may acquit you of the other charge. This business of the necklace is a bit smoky if you ask me.'

'I thank you for acquitting me of the first charge,' Troy said, his tone icy calm. His pride had been dented by Marianne's accusation, but he would have been seriously angry had his father not dismissed the possibility. 'I shall tell you, as I did Marianne, that I am guilty on neither count.'

'Then why were you there?'

'That is something I am not at liberty to disclose,' Troy said, his face set stubbornly rigid. He had no intention of betraying his friend. 'I am sorry, Father, but you must take my word for this.'

'And if I choose not to?'

'Then you must believe the worse of me,' Troy said. 'I have told you everything I can, because you have the right to know. What you choose to do now is up to you.'

'Trenwith is one of my best friends, damn it! We've known each other for years.'

'Yes, I am aware of that ... it was probably the reason...' Troy broke off, for it would be ungenerous of him to say that he was feeling relieved to be free of an engagement that he had known was a mistake almost as soon as Marianne had accepted him. He had enjoyed the chase, because she was beautiful and popular. He had liked it that she chose him over a dozen others she might have taken, but he hadn't been in love with her. However, he would never have dreamed of jilting her; it would not be behaviour befitting a gentleman. 'Surely he will understand? I didn't jilt her, Father. It was Marianne's choice.'

His father frowned. 'Yes, I realize that. I believe you are too much the gentleman to have thrown her over, but it is still awkward.

Trenwith will take his daughter's side. He will think you have done something to upset her ... and he is a difficult man when he believes his honour may be in question. He will not like this business of the necklace one bit.'

'I shall speak to him before I leave—'

'No! I forbid it. You have done enough harm, Troy. Leave Trenwith to me. I shall speak to him myself. We must both leave of course. I shall go down to the country. It might be best if you took yourself off elsewhere for the time being. You must not be thought to be sulking. Far better to show yourself and act naturally.'

Troy inclined his head. 'I have instructed that my trunk be sent to Pelham Place in London. That is where I intend to head immediately, but I may go to stay with friends for a while.'

'You are of an age to please yourself,' his father said, 'and independent of any threat I might hold over you. I shall expect to see you when we go up to London in the spring.'

'Of course. I shall hope by then that both you and Trenwith will have learned to forgive me.'

Troy walked from the room with his head high. At least his father hadn't believed he was a jewel thief, but he probably imagined that Troy was involved with Margaret Hastings in some way. It was ironic that he had always avoided her net, and that she had taken Barney as a lover out of pique. It wouldn't surprise him in the least if the story of the missing necklace was a complete lie to punish whoever had taken the letter. Margaret was clever enough to have worked it out that he was the most likely culprit: Barney simply didn't have the nerve for it.

Either way, she had made things awkward for everyone. Most of the Trenwith servants were up in arms over it, and it was possible that some of them would leave, causing a domestic crisis for Lady Trenwith. But that wasn't his concern. In a few minutes he would be on his way to London, and he couldn't help feeling as if he had thrown off his chains – chains of his own forging, perhaps, but they had weighed on him heavily. He could almost welcome the scandal because he knew that he had escaped lightly. Marriage to Marianne Trenwith would have meant a lifetime of regret.

As he went up the stairs and turned towards the east wing, he saw that Lord Hastings was about to go down, and judging from his expression he was very angry about something.

'Thank you for seeing me,' Lord Hastings said when the two were closeted in Sir James's study. 'I am sorry for this awkwardness, Trenwith.'

'I welcomed the chance to apologize,' Sir James said, his face a little red from embarrassment. 'I don't know how it could have happened. We made a search of the servants' rooms but nothing was found. I have been waiting for you to tell me what you wished me to do before contacting the police.'

'Then you have not done so?' Lord Hastings said, and looked relieved. 'That was very sensible of you, Trenwith. I am enormously grateful. You see, it has all been a dreadful mistake...'

'I am sorry, I do not understand you,' Sir James said. 'I imagined you might be insured but you will need to let the police know of course.'

'That is just the point,' Hastings said. 'The necklace wasn't stolen. My wife didn't bring it with her. She could not have done so for it was at the jeweller's ... being cleaned.' He cleared his throat and could not quite meet his host's eyes, because the whole thing was a damned lie. Margaret had sold the wretched necklace, but when the proprietor of the shop looked at it later, he had recognized it as a family piece and informed the rightful owner. Having redeemed it, Hastings had intended to confront his reckless wife and he had been furious when he discovered what she had done. 'It was foolish of her not to have noticed and I cannot apologize enough for the trouble she has caused.'

Sir James knew that Hastings was a gentleman of the old school, and he realized that there was more to this than met the eye, but there was no need to go into unnecessary details. It could all be settled between gentlemen and forgotten.

'I am relieved to hear it,' he said. 'I was most anxious that she should not have suffered such a loss due to any carelessness on my part.'

'No, no, my dear fellow,' Hastings said. 'All a regrettable mistake. If anyone should apologize it must be me. I am more distressed about this

36

than I can say, especially as your people had their rooms searched. It is so difficult to get good staff these days, and your wife will be wishing us to the devil. We shall be leaving almost at once.'

'You will stay for luncheon, I hope?'

'No, I think not,' Hastings said. He wanted to get his wife home so that he could tell her exactly what he thought of her behaviour. 'But we shall be in town for the season. You must visit us then...'

He inclined his head and walked to the door. Sir James frowned as he sat at his desk. He would have to speak to Harding and ask him to apologize to the rest of the servants. A most unpleasant business all round. He was about to reach for the bell to summon his butler when someone knocked at the door.

'Please come in,' he said and looked up as Lord Pelham walked in. From the expression on Pelham's face there was more trouble on the way. 'Ah, nice to see you. I have some good news to announce. It seems that the business of the necklace was all a mistake——'

'That is excellent,' Lord Pelham said, 'but it seems you have not heard the latest, which is, I am afraid, not good news at all...'

'Marianne!' Lady Trenwith looked at her daughter in horror. 'Why did you do such a thing? Surely you know what a scandal it will cause? No one likes a jilt, my dear. People will look at you differently now.'

'Please don't scold me, Mama,' Marianne

said. She had washed her face in cold water but she could not disguise the redness of her eyes and nose. She felt wretched and had wished a hundred times that she had not lost her temper. Troy had been so disobliging! She had not expected him to go off without trying to win her back. 'I had to – he was so awful to me.'

'What do you mean? Did he hit you or try to ... he didn't seduce you?' Lady Trenwith was shocked.

'No, Mama, of course not,' Marianne said. 'Nothing like that. I should hope he would know better than to try – but he was cold and angry. I saw him leaving Lady Hastings's room last evening, at least I thought that was where he came from, and he admitted it when I challenged him.'

'You didn't ask him if he had stolen the necklace?' Lady Trenwith was horrified as she saw the truth in her daughter's eyes. 'Oh, Marianne! I am not surprised he was angry. You couldn't have thought ... besides, it was all a mistake. The necklace wasn't stolen at all, merely being cleaned. Lord Hastings has apologized to your father.'

'Oh ... but he went there for some reason, Mama,' Marianne said. 'So it must mean that he was ... well you know...' she blushed as her mother gave her a look of reprimand. 'I asked him to deny it but he refused.'

'I am not surprised,' her mother said and gave her a quelling look. 'Ladies do not ask gentlemen that kind of question. I told you when you asked me if you should accept him,

Marianne. Some gentlemen are inclined to amorous affairs outside marriage, but a lady does not notice. She cares for her home and her children, and after a while may feel relieved that her husband does not stay with her at night as often as he once did. You will have to accept such things unless you are very fortunate in your choice of a husband.'

'But we are not even married and it is humiliating...' Marianne said, her face flushed with temper. Her pride had been hurt and she felt bruised and angry. 'I was angry and I spoke hastily but I really could not tolerate such behaviour!'

'Then you should not have chosen a man like Troy Pelham,' Lady Trenwith said. 'If you want a husband that you can lead around on a string, you must look for another kind of man entirely.'

Marianne was thoughtful. 'Do you mean like Barney Hale?'

'Perhaps...' her mother said and frowned at her. 'Is there no chance that Troy would forgive you and take you back? If you apologized sincerely he might accept it, Marianne.'

'I am not sure that I want to marry him!' It was said in a moment of pique, but in her heart she knew she had made a terrible mistake.

'You may not get a chance to marry anyone else,' her mother said, giving her a severe look. 'You were very popular, Marianne, but even if people think Troy has done something wrong, a lot of people will blame you. Having a mistress, especially before marriage, is quite acceptable. Many of our friends will think you immature and silly. I daresay we shall still be received, but you may find that some ladies will look askance at you, and the gentlemen may not flock round as they did before.'

'Have I ruined myself, Mama?' Marianne was crushed by her mother's censure, her hopes of finding someone else quite deflated.

Lady Trenwith was silent for a moment. 'We may brush through this scandal, but my advice to you, Marianne, is to be very nice to the next gentleman who courts you, and if he offers make sure that you get his ring on your finger as quickly as you can.' She turned towards the door. 'Several guests are leaving early. I must go and say goodbye to them. I suggest that you come down in a few minutes and behave in a ladylike manner...'

Sarah saw her mother leaving Marianne's room. She knew that the house was in turmoil. Several of their guests were leaving early; Lord Pelham and Troy of course, also Lord and Lady Hastings – which was a relief to all of them – but one or two others had invented excuses why they had to get home sooner than planned.

It was unfair on her mother, Sarah thought, because she had had to soothe ruffled feathers – not only amongst the guests, who had felt that a cloud of suspicion hung over them, but also the servants. Rose had told Sarah that one of the parlour maids had already given in her notice.

'Julie is going to work in a dressmaking establishment,' Rose had told her. 'Her aunt is the head seamstress there and she has been asking Julie to join her for a while. She wouldn't leave because she says the hours are even longer there than here, but now she has changed her mind. And that means Ronnie Simmons is going too. Jack says he's one of the best workers they've got at the stables and that they will be lucky to get anyone as good in his place.'

'That's a shame,' Sarah said. 'And it was all a mistake. Won't Julie change her mind if Mama asks her?'

'I doubt it,' Rose said. 'She's been talking of leaving for a while, and it only took a bit of upset to make her decide.'

'I hope you won't leave us, Rose?'

'Not just yet,' Rose said. She had thought about it, but she wasn't sure what she wanted to do, and Jack liked working for the family, so she had decided to stay for the time being. Besides, her mother lived in the village and it was easy just to walk down on her day off.

Sarah dismissed the rest of their conversation from her mind as she went to her sister's door. She knocked and this time she was invited to enter.

'Are you all right?' she asked, looking at Marianne unhappily.

'Of course, why shouldn't I be?' Marianne said, tossing her pale tresses back from her shoulder. She had changed into a fresh gown of striped linen and put on the merest touch of face powder to cover the red around her eyes.

41

'I made a mistake, that is all. I spoke hastily, but it was Troy's fault. He was so cold and unpleasant.'

'Do you wish you hadn't jilted him?'

'I dislike that word,' Marianne said, and her expression was icy as she looked at her sister. 'I broke off my engagement because I discovered that we did not suit. Troy Pelham isn't the man I thought he was. He has behaved badly towards me.'

'But he told you that he was innocent of any wrongdoing – and he couldn't have stolen the necklace, because it wasn't stolen at all—'

'Then why was he there?' Marianne demanded, her tone petulant. 'I would almost prefer that he had taken the necklace, perhaps for a practical joke or something...'

'You don't think that he was having an affair with her?' Sarah stared at her sister in disbelief. 'Surely you know he wouldn't, not under Father's roof and just after you were engaged? Besides, I think...' She broke off as Marianne looked at her, because she couldn't tell her that she thought Barney Hale had been involved with Lady Hastings. 'Troy has gone, you know. He was very angry ... insulted I think.'

'How do you imagine I feel?' Marianne snapped. 'But you never consider my feelings. No one appreciates how my nerves have been affected by all this horrid business.'

'How do you feel?'

'As if I would tell you,' Marianne said. 'Run away and find Lucy. I really do not want to speak to you at the moment.'

Sarah left the room without another word. She was angry with her sister for throwing away Troy's love, and for hurting him. She didn't mind that Marianne had been sharp with her, because it was her sister's way and she was used to it, but she minded very much for Troy. She wished that there was a way for her to see him, to tell him that she was completely on his side, but she knew that she was unlikely to meet him for months. They were going to London in April, but that was ages away, and in the meantime there was nothing she could do – unless Barney would be seeing him sooner. She could write a letter telling Troy what had happened after he left and that she hoped they would meet in London.

Feeling a little better, Sarah went in search of Barney. She found him in the games room, knocking a few balls about on the billiard table. He looked miserable and she wondered if he was blaming himself for what had happened over the necklace and Troy's broken engagement.

'Will you teach me to play?' she asked, giving him an inviting smile. 'It looks fun and I've often wished I might.'

'Yes, if you would like me to,' Barney said, looking at her awkwardly. 'I was wondering if I ought to leave ... with all the bother...'

'Do you want to?'

'No, not particularly,' Barney confessed. It was actually the last thing he wanted, because he kept thinking about Marianne and the fact that she was no longer engaged to Troy. And, despite feeling guilty, he couldn't help wondering if he might stand a chance with her now. 'Wasn't sure if I would still be welcome – Troy's friend and all that...'

'I cannot think that anyone would hold it against you,' Sarah said. 'My mother is upset by all the turmoil. I think she would be glad if you continued your visit. I know the Forresters are staying on and my cousin Lucy has just arrived for a few weeks' visit. Besides, Marianne is unhappy. You might make her feel better if you make a little fuss of her.' It had not escaped Sarah's notice that Barney was head over heels in love with her sister. 'She will need her friends – it isn't very nice to be known as a jilt.'

'No, but of course it wasn't her fault,' Barney said loyally, and then flushed as he realized that he was implying it was Troy's fault. 'No one's fault really, I suppose...'

'I think Marianne ought not to have accepted him in the first place,' Sarah said, uncertain why she was meddling in her sister's affairs. 'She needs someone different ... someone who really cares about her ... like you.'

Barney went bright red and Sarah smiled as she turned away to pick up a cue. 'You had better show me what to do,' she said. She had given him a little push; it was up to him now. 'I think you use the narrow end, don't you – but what do you do next?'

'Do you think Marianne really loved him?'

44

Lucy asked Sarah as they were sitting in the library. It was cold out, though the weather was crisp and bright, and through the windows they could see Marianne and Barney Hale walking together in the garden. 'The way she has been making up to Barney this past week makes me think her heart isn't broken the least little bit.'

'That's good, isn't it?' Sarah said. 'I mean, I wouldn't want her to be miserable, and she was for a couple of weeks. I thought she really cared, but then she started smiling at Barney – and he is mad about her. He always has been. In fact I've wondered ... but of course he wouldn't have ... not on purpose, because he couldn't have known that she would see him...'

'What are you talking about?' Lucy asked. 'I know Marianne thinks that Troy was having a thing with Lady Hastings, because I heard Aunt Helen discussing it with Uncle James.' She blushed as Sarah looked at her, her fine brows arched. 'Well, yes, I did listen at the door. I know I shouldn't but it is the only way to find out what is going on. You know how the grown ups are – they never tell you anything until you are out. And I do like to know, don't you?'

'Yes, of course. Well, I can't tell you all of it,' Sarah said, and laughed as her cousin's eyes widened. 'As a matter of fact, I overheard something here in the library one morning. Troy and Barney were talking; they didn't know I was here behind the screen and Barney

45

asked Troy to get something from Lady Hastings's room. I think it was a letter she was using to blackmail Barney, but I'm not completely sure.'

'Sarah!' Lucy's mouth formed a perfect 'O' of surprise. 'Why didn't you tell me before?'

'Because it wasn't my business. I shouldn't have told you now, and you mustn't tell anyone else … cross your heart and hope to die?'

'Oh, absolutely,' Lucy said, looking thrilled, because she adored secrets. 'Do you think Barney planned it all so that Marianne would break off her engagement and turn to him?'

'To be honest I don't think Barney has the brains to plan anything that devious,' Sarah said, and chuckled as her cousin nodded her agreement. 'Besides, he really likes Troy and he felt awful about what happened – but he has seen his chance now and he intends to make the most of it. If he asks her, I think Marianne will agree to a short engagement and marry in the spring or summer. Mama is taking me to London for a season this year and Marianne won't want to risk being ignored or less popular than she was before. If she is engaged to Barney, she won't feel left out if she doesn't get as many admirers as last time.'

'Are you hoping she will marry him?' Lucy looked at her intently.

'Well, I think it would be the best thing for her, don't you?' Sarah glanced down at her hands, wondering guiltily if she had pushed her sister in Barney's direction for the right reasons.

46

'Yes, I do in the circumstances,' Lucy said. 'After all, she jilted Troy and I doubt very much if he would take her back after that. From what I've seen of him, and I know it isn't that much, I think he is far too proud.'

'Yes, I agree with you,' Sarah said, and wrinkled her brow in thought. 'I spoke to him before he left and he was very angry. I think he felt that Marianne had insulted him by believing that he might be a thief – or a seducer, which is just as bad.'

'He did steal the letter, though,' Lucy said, and then as she saw Sarah's quick frown, 'but that was different, because that horrid woman was using it to blackmail Barney, of course.'

'And she made up the tale of her necklace being stolen,' Sarah said. 'I think she did that on purpose, to punish whoever had taken the letter. Mama said Lord Hastings was most apologetic, but he is really staid, a perfect gentleman. I am surprised he doesn't divorce her.'

'Oh, he couldn't do that,' Lucy said. 'Think of the scandal! It would be awful and she would be ruined.'

'Well, I think she deserves it,' Sarah said, and then realized that she sounded unkind. 'Or perhaps not – but she isn't very nice, is she?'

'No, she isn't,' Lucy said, and glanced out of the window. 'Oh, do look, Sarah – Barney has just kissed Marianne. Do you think that means he has proposed to her?'

'I don't know.' Sarah wrinkled her brow. 'It is a little bit soon for that – look, she is smiling and shaking her head. No, I don't think they have settled anything yet, but I am sure they will soon.'

She picked up a fashion magazine from the table behind her. They had been looking at some of the outrageous designs of Paul Poiret. He was the man responsible for introducing that wicked instrument of torture, the hobble skirt that made it almost impossible for ladies to walk and had been banned in the Trenwith household. His designs were wildly popular but held to be outrageous by many, for he dressed his followers in rich and exotic clothes, some of which were uncomfortable to wear.

'I don't think Mama would let me wear anything like that,' Sarah said, and giggled, turning the subject from her sister. 'But then, I am not sure that I would want to – are you?'

'Sir James told me that Lord Hastings was most apologetic,' Lord Pelham said to his son. They were in the study at Pelham Place, a tray of brandy and glasses on the desk where he sat, Troy standing before the fire, one foot on the steel fender as he stared into the flames. 'If Marianne suspected you of theft I am sure she would wish to apologize now.'

'As a matter of fact, she did write to apologize a few days after I left,' Troy told him. 'She said that she might have made an error of judgement and that if she had wronged me, she was sorry.'

'I see … not a fulsome apology, but you might have received a warmer one if you had gone down to see her.'

'I neither wish for a further apology nor expect one,' Troy said, his nostrils slightly flared, which was a sign that he was still angry. 'It is a matter of trust, Father. I see no future for a marriage when the woman involved does not trust me. It would be a recipe for unhappiness for us both.'

'Perhaps you are right,' his father agreed. 'I was sorry for it, though. Marianne is a nicely behaved gel. You might have done worse.'

'Yes, perhaps,' Troy said. 'I do not think it will take her long to forget me, however. Barney stayed on after I left and he has written me a long and foolish letter about betraying my trust but not being able to help himself. It appears that he intends to propose to her soon, and believes that she may accept him.'

'I had heard something, which is why I came up. I thought you might wish to speak to her...'

'Well, you wasted your time, Father,' Troy said, his eyes glinting in the firelight. He had not yet completely forgiven his father, and he was still smarting, both from what he considered the insults to his honour and the way Marianne had turned to Barney so swiftly. Not that he minded who she married, but his pride had suffered a blow from which it had not yet recovered. It was a strange irony that Barney had been guilty of the very thing she had accused Troy of, and he wondered what Marianne would say if she knew. Not that Troy would tell her. Barney was welcome to her if she would have him.

Since coming to town, he had indulged in several drinking bouts with his friends, which had done nothing to restore his ego and had resulted in him feeling wretched for hours in the mornings.

'When are you coming home?' Lord Pelham asked as his son continued to stare moodily into the fire. It was March now and he considered that this estrangement between them had gone on long enough. 'I'm sorry if I offended you over this business, Troy – but it was such a shock.'

'Yes, I expect so,' Troy admitted, and a wry smile played briefly over his lips. He turned to his father. 'I'm going down to Newmarket to stay with Tubby Brocklehurst for a few weeks. He has some horses in training and I'm interested in seeing them. He has asked if I will help fund him for the flat season, and I might if I think the bloodstock is promising. I may come up when the season is under way. If you and my brother are in residence I shall see you both then.'

Lord Pelham realized that this was as much as he could expect from his elder son for the moment. It was a step towards healing the breach, which he was heartily glad of, for he had regretted words spoken in haste.

'I daresay we shall come up for a few weeks,' he said, and cleared his throat. 'It is good to see friends and your mother always came for the season, though I sometimes felt I could do without the rattle and fuss, but I accepted it for her sake. We did pretty well together, Lady

Pelham and I...' He sighed. 'I miss her, but she had become very frail from her illness.'

'We all miss Mama,' Troy said. His mother had contracted a wasting sickness three years earlier and died during a cold winter that had dragged her down. 'I would hope for a marriage at least as happy as yours, sir. That is why I have wished Barney good luck. Next time I shall choose more carefully, I assure you.'

'Well, let us say no more about the wretched business,' Lord Pelham said. 'I shall come up some time in April, and Andrew intends to stay with me before he goes off to train as an officer. You may join us when you please.'

'I always love staying at your home,' Sarah told Lucy as they walked in the park together. Situated on the outskirts of Newmarket, it had extensive grounds, which bordered on the Brocklehurst Racing Stables, and they could see some horses grazing in the meadow beyond. 'Just think, this time next week I shall be in London.'

'Yes, I do envy you,' Lucy said with a sigh. 'I wish I was a year older and then my mother would have allowed me to accompany you and Aunt Helen.'

'Yes, I wish you were coming too,' Sarah said. 'Shall we go and have a look at the horses? I slipped an apple in my pocket before we came out. It is a bit wrinkled but I cut it into four and that will be a piece for each of them.'

'Do you think we ought?' Lucy said. It wasn't the first time they had fed the horses little titbits but she felt guilty over it. 'Mr Brockle-hurst has those horses in training...'

'Well, one piece of apple isn't going to hurt, is it?' Sarah started towards the three-bar fence, putting her foot on the first bar and then straddling it. Her dress caught and she pulled it free, jumping down on the other side. 'Come on, Lucy. They won't hurt you.'

'I'll stay here and watch,' Lucy said; she was a bit nervous of the high-spirited horses. She was used to riding her well-trained and docile mare, but the racing horses were nervous, un-predictable creatures. 'I'm not sure you ought to go right up to them, Sarah.' Previously, they had fed them from the safe side of the fence.

'Oh, they won't harm me,' Sarah said con-fidently. She had been in and out of her father's stables since she was introduced to her first pony. She had hung around the yard to watch the stallion being put to the mare, which had answered a lot of questions for her that she would never have dared to ask her mother. 'I've fed them several times now. They know me...'

Lucy watched anxiously as her bolder cousin walked towards the horses. All four had their heads down, grazing the lush grass, but as she approached the black mare with a white star on her forehead put her head up, her eyes rolling as she sniffed Sarah's scent.

'Here you are,' Sarah said in a soft, coaxing voice. She took a piece of apple from her pocket, offering it on the palm of her hand for the mare to take, and smiled as the soft lips tickled her hand. The mare looked at her expectantly, waiting for more, but Sarah was determined to share the apple equally. She took another piece from her pocket and approached the next horse, but the mare did not approve and as she held out the offering, it charged the other horse, knocking Sarah to the ground in the process. She saw the two horses jostling and had just managed to roll away out of danger of the flashing hooves when she heard a shout from behind her. In another moment two men came running towards her. While one of them tried to stop the horses from damaging each other, the second, rather plumper than his friend, helped her to her feet.

'Are you all right, miss?' he asked, looking anxious. 'You really ought not to get too close to them, particularly when Diamond Star is coming into heat. She is very temperamental just at the moment...' He flushed as he realized what he had said to a young lady. 'Excuse me ... I ought not to have said such a thing to you.'

'No, you ought to have told her she was a damned idiot and had no right feeding your horses at all!' The second man had managed to sort the horses out, sending them cantering off across the field in opposite directions. 'What the hell did you imagine you were playing at?' He glared at her and then did a double take. 'Sarah! What the blazes are you doing here?'

'I am staying with Lucy,' Sarah replied, hanging on to the shreds of her dignity by a thread. 'I am sorry if I have upset the horses, Mr Brocklehurst. I have fed them quite safely before, though I must admit it was from the other side of the fence.'

'And that is where you should have stayed,' Troy said, his voice still harsh, though less outraged than it had been. 'Not that you should be feeding them at all. What did you give the mare? I hope it wasn't sugar or anything stupid?'

'Just a piece of apple,' Sarah said, showing him another piece from her pocket. 'I didn't think it would harm them.'

'It won't,' Tubby said, because he didn't enjoy getting one of Troy's set-downs himself, and he liked the plucky young girl. 'The main thing is that you aren't hurt, miss ... I am sorry, I don't know your name, though I have met Lucy, of course.'

'I am Sarah Trenwith,' she replied, smiling gratefully at him. 'I am sorry I gave you a fright, sir. I shan't be that foolish again – but may I give them apple from the other side of the fence?'

'No harm in that, is there, Troy?'

'As long as you stick to a slice of apple and don't start feeding them sweets or sugar. These horses will be in training soon, apart from the mare, which may be breeding – if we are lucky.'

'Thank you,' Sarah said. 'I suppose I've blotted my copybook now. You won't want to show me around the stables?'

'Oh, I think we can do that,' Tubby said, before Troy could jump down her throat, 'but under proper supervision. Not this afternoon, because we have a few things arranged that wouldn't be suitable for young ladies to watch

54

– but if you would care to call in the morning? I am sure that my mother would be delighted to receive both you and Lucy to lunch afterwards.'

'Oh, I should have loved that,' Sarah said, 'but I am afraid that this is my last day here. I'm going home in the morning. My mother is taking me to London next week and I have to have some fittings for new dresses. I shall buy most of them in town, of course, but I need one or two before I'm fit to be seen. At least, that is what my mother says...' It had actually been her sister who had told her she wasn't fit to be seen in polite company, but Sarah worried that Troy might still be suffering from a bruised heart, and so had substituted her mother for Marianne. 'I may be allowed another visit with Lucy in the summer – perhaps next time?'

'Yes, rather,' Tubby said, liking her more each time she spoke. 'I shall be popping up to town with my mother in a week or two. Perhaps we shall see each other then?'

'Yes, I hope so,' Sarah said. 'And it was very decent of you not to grumble at me for upsetting your horses, sir.'

'Wouldn't dream of grumbling at a young lady like you,' Tubby said gallantly. 'You don't want to take notice of Troy, he's in a bit of a mood, you know...' The penny suddenly dropped and he realized that Sarah must be Troy's ex-fiancée's sister. 'Yes, of course, you do know...' His neck flushed bright red, and he was clearly embarrassed.

'I was angry with Sarah for risking injury to

herself and the horses,' Troy said, his eyes narrowed as he looked at her. 'It had nothing to do with the fact that Marianne jilted me.'

'No, of course not,' Sarah said, and gave him a brilliant smile. 'I thoroughly deserved every word. And I am truly sorry.'

Troy nodded. 'I might have asked if you were hurt?'

'No, I managed to roll out of the way – but I could have been if you had not arrived so opportunely. I have to thank you for your prompt action, Troy. You risked injury yourself for my sake.'

'I would have done it for anyone,' Troy said, but his eyes were no longer cold as he looked at her. 'That was quick thinking, Sarah. Well done! Most of the ladies I know would have been screaming their heads off or fainting if they had experienced anything as unpleasant as that little incident.'

'Oh, I've been thrown a few times, and my father's stallion gets a bit out of hand at times, but I don't fear horses. I adore them.'

Tubby gave her a look of such approval that Troy snorted. His friend was already halfway to being caught in Sarah's toils. It seemed that the Trenwith sisters only had to smile at a man to have him begging for more.

'You should return to your cousin,' he said, his voice harsh once more as he thought of his friend's probable disappointment. 'And please remember not to get too close to highly-strung horses in future. Next time I might not be around to save you.'

Sarah noticed the flash of anger in his eyes and turned away, feeling hurt. Why did he have to be so cross about it? The horses were not his, and Mr Brocklehurst had been so generous to her. Perhaps Troy was still angry because Marianne had jilted him, even though he was pretending that it didn't matter?

She joined her cousin, who had watched the whole thing anxiously from the other side of the fence. Lucy immediately pounced on her, looking at the tear to her gown and the muddy patch where she had rolled on the ground.

'Are you all right, Sarah?'

'Yes, fine,' Sarah said. 'I might have a bruise on my thigh where I fell, but otherwise I'm all right. Don't make a fuss, Lucy. It is all over.'

'It might have been different if Troy Pelham hadn't come when he did,' Lucy said. 'It was him with Mr Brocklehurst, wasn't it?'

'Yes,' Sarah said. 'He was cross with me for upsetting the horses – but Mr Brocklehurst was very kind.'

'I told you not to do it,' Lucy said. 'I was so frightened. I thought you were sure to be killed.'

'Well, I wasn't,' Sarah said, feeling that her dignity had been bruised more than her body. 'It's over and I would rather not talk about it. Let's go back to the house. I need to change my dress before anyone sees it – and I want you to promise not to tell anyone, Lucy. If your mother mentioned it to mine, I might not be allowed to go to London.'

'I shan't tell anyone,' Lucy promised. 'If

Mama sees your dress, we'll just say you slipped on a patch of mud – all right?'

'Yes, thank you,' Sarah said, and linked arms with her. 'You are my best friend, Lucy. I wish you were coming to London with us, but I don't suppose your mother will relent if we ask her.'

'Not a chance,' Lucy said, and smiled ruefully. 'I've got to wait until I am eighteen, and that's her last word on the subject – but you can write and tell me all about it, and perhaps you can come and stay again.'

'Yes, I shall write to you,' Sarah said. 'I would like to visit again in the summer but we shall have to see what happens in town...'

She knew that her mother might be hoping she would become engaged, though of course in the circumstances it might be better if Marianne were to be married first.

Sarah didn't mind waiting. There was only one man she wanted to marry, and Troy wasn't interested. After what had happened that morning, Sarah wasn't sure that Troy liked her at all.

Three

'Yes, Sarah, that dress suits you very well,' Lady Trenwith said as she looked at her younger daughter in the buttercup-yellow silk gown they had commissioned from a fashionable modiste as soon as they reached town. 'I think you were wise to choose deeper colours rather than the pastels that look so well on Marianne.' She turned to her other daughter, a vision in white, a slight frown crinkling her brow. Lady Trenwith had expected that Marianne would be engaged to Barney Hale by now and was a little disappointed that it had not happened. 'You look beautiful as usual, Marianne.'

Sarah knew why her mother was annoyed with Marianne, but she also knew why her sister had held Barney off for the time being. Marianne wouldn't admit it but she was regretting her hasty dismissal of Troy. Sarah felt a little sorry for Barney, because Marianne had him dangling on a string; she hadn't said yes and she hadn't said no. It would be unseemly to be in too much haste, and she wanted to be certain of her feelings this time – that was the excuse she had used, because Barney had told Sarah so in a fit of the blues.

'Just keep being nice to her,' Sarah had

replied encouragingly. 'I am sure she will make up her mind eventually.'

Sarah sometimes felt a twinge of guilt when she thought of poor Barney. He might not have stayed on at Trenwith Hall that time if she hadn't encouraged him, and he would probably have given up on Marianne long before this without Sarah's encouragement. Sarah knew that her motives were less than pure, for she could not help hoping that perhaps Troy would turn to her one day. Not that her recent encounter with the horses had done anything to improve her chances! He must think her all kinds of a fool now.

'Come along then, girls,' Lady Trenwith said, a little sigh on her lips. 'I think Mrs Blundell's dance will be pleasant.' It was just a small affair and not one of the most prestigious taking place that evening. However, the invitations had been slow in arriving and they had accepted before the Devonshires' card had arrived. It would have been the height of rudeness to cancel Mrs Blundell's dance at this late stage, especially as she was a particular friend of Lady Trenwith. 'It is time we were on our way. The carriage is waiting.'

Marianne pulled a face behind her mother's back as they followed her down the stairs of their London house.

'Barney says his father has bought two of the latest automobiles,' Marianne whispered to Sarah. 'Why we have to cling to a carriage and horses I do not know. A luxury car is far more comfortable.'

'Papa did suggest it, but Mama does not like the idea,' Sarah told her. 'I think he will win her over in the end, but you know how old-fashioned she is about some things.'

Marianne pulled a face, but Sarah noticed that she claimed more than her fair share of the seat in the carriage, spreading the skirts of her diaphanous white gown, which was made of tulle Arachne over silk, on either side of her – something she would not have been able to do in the motorcar she claimed to favour.

Sarah had kept an open mind about the evening in front of them. It would probably be rather boring, for she could not think that Mrs Blundell would have captured anyone of note, which meant that Troy would not attend. They had been in town for three days now, and this was their first engagement. So far she had seen nothing of him. She was not even sure that he would be in town, though Barney had assured her that he was coming.

There was a blaze of light outside the Blundells' house. It seemed that Mr Blundell, who was a wealthy businessman and prospective candidate for the Tory party, had invested in electricity and was showing off its benefits for the comfort of his guests.

It seemed very bright to Sarah as she followed her mother and sister inside. At home in the Hampshire countryside they were still using oil lamps and candles, though they had gas in the London house. Her father had spoken of converting to electricity at home, but her mother had yet to be persuaded of the benefits of the

61

twentieth century.

Mrs Blundell greeted them cordially, complimenting both girls on their dresses, though she was rather warmer to Sarah than to Marianne. Sarah wondered about it, for she had thought that most people had accepted what had happened as being Troy's fault in some way. However, as they went through into the gallery, where the dancing was about to begin, she understood the reason for their hostess's odd looks at her sister. Troy Pelham was already there, drinking champagne as he talked to his host, Tubby Brocklehurst and Barney Hale, as well as three other gentlemen who were not known to Sarah.

She saw that Troy had noticed their arrival, because his expression tightened. She wondered if he had chosen the Blundells' affair over the more prestigious one taking place that evening because he imagined they would be attending the Devonshires' dance.

For a few moments the Trenwith party stood by themselves. Sarah shot a look at her sister and saw that Marianne was looking pale, which was not surprising because she had always been used to being the centre of attention at any affair she attended. Sarah felt quite sorry for her, especially when the first people to actually come and speak to them were all older ladies, friends of Lady Trenwith. It looked as if Marianne was being given the cold shoulder, because even her mother's friends had a warmer smile for Sarah than her sister.

And then two gentlemen began walking

towards them: Troy and Mr Brocklehurst. Sarah knew they were coming to them, and her breath caught. Who would Troy choose to dance with – her or Marianne? Her heart sank as Troy bowed to Marianne.

'Good evening, Miss Trenwith,' he said. 'Would you give me the pleasure of this dance, please?'

Marianne accepted with alacrity, her face lighting up. She looked so beautiful that Sarah's hopes zoomed to nothing. If Troy had forgiven her, he would probably ask her to resume their engagement.

'Miss Sarah – would you be kind enough to favour me with this dance?'

Sarah smiled at Tubby as he led her on to the dance floor. He was a little heavier of build than Troy, but exceptionally light on his feet and she soon found herself enjoying their dance immensely, so that when he asked if he could reserve two more during the evening, she accepted with pleasure, telling him to write his name where he pleased on her card.

'You are the most delightful girl, Miss Sarah,' Tubby said, looking at her adoringly. 'I shall anticipate our next dance with pleasure.'

He returned her to her mother, just as Marianne had accepted Barney's invitation to dance next with him. Sarah caught a look of petulance on her sister's face but did not know what had caused it, but then, as she hesitated, Troy's voice spoke from behind her.

'Will you dance with me, Sarah – if you haven't promised all of them to Tubby?'

'You know I could not do that,' Sarah said, her heart fluttering. 'It is kind of you to ask me, sir. We were not sure that you would wish to acknowledge us publicly.'

'I would rather you called me Troy,' he said, as he led her towards to dance floor. 'I asked your sister to dance because I wanted to show everyone here that both Marianne and I are civilized. We may have decided we do not wish to marry, but we can still be polite to each other.'

'Oh, I see...' she said, though of course she didn't. 'Then you aren't ... it isn't on again?'

'No,' Troy said, and the set of his mouth left her in no doubt that he meant it. 'However, we are bound to meet each other everywhere, and it would be awkward if we were not seen to have made up our differences.'

Sarah gazed up at him as they danced. She had enjoyed partnering Tubby, but this was like floating on a cloud, like dreaming. She had never felt so happy in her entire life!

'I think that is very ... gallant of you, Troy. I thought for a moment that Marianne was going to be frozen out...' And so had he, she realized, which is why he and Tubby had acted so swiftly. 'Or was it Mr Brocklehurst's idea?'

'I leave that to you to decide,' Troy said, an enigmatic expression on his face. 'Am I a hero or a villain – believe as you will, Sarah.'

'Of course you are not a villain,' Sarah said hotly. 'I have never thought that for one moment – and you should know it. I wrote to you, even if you threw my letter away without

64

reading it.'

'Now what makes you think I would do that? It was a source of solace to me in the darkest hours.' His smile teased and mocked her.

'You wretch,' Sarah said, her eyes flashing mischief at him. 'I suppose you think I am the world's biggest idiot for going into the field to feed the mares?'

'The jury is out on that one,' Troy said. 'I hardly know you, and you do seem to be accident prone.'

'You mean my ankle ... and then the horses. How was I to know she was coming into season, poor thing? It is such a wretched time for all females that I would have understood not to approach her, if I'd known...' She saw the laughter in his eyes and, without thinking, stuck her tongue out at him. He laughed out loud then and she flushed. 'And that was most unladylike and will earn a reprimand from Mama if she saw me.'

'On two counts I imagine,' Troy said dryly. 'You are an unusual girl, Sarah. I promise that your mama shall not learn of your unruly tongue from me.'

Sarah glowered at him, but reined in the retort that trembled on her lips.

'I did not expect to see you here this evening, sir.'

'Barney told us you were coming,' Troy said. 'Naturally, Tubby wanted to come and I decided that I would sort any awkwardness out from the start. By the way, I happen to be very fond of Tubby. I should be most distressed if he were hurt...'

Sarah understood what he was saying to her and nodded. 'I should also be sorry to hurt Mr Brocklehurst. I like him very much as a friend, and I shall try to maintain our friendship.'

'Ah, I see. It is as I thought,' Troy said. 'I must steer his attention elsewhere. It is a pity your cousin Lucy is not here – though she does not share your passion for horses.'

'Lucy likes horses. She just prefers them to be well trained and gentle.'

'And I suppose you prefer something with more mettle?'

'Yes. I like spirit in anything, sir – horses, dogs and people.'

Troy's eyes caught fire as he saw the mischief in her face. 'Poor Tubby,' he said, and sighed. 'He will suffer if you reject him, but I think he would suffer far more if you did not.'

Sarah arched her brows at him, but he shook his head. The music had ended and he escorted her back to her mother, bowing his head to both of them. He did not ask Sarah for a further dance, and some minutes later she learned that he had not asked Marianne either, which was the source of her sister's petulance.

However, his gesture had broken the ice, and both girls had a ready supply of partners, though Sarah did not sit down all evening, apart from supper, and her sister was forced to sit at least three dances out. Sarah felt sorry for Marianne, because she knew that in the past the gentlemen would have queued up to be her partner.

66

It did not surprise her that Marianne accepted Barney's invitation to eat supper with him, though Sarah might have chosen from half a dozen eager to wait on her. It was being whispered that she was by far the best of the Trenwith girls, perhaps not quite as stunning to look at as her sister, but she had a ready smile, a sense of humour and a gentle kindness – something Marianne lacked.

Sarah chose Tubby to dine with but included her mother in the acceptance, hoping to show that she was pleased to be his friend, but wished for nothing more. However, once they were seated, several other gentlemen brought their sisters or friends over to join them, and Sarah was soon the centre of a large circle. It was a little disappointing that Troy was not amongst them. She thought that he had slipped away earlier, perhaps to his club where he might spend the evening playing cards or billiards.

She was aware of a sense of loss, but contented herself with the friends she had, giving no sign that the evening had lost its sparkle for her. She was rewarded with a deluge of invitations, from card parties, trips to the theatre in a group – properly chaperoned, of course, to drives in carriages and automobiles. She referred most of the invitations to her mother, though accepted an engagement to go shopping with Miss Mary Harris and to drive out in Tubby's new Daimler Phaeton, of which he was inordinately proud.

When the evening finally ended, she felt that

it had been a success, and was pleased with her mother's words of praise on the way home.

'You behaved very well, Sarah,' Lady Trenwith said. 'I was proud of you, my dear. I think it not unlikely that you may receive more than one proposal this trip, but if you should wish to accept any of the gentlemen, you must bear it in mind that I could not sanction a marriage before Christmas. So you should ask for a little time. I do not think long engagements are necessarily a good thing.'

'I am not in any hurry to become engaged, Mama,' Sarah said. 'I would rather get to know someone first.'

'Sensible girl!'

She heard Marianne sniff, and then her sister announced defiantly that she had accepted an offer to marry Barney Hale.

'Marianne!' Lady Trenwith looked at her sharply. 'Is that not rather sudden? I thought you had not made up your mind?'

'Well, now I have,' Marianne said. They had arrived home and were helped down from the carriage by a groom. Marianne maintained her silence until they were in the front parlour, and then looked at her mother and sister defiantly. 'Barney asked me again, and I said that I would marry him quite soon. I see no point in waiting, Mama. I like him better than ... anyone else I have met and I think I should like to be married.'

'Well, perhaps that would be for the best,' her mother said. 'If you are certain this time? I do not wish for a repeat of that last unpleasant business.'

'I am certain,' Marianne said. 'I cannot imagine why I ever said I would marry Troy Pelham. He has a sarcastic tongue, and I do not truly like him. I shall be much happier married to Barney.' She could twist him around her little finger, and she had always been a little bit afraid of Troy, even when he had been nice to her. That evening he had been polite but distant, making her feel as if she were someone he had never met before. Having hoped for a passionate declaration of regret and a desire to renew their relationship, she had felt rejected and humiliated when he did not ask to dance with her more than once. 'Barney loves me. I do not think that Troy really cared for me at all.'

Sarah smiled and kissed her sister on the cheek. Inside, she was feeling wildly happy, but she tried to conceal it. 'Are you sure you want to marry Barney?' she asked. 'Even if you don't want Troy, there are lots of other pleasant gentlemen out there.'

'Yes, of course I know that,' Marianne said sharply. She had not enjoyed seeing most of them clustered around her sister that evening. She had been used to considering herself the beauty of the family, and it did not suit her to be obliged to sit out while her sister danced. Once she was engaged to Barney she could dance with him as often as she wished. It had been made clear to her that Troy was not interested in her, and she had found that most of the gentlemen who had asked her to dance had kept their distance. She would not receive a string of proposals this time, and so she had decided to settle for Barney. He would inherit his father's title and his property one day, and she believed it was the best she could do in the circumstances.

It was all Troy Pelham's fault! If he had told her the truth she might not have lost her temper and broken their engagement. It wasn't that she was breaking her heart for him, but her pride had received a damaging blow, for she knew that she owed her success that evening to him, and that rankled.

Having achieved what he had set out to do, Troy left the Blundells' house before supper. He walked to his club, which was a mere stroll away, feeling pleased with himself. He had done his duty, as he saw it, which was to publicly heal the breach between himself and the Trenwith family. Lady Trenwith had been a bit stiff with him, but she had seen the sense of what he was doing and put on a polite manner that fooled those who did not know her well. It would go some way to stemming the gossip, and perhaps make things easier for both Marianne and Sarah...

A little smile played about his mouth as he thought about Sarah. She was very different from her sister, and he had been highly amused by her comments about Tubby's mare. Her behaviour would have shocked her mother and the old tabbies who imagined they still ruled society, though in truth their reign was almost done. Things were changing swiftly, despite the way some clung to the old rules. He knew quite a few young ladies who were willing to flout them; they considered themselves suffragettes, pioneering women who were fighting for women's rights. Some of them were willing to chain themselves to railings or suffer the indignity of being sent to prison, and force-fed if they went on hunger strike. He could just see Sarah chaining herself to the railings outside Buckingham Palace, and it made him chuckle. He wondered if Lady Trenwith had any idea of her daughter's true nature. He doubted it, for he had seen little of it when he was courting Marianne.

Would it have made a difference if he had? Troy frowned as he reviewed his own thoughts. He had pursued Marianne because she was the season's prize, and he had been exhilarated by the chase. It was unlikely that anything would have deflected him, though he had soon realized his mistake once his ring was on Marianne's finger.

He was in no hurry to put a ring on anyone else's finger, he decided. Another year or two of freedom wouldn't hurt...

The invitations arrived thick and fast after the evening of Mrs Blundell's ball, and Sarah knew that her mother was very relieved. Troy's action had lifted the slight cloud that had hung over them as a family, for it seemed that many of the more important society hostesses had taken his side. The Trenwiths would not have been ostracized, but were unlikely to have been invited to some of the most prestigious affairs had he pointedly ignored them. Lord Pelham and his two sons, Troy and Andrew, were extremely popular, as well as influential, for Pelham was a personal advisor to a member of the royal family, and often at court. It was hoped that Troy would opt for politics or the law, though Andrew had already decided on a military career and was due to enter the Royal Military College at Sandhurst. Troy had himself been interested in entering the forces, but as the heir it had not been considered suitable.

Sarah had met Troy on several occasions since the Blundells' dance: a dinner at Lady Markham's house; Mrs Wrexham's soirée; and a card party hosted by Tubby Brocklehurst's aunt Millicent. However, she had not attended another dance until this evening. It was perhaps the most prestigious affair so far that season, and would be attended by everyone of any consequence.

When Sarah entered the already overflowing reception rooms with her mother, sister and Barney, she looked eagerly for Troy's commanding figure, but was disappointed to find that he was nowhere to be seen. Nor, it seemed, was Tubby, and that was a surprise for he was usually at every function she attended.

However, Sarah did not lack for partners and her card was soon filled. She loved dancing and the pleasure it gave her soon helped to alleviate her disappointment. However, after supper, she saw that Troy and Mr Brocklehurst had just arrived. There was a burst of cheering and several of the gentlemen were slapping them on the back or shaking their hands.

'What is all that about?' Sarah asked Barney as he came to remind her that she had promised him this dance.

'Oh, they had a horse running at Newmarket and it won by several lengths,' Barney said. 'I won a hundred guineas on it myself, because the last time it ran it came in a poor fourth and the odds were high. Tubby swears it is because of the new regime Troy has imposed on his stables, and they both won a packet.'

'Oh, I see,' Sarah said, and laughed. 'They have been to the races. No wonder they are late. The ball of the season cannot match up to a good race on the flat.'

Barney looked at her and then grinned, because Sarah was such an easy companion, so different from her sister. 'We men are such fools, are we not?' he said. 'To put racing above the company of beautiful ladies.'

'You did not,' Sarah reminded him.

'No ... but that is different,' Barney said, and looked slightly rueful. 'I could not disappoint Marianne.'

'No, of course you could not,' Sarah said, and then looked up in surprise as someone tapped Barney on the shoulder. 'Troy...'

'You don't mind me cutting in, old fellow?' Troy said, and whisked her away before Barney could answer.

'That was not kind of you,' Sarah said in mock reproof. 'It was Barney's dance – his only dance with me.'

'Precisely,' Troy said, a wicked gleam in his eyes. 'I don't think I could get away with it with Marsham or Barrington, and I have only looked in for the chance of seeing you. I wanted to tell you that we won today. Do you remember the piebald that you tried to feed the apple to that day? The one the broody mare went for?' Sarah nodded. 'That was the one. I thought you might like to know. We have quite a few chances of winning this year, but we shan't get odds like that again – they'll be ready for us in future.' His eyes were alight with devilment and the lust for life, and Sarah felt his excitement as if it were her own.

'It must have been very exciting for you. I should have liked to be there to see it win.'

'Perhaps you'll be at Royal Ascot in June? We have an entry for the Gold Cup.'

'Oh, I should like that,' Sarah said. 'But I don't know if we shall attend. Mama will be preparing for Marianne's wedding when we go home, and I suppose there won't be time.'

'If you could wangle a few days with your cousin, you could come with us,' Troy said. 'Lady Brocklehurst will be one of the party and some other ladies. I could ask them to invite you and Lucy.'

'I should love to come,' Sarah said. 'I know Father likes to attend sometimes, but Mama does not care for racing and she will make an excuse if she can.'

'Escape to your cousin's,' Troy said, and then bowed his head to her as the music ended. 'I know I must relinquish you to your string of admirers now, but I shall be at Lady Endicott's card party tomorrow – do you go?'

'Yes, I believe so,' Sarah said. 'Thank you for … you know…'

He winked at her and walked away, pausing to talk to a few of the gentlemen before leaving the room. Sarah's heart skipped a beat. He had come to the ball only to speak to her and he had not danced with anyone else. Surely that was a sign that he was interested in her?

She smiled to herself, nursing her pleasure as she waited for her next partner to claim her. If she could just persuade her mother to let her visit Lucy she might spend a lot of time in Troy's company, and who knew what might happen then?

'You should be careful,' Marianne said to Sarah the next morning. 'People are beginning to talk. If you are not careful you will become an object of ridicule.'

'What are you talking about?' Sarah was in her bedchamber looking through her dresses as she tried to decide which she should wear that evening. She could not decide between a pink silk and a pale blue satin with a tulle overskirt.

'I mean the way you are making eyes at Troy Pelham,' Marianne said, her mouth drawn into a thin, spiteful line. 'I should have thought you would be more aware. He will end by breaking your heart. Surely you have learned from the way he behaved towards me?'

'I believe it was you who made the mistake,'

Sarah said. 'You threw away what you had and now you regret it – don't you?'

Sarah saw a flash of temper in her sister's eyes and knew that she had gone too far.

'You are a stupid little girl,' Marianne snapped. 'He was having an affair with that Hastings woman, and we had only just become engaged. What kind of a husband do you think he would make? You could never be certain he was faithful to you.'

'I don't know what kind of husband Troy would make,' Sarah answered honestly. 'He might have affairs, I suppose. A lot of men do, don't they? I think Papa had a mistress for some years, though Mama pretended she didn't know. I wouldn't like that, but I think it happens in a lot of marriages.'

'Well, he won't marry you,' Marianne said. 'He is just making a fool of you to spite me. I jilted him and he hates me for it so he is making a play for you, but it won't come to marriage. You would be foolish to expect it.'

'You don't know what is in his mind,' Sarah said, fending off her sister's ill temper, 'and you don't know what is in mine. I'm not in any hurry to get married. I like Troy but I like several other gentlemen – and I'm allowed to dance with anyone I please, as long as I don't show any partiality for them or behave badly.'

'You were laughing with him like a silly little girl!'

'Was I? Well, he was making me laugh. Troy has a wonderful sense of humour, don't you think?'

76

Marianne stared at her. She had never known when Troy was jesting and when he was serious. It was one of the things that had made her uncomfortable.

'Well, you won't be warned,' she said. 'But be careful, Sarah. If people start to talk, Mama will not be pleased with you.'

'Perhaps she will if Troy does ask me to marry him.' A little devil sat on Sarah's shoulder, prompting her.

'Neither Mama nor Papa would hear of it,' Marianne said. 'They were furious with him for going off the way he did and not trying to put things right. They would say no if he asked their permission.'

'Why should they?' Sarah sensed that her sister was jealous of her, even though she would be married within a few weeks. 'If Troy wanted to marry me and I said yes – why should they deny us?'

'Because it would cause another scandal,' Marianne said. 'People would suspect it had been going on all the time – and they might think you had behaved in a way you ought not...'

'No!' Sarah was horrified as she realized what Marianne was implying. 'You are wicked to say such a thing! And I shan't take any notice of you. I shall speak to Troy when I please – and if I want to marry him I shall...'

She walked out of the room, leaving Marianne to stare after her in frustration.

They were making up fours at whist and Sarah

felt a flutter of delight as Troy told her that he had requested her for his partner that evening. They were playing against Mr Brundle and Lady Ardingly, and Sarah found herself being received with smiles and friendly words.

'I do hope I shan't disappoint,' Sarah told him. 'I enjoy playing, but I am not sure I am up to the standard you and your friends would expect.'

'Just follow my lead,' Troy said. 'I daresay we shall take our share of tricks. Besides, winning isn't the object of the evening – it is having a good time and enjoying the company of friends. If I wanted to gamble seriously I should go to one of my clubs.'

'Oh, I see,' Sarah said, and felt better. 'Then I think we shall have a nice evening together, Troy.' She gave him a shy smile, feeling her heart leap when he smiled back at her.

It was a very enjoyable evening, for Sarah found that by watching Troy's lead and what the others had played, she was able to help her partner win several tricks. In actual fact, the honours were almost even when they abandoned play to go into supper, and Lady Ardingly suggested that she and Sarah join forces afterwards and challenge the men.

Sarah found the idea stimulating, and they made a fearsome partnership, beating the men by four games to two, something that Lady Ardingly insisted on telling everyone when they finally broke up for the evening. Lady Ardingly was one of the most fashionable ladies present, her gown elegant with a touch of the oriental style that the French designer Paquin had made so popular. It looked as if it might have come from the designer's own hands, which would not be surprising, as the lady was extremely wealthy.

'You must visit me one day at home,' she told Sarah before they parted company. 'Come and have tea with me – just you. Would your mama allow it?'

'Perhaps if you asked her,' Sarah said, feeling pleased to have made a new friend. 'I should like it very well, ma'am.'

'You must call me Fenella,' the lady said and smiled. 'Come tomorrow if you can. I shall ask your mama.'

Sarah was a little surprised that her mother agreed, but she was preoccupied with Marianne's bridal clothes and she had arranged for fittings throughout the next day, which would have meant Sarah had little to do but stand around and watch.

'Yes, of course you may go. I shall send you in the barouche and the coachman may wait for you. I shall not be needing a carriage until the evening.'

'Thank you, Mama. That is very kind of you.'

'Lady Ardingly has a nephew she is very fond of,' Lady Trenwith said thoughtfully, when they were alone later. 'There are no children of the marriage and the nephew will inherit everything, I imagine. You may use your time profitably if you choose, Sarah. I am afraid that we shall have to go home sooner than I had planned. I may take you somewhere else after the wedding – but that must come first. There is plenty of time for you, after all. You are still only eighteen.'

'Yes, of course, Mama,' Sarah said. 'I know that Marianne's wedding must come first.'

'You are a sensible girl,' Lady Trenwith said. 'Your sister is lucky to have come through this awkwardness unscathed, but I shall be happier when she is wed.'

Sarah dressed in a pale peach tea-gown for her appointment the next afternoon. She wore a large chip straw hat with tulle veiling, and allowed her hair to flow freely on her shoulders. Her shoes were elegant and fashioned of a soft kid, her gloves white and her parasol a shade darker peach than her gown. Because it was a beautifully warm afternoon, she asked the coachman to leave the top down, enjoying the fresh air as they made the journey out to Lady Ardingly's home, which was situated on the road to Richmond.

It was a large house, imposing and set back in good grounds with a crunchy gravel drive leading up to the front door. A maid was waiting at the door to admit Sarah and show her into the drawing room, and as they approached she heard the sound of male laughter. She had imagined it was just a tête-à-tête and hesitated uncertainly before she entered the room.

There were several other guests already seated on various chairs and sofas arranged tastefully in the huge room. Sarah saw at once that Troy was one of the guests, also Mr Brocklehurst. She had the oddest feeling that she had been invited especially for Troy's sake.

'Ah, there you are, dear Sarah,' Lady Ardingly said as she saw her. 'I am so glad you have come, I was feeling outnumbered amongst all these gentlemen. Please, come and sit down. I think you may not have met my niece, Miss Manley. Selina, say hello to Sarah Trenwith.'

There were just three ladies and six gentlemen, which made Sarah feel a little awkward initially, but then Troy stood up and invited her to sit by Selina Manley, standing by the fireplace to survey the room the better. Standing up he was even more impressive and seemed to impose his personality on the room. Sarah thought he was the most vibrant, most vital man she had ever met.

'Sarah,' he said, his gaze intent on her, 'yours is a fresh opinion, because you have heard none of the nonsense that has gone before – so tell me what you think of the suffragette movement?'

'That's hardly fair, Troy,' Tubby Brocklehurst protested, 'throwing her in at the deep end when we've all had our say before she arrived.'

'I don't mind giving an opinion,' Sarah said. 'I thought it quite disgraceful of Asquith to bring in the Cat and Mouse bill – to release a woman who has been on hunger strike for her health's sake, but to have the power to re-arrest her if the government considers she has done something unlawful cannot be right or fair. Poor Sylvia Pankhurst. I think she was treated appallingly.'

'Hear, hear, you are perfectly right,' Lady Ardingly said. 'I am glad that you are prepared to speak your mind, Sarah. We must support those brave ladies who are willing to suffer so much for our freedom.'

'You have never been anything but free, Fenella,' Troy said with a challenging look. 'All I am saying is that women should respect the law as far as it goes. I agree that it needs to be changed, but there are men with more fore-sight than Asquith, and it will be changed in good time.'

'But what is good time?' Selina Manley asked. 'Do you not think that the time is now, sir? Women have waited throughout the centuries for the rights that have been denied them. It is true that Fenella and others like her have always lived much as they pleased, but there are many women chained to brutal husbands with little recourse to the law, and all kinds of inequalities that need to be addres-sed.'

'She is right,' Tubby said. 'I applaud those women who chain themselves to the railings, knowing that they will probably be sent to prison, and treated shamefully. And some of them have been treated shamefully. You cannot deny that, Troy.'

'No, I would not deny it,' Troy said, a smile of wicked delight on his lips. 'I merely think it is undignified for ladies to behave in such a manner...'

He was howled down by the other gentlemen

present, and Sarah was amused, because she knew that he had chosen to play devil's advocate purely for the sake of mischief. When he had them all up in arms against him, he laughed and gave in gracefully. The conversation then turned to the performance of Mrs Patrick Campbell in Mr Bernard Shaw's play *Pygmalion*, in which she used an expletive that had now become all the rage.

They were such a lively, informed group that Sarah found herself listening more than she talked, but she enjoyed herself immensely, and the time rushed by so that before she knew it, everyone began to leave.

'It was lovely to have you here with us,' Lady Ardingly said as Sarah prepared to take her leave. 'I do hope we have not shocked you with all our silly arguments?'

'I did not think them in the least silly,' Sarah said, for some of the subjects the company had touched upon were controversial and not at all what she would hear at home. 'I have enjoyed myself very much, ma'am.'

'No, no, you must call me Fenella,' she said, and smiled. 'Ma'am or Lady Ardingly are both so formal, so ageing...' She laughed for she was not above five and thirty, and an extremely beautiful, elegant woman. 'Do come and visit us again. I am always at home on Tuesdays and Thursdays.'

'Unfortunately, we are going home sooner than we had planned for my sister's wedding,' Sarah said.

'Well, there is always the future. You will

come to town in the future, Sarah, perhaps when you are married and you may please yourself. You will not always be accountable to your mother – and if you choose wisely your husband will wish to please you. Is that not so, Troy?'

'Of course,' he said, and smiled at her. 'You are always right, Fenella. Would I dare to disagree even if you were not? May I escort you to your carriage, Sarah?'

Sarah inclined her head. She had been hoping for a few minutes alone with him, and she was very glad for him to walk her outside.

'So you liked my friends?' Troy's eyes quizzed her. 'You did not find them too outrageous?'

'I think you are the most outrageous of them all,' she told him, and saw the spark of laughter in his eyes. 'Tell me, what is your true position on the suffragette movement?'

'I support the motivation if not always the actions of various members. It was foolish of Emmeline Pankhurst to become involved in the use of arson, for instance. She can do her cause no good from prison. Several other incidents of a similar nature have taken place recently, and all it does is turn reasonable men against the perpetrators, while they end in prison.'

'But surely these ladies are martyrs to the cause?'

'Perhaps – though I think a more sensible course of action would bring swifter reform. Sylvia Pankhurst and her supporters must negotiate with those who truly wish to help them, and stop blowing things up. If they are not careful this foolishness will end in tragedy. And I do not forget that poor tragic woman who was killed when she threw herself in front of the King's horse at the Derby last year. That was a waste of a life – and the ruin of a damned good race!'

'Yes, perhaps you are right,' Sarah agreed, though she shook her head over his last remark, which she knew was meant to lighten their conversation. 'I think you would make a very good politician, sir – if you chose to be serious long enough to win your seat.'

'In a few years,' Troy said, with a shrug of his shoulders. 'For the moment ... I should have liked to join the army but Father does not approve.'

'You are his heir. He would not have you put yourself at risk should we be at war in the future.'

'I daresay you are right,' Troy said, and frowned. 'Sometimes I believe that may not be too far off, despite all the denials. This trouble in the Balkans may boil over and we shall be dragged into it.'

'Oh, surely not?' Sarah said, quite alarmed by the turn their conversation had taken. 'You do not seriously think that we could be involved in such a war?'

'No, no, of course not,' Troy said, seeing that he had distressed her. 'It is mere speculation, a moment of foolishness, Sarah. Forget that I said anything.

'You told Fenella that you were returning

home soon. Do you feel that you will be allowed to visit your cousin before the wedding?'

'Perhaps. Mama is wrapped up in Marianne at the moment. She might be pleased to get me out of the way for a while.'

'Then I shall hope to see you in the near future,' he said, and took her hand, lifting it briefly to his lips. 'It was a delight talking to you, Sarah. I hope we may talk again soon.'

In the carriage, being driven home, Sarah wondered what had made Troy speak of war. She knew that the papers had been printing reports of unrest in the Balkans for some months now, and she had read of various treaties and pacts. There were also rumours of an arms race in Europe, which the paper had said could end in war, but all that had seemed so far away that she had not given it a thought. Clearly the possibility had registered in Troy's mind, and she wondered what he would do if it were to happen. Yet she need not wonder, for instinctively she knew that he would be one of the first to answer the call to arms.

It seemed to Sarah then that a black cloud hovered over them and she shivered as she remembered things that had happened during the Crimean War, which she had read about in her father's books. Could something as cruel and terrible as that be about to happen again?

No, no, it could not! Sarah found it too horrible to contemplate. She did not want either Troy or his brother – or any of the other young men she knew – to be caught up in something like that...

Four

Sarah had been right to think that her mother would be too wrapped up in Marianne's needs to bother much with Sarah for a few weeks, and her request to be allowed to stay with her cousin was granted easily.

'It will be just as well if you do go for a visit,' Lady Trenwith said when asked. 'I have my hands full with your sister's wedding. You must return for that, naturally, but I have noticed that Marianne is irritated with you, and you will be best out of the way. I do not want her having a fit of the vapours and jilting Barney.'

'I am sure she would not, Mama, but I should like to visit Lucy again.'

'I shall send you in the carriage tomorrow. Your aunt told me you were welcome at any time and I have written to tell her to expect you.'

'Thank you, Mama,' Sarah said, and kissed her cheek. 'You are very good to me.'

'It has not escaped my notice that you enjoy Troy Pelham's company,' her mother said, giving her a sharp look. 'I have no objection to a friendship between you, but I would advise you not to become too friendly with him. I think your father would not approve of anything further between our families after the way he behaved.'

'But surely it was Marianne who jilted Troy? He has behaved very well to her, Mama. You must admit that, I think?'

'I do not fault him as a gentleman,' her mother said, looking stern. 'But if you became involved with him it might cause a scandal – and it would hurt your sister's feelings. I am sure you would not be so unkind as to deliberately cause your sister distress?'

Sarah was silent, because it was unfair of her mother to blame her for Marianne's situation. Marianne had made her own choice, and if she now regretted it she had only herself to blame. However, it was useless to protest, because Sarah had no idea of whether or not Troy was interested in her other than as a mere acquaintance. Sometimes when he looked at her in that provoking way of his, she thought that it was sheer devilment on his part, but at others his smile made her heart race and she felt that he cared for her deeply.

She turned away, the rebellion churning inside her. She must be careful, for her mother could forbid the visit with Lucy if she chose. However, if the chance to be with Troy came along Sarah would take it, and if he asked her to marry him she would say yes. She could not think beyond that, because it would be too awful if her father forbade them, and yet she felt that she was ready to defy even him to be with Troy.

Sarah looked out of her bedroom window. A period of sustained good weather had begun when she arrived to stay with her cousin, and it was going to be yet another lovely day. The hour was early. Sarah knew that both her aunt and her cousin would probably still be sleeping, but she was restless. She had walked to visit the horses at least once a day for the past four days, but so far she had seen no sign of either Troy or Tubby. She was beginning to wonder if they had gone off to another part of the country, to race their horses.

Dressing in a simple linen dress that would not take harm on a country walk, Sarah slipped the carrot she had wangled from the kitchen the previous day into her pocket. It was a little woody, for it had been stored throughout the winter and was past its best, but the horses would look for something and she did not like to disappoint them.

The servants were already about their work when she went downstairs. Sarah smiled at the maid dusting in the hall, and the footman left his brass polishing to open the door for her. They were not surprised to see her up and about before the rest of the household, because she often slipped out for a solitary walk when she stayed there.

Outside, it was warm despite the early hour, and the sun was already washing the fields with its golden warmth. Sarah could see men in a field a little distance off as they began to scythe, cutting the long grass so that it fell in neat rows where it would lie until it was gathered in. The smell of new mown grass was strong and one of the pleasures of early summer. Above her head a lark soared in the sky, trilling its sweet song. She was feeling happy and when she heard the sound of hoof beats behind her, something told her that she was about to see the man she had hoped to meet. She turned to watch as he approached, waiting on the grass verge to one side of the lane for him to reach her.

'Sarah,' Troy said, as he brought his horse to a halt. He gazed down at her, a smile of satisfaction on his lips. 'Tubby told me that you were staying. I believe his aunt is giving a dinner this week, and your cousin's family is invited. Your visit is for more than a few days, I hope?'

'I have another three weeks,' Sarah said, and her heart began to race as she looked up at him. 'I do not go home until the week after Ascot – if you still mean to invite us?' She did so hope he would!

'Tubby's aunt is already sending invitations out for a party,' he replied. 'It will be an interesting day out for all of us. The ladies may parade in their finery and drink champagne in the marquee. If they do not wish it, they need hardly see a horse at all.'

'What a waste of a day at the races,' Sarah said honestly. 'I mean to watch every race and I shall pick my horses – but you must place my money for me, because I should not know how to do it myself.'

'It would be quite shocking if you did,' Troy

said, with a teasing grin that belied his words. 'But then you do not care for the conventions much, do you, Sarah?'

'Some of them are so silly,' Sarah said, and laughed, because she knew he was trying to provoke her. 'This is the twentieth century, is it not? Mama still thinks we are all Victorians. She has no time for the suffragettes or anything remotely new. She will cling to her horse and carriage even now that there are trains and automobiles.'

'She belongs to a more elegant age, a different way of life,' Troy said, gazing down at Sarah's eager face. She felt that he approved of her even if he pretended to be shocked. 'Things are changing fast, Sarah, and one day your mother will have to wake up to the fact that life moves on. Indeed, we all shall unless we wish to become dinosaurs.'

'Yes, perhaps,' Sarah replied, though she thought that her mother was unlikely to change for anyone. She watched as Troy dismounted, holding his horse lightly by the reins. 'I was going to walk down and look at the horses – shall we go together?'

'I hope you know better than to go into the paddock and offer food?'

'Oh yes, I stay outside the fence. I have a rather old carrot in my pocket. I do not know whether it will tempt them.'

'As long as you do not feed them bread or sugar,' Troy said. 'It is not good for them when they are in training.'

'I have heard that your horses are doing well?'

'We've had several winners, and some failures, as is always the case,' Troy said. 'How is your family? I know Barney says the preparations for the wedding are taking over his life. He said he is drowning in petticoats and ribbons.'

'Yes, my mother can think of nothing else but clothes and the reception. She was relieved to send me to my cousin for a few weeks. Marianne is not pleased with me...'

'What have you done to upset her?' Troy asked, the light of mischief in his eyes once more.

Sarah blushed under his scrutiny. 'Oh, it is just irritation of the nerves, I think. Tell me, what do you think of the news?'

Troy raised his eyebrows, because he could guess what she would not say. Marianne was marrying well, but not as well as she might have, and she would not wish her sister to outshine her.

'Do you speak of the trouble in the Balkans or the attack on Buckingham Palace by the women's movement?'

'I suppose I meant the suffragettes,' Sarah said, and frowned. 'I know there is a great deal of unrest abroad, but it cannot affect us here – can it?'

'Who knows?' Troy replied. 'We have treaties that would draw us into a war if it happened.'

'Please do not speak of war,' Sarah begged. 'It surely cannot happen. Why should it?' She did not know why but any mention of war made her uneasy, as if a black cloud hung over her world.

'Why indeed?' he said, and smiled at her. He hesitated and then reached out, touching her cheek with the tips of his fingers. For a moment Sarah thought he would kiss her and her heart raced, but it did not happen. Troy's hand fell back to his side, as if he had thought better of it. 'I think I must leave you to your walk, Sarah. Tubby has spoken of calling on your aunt this afternoon. I daresay you will see us both later.'

Sarah stood back as he remounted. She watched him ride away, thinking how well he sat his horse. She knew he was an excellent horseman, but then he did everything well and was accounted an accomplished sportsman. She was thoughtful as she considered his last remark in response to her question. Clearly it had been meant to reassure her, but it was not his opinion. Troy felt that England would be drawn into any war in Europe. She could only pray that it would not happen, because she knew instinctively that it would cast a shadow over all their lives.

Sarah wore one of her favourite gowns that afternoon. It was a pale primrose silk and suited her colouring well. Her aunt's maid had helped her to swirl her thick hair into a smooth knot at the back of her head, and she looked grown up, elegant and quite different to the girl who had gone hatless for her walk that morning.

They were all sitting in the parlour when the

gentlemen were introduced. Sarah's heart raced as she saw Troy come in, followed by his friend. He was so very good-looking, and each time she saw him she found herself more attracted to him. Had she been inclined to heed her mother's warning it would have been impossible to contemplate a future with him, but since she had decided that she would not let Marianne's spite stop her finding happiness, she shut all doubts firmly from her mind. Troy liked her. If he made her an offer, she would accept him. Her father would not refuse once he knew that they were in love. Once Marianne was safely married all the unpleasantness could be forgotten.

Of course, she did not yet know if Troy's feelings matched her own. It might be that he was merely flirting with Sarah to pass the time. However, he sat close to her when tea was served, and although the conversation was general he managed to include her, listening to her opinions with interest and taking them seriously, which she took as a compliment.

It was agreed that they were to dine at Lady Marlowe's house in two days' time, and a picnic luncheon was arranged for the following day. Sarah felt a warm glow inside, because it seemed that for the next three weeks she would be seeing Troy as often as she wished.

'We may as well make the most of the fine weather,' Lucy's mother said. 'We shall have our picnic in the garden. I shall have the servants set up the croquet hoops and anyone who cares to play may do so.'

Everyone agreed it was a splendid idea and the gentlemen said that it was time they were leaving, for they had an engagement that evening. Sarah and Lucy went to the door to see them both off.

'Until tomorrow,' Troy said, and took the hand Sarah offered, but instead of shaking it politely, he lifted it and dropped a kiss within the palm, closing her fingers over it. 'I shall look forward to seeing you both.'

Sarah's heart raced, for the expression in his eyes told her that his words were all for her. She held her hand closed, wanting to capture the kiss and hold it for as long as she could. The two gentlemen got into Tubby's automobile and set off, the engine making little popping sounds that they could hear until it was out of sight. Sarah felt that Troy had been telling her something when he kissed her hand that way, and she felt like shouting her joy aloud. She was sure he felt more than friendship for her. Was it possible that he had begun to fall in love with her?

As the two girls went back to the house, Sarah nursed her secret hopes and smiled inwardly. She had loved Troy ever since he had so gallantly swept her up to her room that day when her ankle was sprained, but it had seemed hopeless. She had believed him in love with her beautiful sister, but Marianne was marrying someone else. And Troy was noticing Sarah, not just as a pleasant girl he knew – but as a woman he liked.

Sarah was aware that there could be problems ahead for her. Troy might only be flirting with her, and her parents might not be pleased even if he did ask her – but she would find a way to be with him even if they forbade the marriage.

For a moment it seemed as if a dark cloud hovered, but she pushed it away. If Troy loved her she would do whatever was necessary to make her family understand how she felt, and if they refused ... Sarah shook her head. She would face that when the time came!

In the meantime she was going to make the most of her visit with Lucy. She would see Troy every day and she would let him see that she liked him. The rest was up to him.

The picnic had been such fun! Sarah and Tubby had teamed up against Troy and Lucy to play croquet, and of course Troy had managed to carry Lucy through to the winning post.

'We might have known he would win,' Tubby said ruefully, and threw himself down on the rug spread beneath the shade of an ancient tree. He accepted a consoling glass of wine from his hostess's hand and sipped it. 'He always wins at everything. Mere mortals don't stand a chance against Troy! I swear he was well named, for he is beloved of the gods.'

From the look he directed at her, Sarah wondered if he were complaining about more than the game, but as yet he had not said or done anything to make her think she was more to him than an acquaintance. She hoped he wasn't falling in love with her, because she liked him as a friend and would hate to hurt him.

Troy laughed and winked at his partner. 'We beat them fair and square, Lucy. Don't let him tell you any different.' He glanced at Sarah as she stood under the tree seeking a little shade from the sun. 'Would you like to walk, Sarah?'

'Yes, thank you,' she replied. 'It would be nice up by the lake.'

'You young ones have far too much energy,' Lucy's mother said. 'I shall just stay here and relax.'

Sarah smiled and shook her head, falling into step beside Troy as they strolled away in the direction of the lake. She had enjoyed pitting her skill against him on the croquet green, but now she was content to walk in silence. Troy seemed in a similar mood and did not speak until they had left their friends far behind.

'Barney asked me to the wedding, but I do not think I shall come.'

Sarah turned to look at him. 'It was his fault all this happened. If he had not asked you to take the letter you might be marrying Marianne. I always knew that you were innocent of any wrongdoing, and my sister ought to have known too.'

'I have that to thank him for,' Troy said, his dark eyes intent on her pretty face. 'It would have been a mistake, Sarah. I was not in love with Marianne. I think I knew it almost as soon as the engagement ring was on her finger. She is beautiful, and desirable – and I enjoyed the chase. When something is denied me I find it amusing to go after whatever it is and take it, but often become bored as soon as it is mine ... do you think that shallow of me?'

'It isn't a particularly nice trait,' she told him. 'But I suppose it is a part of your nature – of what makes you the man you are.' Barney was right. Troy was one of the golden ones; strong, clever, accustomed to receiving the prize.

'Yes, perhaps. I would have kept to my bargain if Marianne hadn't jilted me. I am not that much of a cad – but we shouldn't have suited. I know she expected me to forgive her, but I was not prepared to take her back. Your father may not forgive me for that...'

'It would be difficult for him to forgive, but once she is married he may relent.'

'Yes, when she is safely married,' Troy agreed, and smiled at her. He reached out and took her hand, playing with the fingers. 'If we discovered that we liked each other rather a lot ... if we became more than friends ... your father might be persuaded in time. Do you not think so, Sarah?'

Sarah's heart leaped with excitement as she gazed up at him. 'I do like you very much, Troy. I always have.'

'Do you, Sarah?' Troy moved in closer, gazing down at her face for what seemed an eternity before he bent his head to kiss her softly on the lips. He stroked her cheek with his fingertips as he withdrew, looking at her intently once more. 'I think I may feel rather more than liking for you, my sweet Sarah – but we have to take things slowly. You are very young and there is no need to rush into anything, is there? We have several weeks in which to meet and enjoy each other's company. I may visit you at your home after the wedding ... would you like that?'

'Yes, I should,' Sarah said, her heart racing. Troy had spoken as clearly as he could for the moment. He wanted time to know her better and they had an excellent opportunity, because the next three weeks seemed to promise so much. 'I should like that very much.'

After that walk, it seemed to Sarah that she was floating on air. She was sure now that Troy loved her and that he would ask her to marry him when the time was right. He and Tubby were in and out of Mrs Trenwith's house every day, and Lucy's mother was always pleased to see them. Sarah did not spend much time alone with Troy; they were always in company with other people and she was content for it to be so. Sometimes their eyes would meet across a crowded room and she would feel suddenly that they were completely alone, but in truth there was little opportunity. They attended dinners; saw each other at the local fête and the show-jumping, where Lucy's horse won a blue rosette; had tea together; went boating on the lake and generally had an enjoyable time.

The visit to Ascot was the highlight of Sarah's summer, for she was taken to the show rings by Troy and given knowledgeable tips on which horses had the best chances in each race. She bet on three she liked the look of and two of them came out as winners, which made her shout with glee when Troy brought her some crisp white notes as her winnings.

'Fifty pounds!' she crowed. 'I have never had so much money to spend in my life. Shall we go and have cream teas in the tent? I shall treat you all from my winnings.'

'We shall have tea and champagne,' Troy said. 'But keep your winnings, Sarah. I shall treat you all, because I did rather better than I expected.'

She smiled up at him as she took his arm and they all trouped towards the large marquee where superior cream teas, champagne and other delicious food was being served to those privileged enough to be admitted. All the ladies were dressed in beautiful gowns and wide-brimmed hats trimmed with silk flowers and ribbons; the gentlemen wore smart coats, tailored trousers and black top hats. Many wore grey gloves and carried silver-topped canes, for Royal Ascot was a formal occasion and everyone dressed properly, especially if they wished to be admitted into the royal enclosure.

It was such a lovely warm day and Sarah felt happier than she could recall feeling before in her life, perhaps because of the way Troy smiled at her. His manner had become more intimate towards her of late, and even the knowledge that she would be returning home for her sister's wedding at the end of that week could not dim Sarah's pleasure.

Her cup of happiness overflowed when Troy handed her a glass of champagne and they went outside in the sunshine to drink it.

'I have enjoyed my visit this year,' he told her, his eyes dwelling on her face as she sipped her drink. 'These past few weeks have been very revealing, Sarah. I have discovered things about myself I never knew.'

'What kind of things?' She looked up at him, eyes wide and clear. In the sunshine she looked beautiful, innocent and fresh: a perfect rose, the embodiment of all that was good about this gentle way of life the English gentry were privileged to lead.

Troy's expression was thoughtful, serious. 'I had no idea so much pleasure could be had from simple things until I met you, Sarah. I've been a gambler, sometimes reckless, taking pretty much what I wanted and giving only as much as I wished – but I've realized that it isn't the way I want to go on living when there is so much more to be had.'

Sarah caught her breath, her pulse racing wildly. 'What are you saying, Troy?'

'I think you know,' Troy said. His eyes were bright with laughter. 'But this isn't the time or place to say what I want to say to you. I think we must wait. I have to go home tomorrow so I shall not see you for a while – but I shall come to your home in two weeks.'

'Do you promise?' Sarah asked. 'You won't go off somewhere and forget me?'

'I shan't forget you,' Troy said, and the expression in his eyes made her heart beat like a drum. 'Your aunt is looking at us. I think she suspects something. We must join the others. I must speak to your father before anyone else guesses the truth of the situation. If he should hear from someone else he would be angry.'

'Yes, of course,' Sarah said, feeling slightly apprehensive. Her parents had no idea that she had been in Troy's company almost every day for the past few weeks. She had to go home and wait patiently for Troy to come. She could only pray that when he spoke to her father he would be received with politeness and understanding. 'Marianne's wedding is next week. Once she is married Papa will not mind us having an understanding, even if he asks us to wait for— Oh...' She blushed. 'I should not have said that for you have not asked me...'

Troy's laughter was warm and mischievous. 'No, I do not think I did, but do not look so embarrassed, my sweet Sarah – it must be perfectly obvious that I shall very soon.'

'Well, I think we all had a pleasant day yesterday,' Sarah's aunt said the next morning. 'I hope you have enjoyed your visit with us, Sarah? I shall be sorry to see you go and I know Lucy will miss you – but we will come for the wedding, and Lucy may stay with you for a few days longer if she wishes.'

'Oh yes, Mama,' Lucy said. 'I always miss Sarah when she goes home. We've had such a good time with Troy and Tubby this summer.'

'Yes...' Louisa Trenwith looked at her niece. 'Yes, they have given us their company most days, which was good of them.' Something in her eyes seemed to say that she believed there was a special reason they had received so many visits and invitations from the gentlemen, but she held her own counsel. She was well aware of the situation, but having a decided partiality for Sarah, she hoped that her sister and brother-in-law would be sensible over what was a slightly awkward situation. 'You know that you will always be welcome to visit with us, Sarah my love. No matter what the situation I should be glad to have you here.'

'Thank you, Aunt Louisa,' Sarah said, and went to kiss her cheek. 'I have loved staying with you and Lucy – and my uncle, of course.'

In her heart Sarah wished that she might continue to stay with her aunt and cousin. She was not looking forward to returning home, because she knew that as the day of her wedding got nearer, Marianne's temper would become even worse. However, Sarah would nurse her secret and that would help her through the days she must endure before Troy came.

'You look lovely,' Sarah said as she helped her sister to fasten her headdress. Marianne's gown was of white, figured silk with a narrow skirt that clung to her slender figure, her veiling gossamer thin and very long. She wore diamonds in her hair and at her throat, also matching earrings. However, her pretty face was marred by a scowl of discontent.

'Your dress is beautiful.'

'What would you know?' Marianne snapped scornfully. 'It is not exactly as I ordered it. That stupid seamstress has made the sleeves too tight and it feels uncomfortable. I shall tell Mama not to pay her!'

'Oh, Marianne,' Sarah said, 'you had several fittings. Why did you not tell her it was tight on your arms? She must have spent many hours working on this dress. You can't ask Mama not to pay her.'

'Oh, be quiet,' Marianne said, a sparkle of tears in her eyes. 'I hate it and I shan't wear it! It's too tight. Oh, I hate everything...'

'Now, Marianne, do not be foolish,' Lady Trenwith said, coming into the room at that moment. 'You are having a silly irritation of the nerves. The dress fits perfectly well, and you may have it altered after the wedding if you wish to wear it again, which I doubt. It will be packed away in a trunk somewhere, I daresay. Everyone is waiting. It is time you came downstairs.'

'No, I don't want to ... I don't want to get married...' Marianne wailed. 'It's all wrong and I hate it ... I hate everything...'

'You will do as you are told,' Lady Trenwith said in a severe tone. 'I have asked you repeatedly if you wished to go through with the wedding and you assured me that you wished to marry Barney. I shall not allow you to shame us all for a second time, Marianne. You will come down and you will smile at everyone – and if you disgrace me I shall be very angry. Do you understand me?' Marianne stared at her

104

sullenly and Lady Trenwith turned to Sarah. 'Go downstairs and wait for you sister, Sarah. I wish to speak to Marianne privately.'

Sarah left the room. She felt upset and guilty, because she had encouraged Barney to court her sister and even though Marianne could have said no before this, it was awful to think of her being forced to marry if she didn't wish to after all. However, ten minutes later Marianne came down to cheers from her assembled family and good wishes from the servants.

She didn't look at Sarah, but she was smiling and seemed to have got over her tantrums. Perhaps it was just wedding nerves after all, Sarah thought, though when she looked at her mother as they went out to the carriages, she was surprised by the severe expression on Lady Trenwith's face.

Sarah helped to carry her sister's train as they walked down the aisle. Barney turned to look at his wife-to-be as she approached, a look of such adoration in his eyes that Sarah felt sorry for him. She knew that he had got Marianne when she was feeling vulnerable and couldn't help wondering what kind of a wife her sister would be to him. Of course, he must know that she didn't love him. Barney Hale wasn't stupid and he must sense that she was marrying him for money, and because she wished to be married, and because she wished to be married in her heart, because otherwise Barney was going to be very hurt one day.

Marianne carried herself well through the rest of that day. No one watching her would have guessed that she was not perfectly content with her wedding. She smiled, flirted prettily with her husband and his friends and appeared perfectly happy. Only the stern expression on Lady Trenwith's face was left to remind Sarah that her sister had given way to tears and tantrums earlier that day.

It was much later in the afternoon that Marianne went upstairs to change. Lady Trenwith sent Sarah after her, telling her to see that Marianne had all she needed for the journey.

When she knocked and then entered her sister's room, Sarah was shocked. Marianne had taken off her wedding gown and thrown it down. Her maid was looking at her in horror, and it was obvious that she had been crying. She turned to glare at Sarah, clearly in a temper.

'What do you want? Have you come to gloat?'

'Why should I gloat?' Sarah asked. 'Mama sent me to see if you had all you need.'

'Shall I bring your carriage dress, miss?' the maid asked hesitantly.

'Oh, get out and leave me alone, my sister will help me,' Marianne said. She threw a satin shoe across the room as the maid fled. 'Silly woman! I am glad that I shan't have to put up with her any longer. As Barney's wife I shall at least have a proper maid to look after my things.'

'I am sure you will have a lot of things you want,' Sarah said. At this moment she felt sorry for her sister. Marianne had married a man she didn't love and she was bitterly regretting it. 'Barney's father is rich. I am sure you will like being married once you get used to it.'

'Please do not patronize me,' Marianne said, her eyes flashing with temper. 'You know I only married him in a fit of pique. You know I wanted Troy Pelham. He had no right to refuse to forgive me!'

'I am sorry you are unhappy, Marianne. You should have told Barney before this if you had changed your mind.' She gave a startled cry as Marianne lunged at her, hitting her hard across the face. Sarah put a hand to her burning cheek. 'What did you do that for?'

'Because I hate you,' Marianne cried. 'You think you will get Troy now, but Mother won't let you marry him. She made me marry Barney, because she said no one else would have me if I jilted him too – but if you think you are safe now you will find out you are wrong. Father hates scandal and Mother will protect him from it whatever you feel.' Her eyes flashed with spite. 'Give me that dress. I suppose I shall have to go down or Mother will come and fetch me.'

Sarah picked up the dark green gown and handed it to her, but made no attempt to help as her sister struggled into it. She wasn't going to let Marianne see that her spiteful outburst had upset her. Besides, she had no intention of taking any notice of anything Marianne said. Her mother might need some persuasion before she agreed to a wedding, but in the end she would come round. She had to, because

Sarah loved Troy too much to give him up.

Marianne was dressed when Lady Trenwith arrived. She gave a nod of satisfaction. 'You may go back to the guests, Sarah. I need to speak to Marianne now.'

'Good luck, Marianne,' Sarah said. 'I hope you will enjoy being married when you get used to it.' She went out of the door before her sister could reply and went back down to the guests.

Barney looked at her anxiously. 'Is Marianne all right?' he asked. 'She has been a while changing...'

'Yes, I am sure she is,' Sarah said. 'I hope you will be very happy, Barney. Marianne can be a little ... hasty sometimes.'

'I know she doesn't love me,' Barney said, looking like a mournful puppy. 'But I adore her and all I want is to make her happy. I would give her anything she wanted.'

'Marianne likes presents and she likes being made a fuss of,' Sarah said, and stretched up to kiss his cheek. 'I think she is lucky to get you and I hope you will be happy.'

'Maybe I'll come to your wedding soon,' Barney said. 'You're a nice girl, Sarah. I wish you happiness.'

'Thank you.' Sarah smiled at him and moved away, mingling with the other guests, who had gathered to watch the bride come down. Marianne was not long in following Sarah. She looked as beautiful as ever and she was carrying her bouquet, which she threw out to the little group of female guests, deliberately turning away from Sarah. Sarah wouldn't have tried to catch it if Marianne had thrown it at her, but a lot of the girls did, laughing and grumbling when it went to one of the older ladies who was already married.

'That is just what she would do,' Sarah heard one of the girls say. 'She thought she would marry the best catch of the year but like an idiot she threw her chance away and had to settle for Barney Hale.'

'Serves her right,' a second girl said. 'And it leaves Troy Pelham for us...' The two girls giggled, passing Sarah without a look in her direction.

Sarah was sorry that her sister should be the subject of such spiteful gossip. She knew that Marianne bitterly regretted her hasty decision to jilt Troy, but once she settled to being married she would enjoy being Barney's spoiled wife.

Sarah wandered away from the guests into the garden. She was trying to dismiss her sister's spiteful taunts, but she couldn't help wondering how difficult it would be to persuade her mother and father that she should be allowed to marry Troy Pelham.

Perhaps when all the excitement had settled and Troy came to ask her father for his permission to marry Sarah it would be different. He had behaved perfectly, helping Marianne to weather the disapproval of certain members of society. Surely there was no reason for Sir James to refuse his request? Sarah hoped her father would be reasonable, because she didn't know what she would do if he refused to see Troy.

Troy frowned as he read the headlines in the paper. He had been aware that the troubles in the Balkans were dangerous and could boil over at any time, but the news of the Archduke's assassination was shocking.

'It will mean a war,' Lord Pelham said. He was sitting at the magnificent mahogany partner's desk in his study, his son in a chair opposite. 'Mark my words, Troy, this could turn out to be extremely nasty before it is done.'

'We shall be drawn into it, of course,' Troy said, returning the paper to his father. 'We can't stay out because of the treaties.'

'Exactly,' his father agreed. 'Your brother is in the army and may be called upon to fight. I thank God that you did not join.'

'But I shall of course if it comes to it,' Troy said. He took out a silver cigarette case and offered it to his father. Lord Pelham shook his head. Troy changed his mind and replaced the case in his inside pocket. 'It is certain to come to a head after the assassination of Archduke Franz Ferdinand and his morganatic wife in Sarajevo. You wouldn't expect me to stay out of it, Father? I couldn't let Andrew go to war while I stayed here and twiddled my thumbs.'

'I would rather you did,' his father replied, and sighed. 'But if it comes to it I suppose I can't stop you.' He frowned as Troy fidgeted with the brandy glass on the desk in front of him. 'Was there something more you wanted to say to me, Troy?'

'I am thinking of asking Sarah Trenwith to marry me.'

'Good grief!' His father stared at him, disbelief mingling with dismay. 'Marianne's younger sister! Are you sure? Have you thought about the consequences? Marianne is hardly married. It will cause a deal of talk, my boy. People will say something was going on before she jilted you.'

Troy shrugged his shoulders. 'It can't be helped, Father. I've fallen in love with Sarah – and it is the real thing this time.'

'Love!' His father snorted. 'What has that to do with anything?' He shook his head. 'I've nothing against the girl, and we can weather the gossip – but I doubt her father will like it. I shouldn't wonder if he digs his heels in and says no. He may demand a period of reflection at the very least.'

'If that happens we shall have to wait,' Troy said. 'I hope it will not happen – but there is nothing else I can do. I take it I have your blessing, Father?'

'Yes, of course,' Lord Pelham replied. 'I hardly know the girl but I shan't take against her. I am sorry the other business happened. It has made things awkward with Trenwith. I don't think he will ever forgive you for not taking her back, but that is his problem. For what it is worth, I think you made the right decision then.'

'Thank you, Father,' Troy said. 'I shall go down to Hampshire in the morning and speak to Sarah's father.'

'I wish you luck,' Lord Pelham said. 'Just be careful what you say to him. He's a decent enough chap but this business over Marianne has made him touchy.' He opened the silver cigar box on the desk and offered it to his son. 'These are a very good sort, Troy – if you care for one?'

'I think I prefer a cigarette,' Troy said. 'But please indulge, Father. There was another little matter I wished to discuss, but it is merely business. I think I should make a will and I was wondering what you thought...'

Sarah was sitting in a small parlour at the back of the house when the door opened and her brother entered. She put her book down and smiled as Luke came towards her, getting to her feet to embrace him.

'When did you get home?' she asked. Luke was three years older than Sarah and had been away travelling for some weeks. 'Mother hoped you would be home for Marianne's wedding, but you didn't come.'

'I didn't get her letter in time,' Luke said. 'It wouldn't have mattered to Marianne. I'll visit her when she returns from her honeymoon and take her a gift. How are you, Sarah? Did you get any of my letters?'

'I got about ten,' Sarah said. 'I kept them all. You've been to so many places. I thought you might never get home.'

'When I left I thought Marianne still wanted Troy Pelham – what happened? Rose told me she married Barney Hale. What on earth possessed her to do something like that?'

'You didn't get my letter then,' Sarah said. 'I wrote to you when you were in Spain to tell you that Troy was willing to acknowledge her but had decided against renewing their engagement and ... I think she took Barney on the rebound because she thought no one else would ask her.'

'She was probably right, because people don't like that sort of thing in a girl,' Luke said. 'No, I didn't get that letter. It must have arrived after I left Spain. I travelled back through France, Austria and Germany.' Luke frowned. 'The situation is precarious out there after the archduke's assassination, of course. I think there will be a war soon by the looks of things.'

'Troy has been talking about that recently,' Sarah said. 'He says the situation has been volatile in the Balkans for a while – but why should we be drawn into a war? I don't really understand it, Luke.'

'It is all a matter of treaties,' Luke said, and frowned. 'But forget that for a moment. If Marianne jilted Troy Pelham, why did I see him leaving the house a few minutes ago?'

'You saw Troy leaving?' Sarah was on her feet. 'When? He promised to speak to Father—' She broke off as her mother walked into the room, her heart thumping. 'Mother...' Her mouth went dry as she saw the expression in her mother's eyes. 'What is it?'

'Do not look at me like that, Sarah,' her

mother said coldly. 'You must be aware of what I have to say to you. Troy Pelham was here earlier. He spoke to your father—'

'Why did he leave?' Sarah cried. 'Mother! Did Father say no? Please tell me he didn't send Troy away?'

'I have no idea what your father said. He wishes to speak to you in his study. No doubt he will tell you what passed between them if he wishes you to know.'

'What is this about, Sarah?' her brother asked. 'I don't understand.'

'Troy loves me and I love him,' Sarah said, lifting her head proudly. 'He came here to ask Father for permission to speak to me.'

'Good grief,' Luke said. 'Father isn't going to like that one little bit. You know what a stickler he is for proper behaviour, Sarah. Marianne has been married only a couple of weeks. It is much too soon to consider an engagement between the two of you. People would talk and they would think the worst.'

'Exactly,' Lady Trenwith said. 'You should have waited for a year at the very least. Your father might have considered it then, but this smacks of indecent haste.' She glared at her daughter. 'You had better go down and see what your father has to say.'

Sarah shot her mother a look of resentment. It was so unfair of her to take Marianne's side all the time. No one cared how Sarah felt! Even Luke had criticized her and he was usually on her side. She lifted her head proudly as she walked downstairs. Her father must be very

114

angry if he had asked to see her in his study. Sir James seldom interfered in his daughters' lives, preferring to leave discipline to his wife.

Sarah's heart pounded as she stood outside her father's door, her mouth going dry as she knocked and waited for permission to enter. When it came she entered, her head held high.

'You wished to speak to me, Father?'

Sir James looked at her with narrowed eyes. 'Were you aware that Troy Pelham intended to visit me?'

'Yes, Father,' Sarah replied. 'Troy told me he would call on you when he could.' She hesitated, then decided she must say what was in her mind. 'Did he ask you for permission to speak to me?'

'No, Sarah, he did not,' Sir James replied, and glared at her. 'It is possible that he intended to but I made it plain from the start that I did not wish for future intimacy with that gentleman. He said that in the circumstances he would not trouble me further and left.'

'That is so unfair!' Sarah cried, without thinking. 'It was Marianne's fault that they broke up. She jilted Troy and she married someone else. Why should I not marry the man I love?'

'Be quiet!' Sir James looked at her with severe displeasure. 'I will not have this, Sarah. Tantrums from a girl of your age are not acceptable. You will behave with dignity, if you please.'

'But I love him, Father,' Sarah said, her throat tight with emotion. 'I love him so much.'

'I have no idea how you became so well acquainted with a man you knew was not welcome in my house, but you will not see him again. I have made my decision. Let that be an end to it, Sarah.'

'You are cruel,' Sarah blazed, refusing to be silent. In the past one word of censure from her father would have made her wish to sink through the floor, but now she was like a wildcat fighting for her young. 'Troy did not take that necklace. He was insulted and ill-used by this family, but in London he went out of his way to mend fences with Marianne so that she would not be cut off by his friends. You should be grateful to him—'

'I have told you my decision. Go to your room now and reflect on your behaviour. When you are ready to apologize you may come down, but until then you will remain in your room. Do you hear me?'

'I hear you,' Sarah said, but there was defiance in her eyes. 'I shall go to my room, but I shall not apologize.'

'You have disappointed me,' Sir James said, looking at her coldly. 'I shall not speak to you again until you come to your senses. Your mother may discipline you as she pleases. Until you learn to behave decently, you are not my daughter.'

Sarah stared at him blindly, tears stinging her eyes. She had always known that he was a stern, harsh man, but she had not realized he was so cold. He did not care that he was break-ing her heart. All that mattered to him was that she behave in a manner he thought fitting. Well, she would not, Sarah thought defiantly, as she turned and walked from the room. She had done nothing wrong! It was Marianne who had brought shame on the family by jilting Troy, but it was Sarah who had to pay the price.

Well, she would not let them part her from the man she loved. Whatever was said or done, she would wait for her chance and one day she would marry Troy.

Five

Troy was furious as he rode away. His reception from Trenwith had left him smarting with a mixture of humiliation and anger. Sarah's father was impossible to deal with; he had refused to listen to anything Troy had to say. In the end Troy had been so angry that he had walked out without asking for permission to speak to Sarah. Clearly it would not be given. Lord Pelham had warned him that Sir James might be unwilling to receive him, but Troy had taken the chance because of his feelings for Sarah. Had he been told that he must wait for some months before becoming engaged to her Troy would have accepted her father's wishes – but to refuse even to listen was insulting!

He had walked out before his rage boiled

over and he said things he might regret, but after a while he began to calm down and wish he had stayed. As things stood at the moment, it seemed that there was no hope of his being accepted as Sarah's fiancé. His only hope was that somehow his father could mend fences between the two families. The men had been friends for many years. It must surely be possible for some compromise to be worked out?

Troy decided that for the moment he must accept the situation. He could hardly go behind Trenwith's back, for that would give Sarah's father reason to forbid them. However, he would write to her and explain, tell her not to give up hope. He would find a way somehow, but for the time being they must be patient.

There were other more pressing things he needed to do, because a war loomed large on the horizon and he had made up his mind to join the army immediately. He would need officer training and it would be foolish to leave it until the last minute. He had been thinking of joining up for some time and he would delay no longer. Sarah would have his letter and understand that he was merely asking her to wait until he could find a way of changing her father's mind. She was still very young and it would do them no harm to wait, though if he had been given the choice he would have married her immediately.

'Have the letters come yet?' Sarah asked as Rose came into her bedroom. She had been confined for the past week, her only friend the maid who visited her each day to bring her food and news of what was going on in the house. 'Is there anything for me?'

'No, Miss Sarah,' Rose said. 'I managed to get a look before they were taken up to Lady Trenwith, but there was nothing for you. Mind you, I don't always see them. I didn't see them the day before yesterday, so something could have come for you then.'

'Mother wouldn't keep a letter from Troy from me, would she?' Sarah frowned as she saw the expression on Rose's face. 'Yes, she would if Father told her to, wouldn't she? It is so unfair. I haven't done anything wrong, except fall in love with the man my sister jilted.'

'It doesn't seem fair,' Rose agreed. 'Master Luke says you have to apologize. Sir James won't relent and in the end he will lose patience with you, miss.'

'Why should I apologize when my father is wrong?' Sarah demanded. 'He is punishing me for what Marianne did, and it isn't just.'

'No, miss, it isn't,' Rose sympathized. 'But it isn't very nice for you stuck up here. You aren't allowed to see your friends and the weather is so lovely. You must want to go out, even if only for a walk in the garden?'

'Yes, I do,' Sarah agreed, because in truth she was sick of being cooped up in her room. She longed to walk in the gardens and go for a wild ride on her horse. 'But I shan't apologize when I've done nothing wrong.'

'Your brother said Sir James is angry because

119

of your attitude. Couldn't you just say you are sorry for being rude to him? Maybe he would relent then and let you come downstairs.'

Sarah got up and walked over to the window, looking down at the garden. It was a beautiful day and she was bored to tears sitting up here with nothing to do, but she was still angry that her father and mother had been unjust. Marianne had brought shame on them. It wasn't Sarah's fault and she was being punished for nothing. Her stubborn nature refused to give in because the punishment was unjust.

'Thank you, Rose,' she said, and sighed. 'I know you are right, but I don't see why I should apologize.'

'Well, I have work to do, miss,' Rose said. 'I'll come up with your tea later. Is there anything else you want?'

'You could bring me a book if you can manage it,' Sarah said. 'And ask Luke if he will visit me, please.'

'Yes, miss, of course I will,' Rose said. She picked up the tray of food that Sarah had barely touched and took it with her, shaking her head. The girl's stubbornness was making for an unpleasant atmosphere in the house, because even the servants were taking sides over it. Rose supported her young mistress, but she knew her brother thought it was all a storm in a teacup. Jack had been talking about leaving to join the army, and if her brother went Rose thought she might go too. To be honest, she had had nearly enough of being a servant in this house. There were other jobs going for a girl like her, and she had heard about a voluntary service where they trained girls to help out in the hospitals.

Jack had told her that the hospitals would need lots of volunteers if the war came, and like most people he was certain it would. 'There're bound to be casualties,' he'd said only that morning. 'You'll be needed, Rose. I'm not saying it's a better job than here, because they are bound to be strict. You have to apply to join the VADs and there's no guarantee they will have you even then.'

'It would be more worthwhile than here, though,' Rose had replied. She had been thinking about it all morning. It was a big step to take to hand in her notice, because her family had always worked on the Trenwith estate, but she didn't like some of the things that went on here. Her mother said this situation was none of her business and she should just do as she was told, but Rose thought that was old-fashioned. Girls didn't have to go into service these days. There were plenty of other jobs, and would be more if there were a war, because a lot of the men would join up. In fact, it was only her loyalty to Sarah that was keeping her here. She didn't like to leave while the girl was so unhappy, but as soon as this unpleasant business had been sorted, she would hand in her notice.

Rose took the tray to the kitchen and then left the house. She needed to speak to Sarah's brother, and she thought the best place to find Luke just now was at the stables. He spent much of his time there, and she would enjoy a little walk to get her out of the house.

Luke saw the pretty maidservant coming towards him and felt a jolt of excitement. He'd had a thing about Rose Barlow even before he went off on his grand tour. It was one of the reasons he'd gone, because he knew anything more than a hasty fumble in the yard was out of the question. He liked Rose too much to take advantage of her, might even have fallen for her hard if he had let himself. However, he knew what his father would say if he were foolish enough to become interested in a girl of Rose's class. But his common sense didn't stop him liking her or thinking that she was pretty, and he grinned at her as she came up to him.

'Were you looking for me, Rose?'

'Yes, sir. Miss Sarah is low in spirits, sir. She asked if you would visit her later.'

'Father told me to stay away until she comes to her senses,' Luke said, and frowned. 'She should know that he won't give in. He is stubborn and she doesn't have a chance of winning this silly argument. Besides, she is in the wrong whether she accepts it or not.'

'I've told her what you think, sir, but she says she has done nothing wrong and she doesn't see why she should apologize.'

'She hasn't done anything *really* wrong,' Luke said, 'but she was rude to Father and he won't stand for any lapse in manners. Sarah knows what he is like. She has to apologize or she will stay where she is for weeks.'

'Could you have a word with her, sir?'

'Yes, all right, I'll go up before tea,' Luke agreed. 'Don't think I blame her for wanting to marry Troy Pelham, because I don't. I think Father is being hard on her, and I might be able to persuade him to think again, but not while Sarah continues to defy him. She ought to know it is the worst thing she could do. The best thing you can do is keep trying to persuade her to see sense, Rose. In her heart she knows what she has to do.'

'I daresay she does, sir – but she is stubborn too.'

'A chip off the old block, I suppose,' Luke said, and sighed. 'They say I take after my grandfather, and he was very different. Well, I'll do what I can, Rose, but I can't promise anything.'

Rose nodded, seeming to hesitate for a moment as if she wanted to say something more, then she turned away and walked back to the house. Her hips swayed enticingly and Luke found that he was breathing hard. Rose was too damned attractive and he had better take himself in hand, because that road led only to disaster! His father thought his work as an artist was a waste of time, God knows what he would say if he suspected his son of lusting after one of the servants!

Sarah's crime would pale into non-existence then! Luke knew he was too much of a coward to fight his father over something like that – or perhaps he just disliked hurting people. Besides, Rose probably wouldn't be interested in

123

an ordinary chap like him. Why should she be when she was as pretty as a picture? No doubt she had half the men in the village after her...

Sarah looked up as the door opened and her mother entered. She had thought it might be Rose with her tea, and her heart missed a beat as she saw the look on her mother's face.

'When are you going to give up this stupidity and apologize to your father? Surely you know that he will not relent?'

'I haven't done anything wrong,' Sarah said. 'Troy loves me and I love him – why shouldn't we marry? Just because Marianne was foolish enough to jilt him it doesn't mean he did anything to make her.'

'As it happens, I agree,' Lady Trenwith said, surprising her. 'Had you waited a few months I might have been able to persuade your father that it was a good match, but he was angry over the whole business. He thought Troy should have forgiven Marianne, and that by not doing so he slighted her. Your father is extremely fond of her and it made him angry.'

'I know she was always his favourite,' Sarah replied. 'But she was the one who jilted Troy. He discovered he didn't love her and he didn't want her back – and then he fell in love with me.'

'Well, I have some news for you,' Lady Trenwith told her. 'Troy Pelham has gone for officer training in the army. Obviously he has accepted the situation and decided to get on with his life. I think you should do the same, Sarah. If you apologize to your father you could go walking and riding with friends again.'

'Troy has gone into the army?' Sarah felt chilled, though she wasn't really shocked. She had known how he felt about the possibility of war and he was always going to volunteer. It didn't mean he had forgotten about her! She turned her face away, changing the subject.

'Rose was telling me some of the girls are joining the Voluntary Services, Mother. They will be trained to help nurse the wounded if there is a war. I think that must be a very worthwhile thing to do, don't you?'

'If you are suggesting that you would like to join something of the kind it is out of the question,' her mother said. 'Your father would not hear of it. He is a stickler for the old ways, Sarah, and you would be mixing with girls of another class in a familiar way. It just will not do. You must remember your background and behave accordingly.'

'So I am supposed to sit at home twiddling my fingers while other people do work that I could do?' Sarah said bitterly. 'This is the twentieth century, Mother. Women do lots of things these days that you never did – look at the suffragettes.'

'I have no wish to look at them or watch their ridiculous antics. In my opinion they should have more self-respect.' Lady Trenwith frowned at her daughter. 'You are so stubborn, Sarah, and it is not a pleasant trait. If you will apologize I might persuade your father to let you go on a visit to my cousin, Amelia Roberts. Amelia wrote asking about you, and she is very sociable. I daresay you would meet lots of young people at her house. It would clear the air if you went away on a visit and gave your father time to forgive you – but I cannot persuade him until you apologize.'

Sarah looked at her mother. Her offer seemed genuine and Sarah already knew that there was nothing to be gained by remaining obstinate, but she didn't want to give in too easily.

'May I have a little time to consider, Mother?'

'I should thought you would have had more than enough time, but if I were you I should make your apology before this evening, Sarah. Your father goes to London in the morning and it will be at least three weeks before he returns...'

Sarah watched as her mother went out of the room. The offer to send her to stay with her cousin Amelia was a generous concession, because Amelia was younger and easy-going. Sarah would be allowed far more freedom there than she could ever expect at home. It would be far better than sitting up here alone brooding. She knew in her heart that sooner or later she was going to have to give in, because her father would never relent unless she did.

She was standing at the window when the door opened once more and her brother entered. He raised his brows at her and Sarah smiled reluctantly.

'Ready to give it up, Sarah?' he asked. 'He won't give in, you know that – and I've got some friends coming tomorrow. I had thought about a picnic and croquet on the lawn?'

'It isn't fair, Luke,' Sarah said. 'Why should I not marry Troy if I want to?'

'No reason as far as I am concerned,' Luke said, and grinned at her. 'He's a decent sort, though he does sometimes lord it over one at times, but then, he is pretty good at everything. I'll try and bring the old man round for you – but you'll have to do the pretty first.'

'Yes, I know.' Sarah sighed and accepted the inevitable. 'I suppose I might as well get it over...'

'That's a good girl,' Luke said. 'Father is off to London in the morning so you will only have one night of avoiding his reproachful looks; he will have forgotten it all when he comes home.'

'All right, I'll change my gown and come down for tea,' Sarah said. 'I'll apologize to Father first ... but I still think he has been very unfair to me.'

'Life is like that,' Luke said, with a shrug, and for a second a shadow clouded his eyes. 'Get it over and forget it – and perhaps it will all work out as you hope.'

Sarah nodded, but she was far from being sure. If Troy hadn't bothered to get in touch with her it might mean that he'd had enough of her family and wanted to forget about marrying her.

The interview with her father had been every bit as bad as Sarah had expected. Sir James had looked at her reproachfully as she apologized. He had not mentioned Troy once, merely telling her that he was disappointed in her and hoped she would learn better manners in future. However, he then accepted her apology, said that she might come down for her meals and see her friends once more.

'Thank you, Father,' Sarah said. 'May I go now, please?'

'Yes, go to your mother. You may thank her for interceding on your behalf, Sarah.'

'Yes, Father, I shall.'

Sarah left his study feeling angry and humiliated. She knew that she had been rude to him, and it was for that she had apologized, but she still felt that she had not been treated fairly. Nothing had been said of Troy and she had no idea whether or not he had tried to contact her. She suspected that any letter he sent her would be confiscated, and her spirit rebelled. Had she been sure that Troy still wanted to marry her she would have written to him at his home in London in the hope that it might be sent on to him. However, she did not feel quite brave enough to do that.

Sarah thought that she might write to Lucy and ask her if she had heard where Troy was stationed for his officer training. He might even have gone to stay with his friend Tubby Brocklehurst. If she had been allowed to go and stay with Lucy she might have met Troy again, but she knew that her mother would not allow that. She had deliberately suggested her cousin Amelia, because Amelia's home was in Hastings in Sussex, a seaside town far away from anywhere that she might bump into Troy Pelham.

Sarah smothered a sigh. It was no use giving way to despair. She was being allowed out of her room now and that meant she could at least talk to friends and go for walks. She would not forget Troy, and if the chance ever came to be with him again she would take it.

The next three weeks were pleasant enough, because Sarah's father had taken himself off to London and then to stay with some friends. The house had a more relaxed atmosphere when he was absent, and with Luke at home there were always plenty of visitors. Luke had lots of friends, both female and male, because he was an easy-going, popular young man, and Sarah found that several of the young men went out of their way to be nice to her. She smiled and talked to them, giving a good performance despite the ever-present ache in her heart. It was good to be with friends again and she liked most of the young men, but no one made her heart race the way Troy Pelham did when he smiled.

There were garden parties, picnics, dinners, card evenings and even a small dance, which she thoroughly enjoyed because she did not sit out the whole night. She was very surprised when she discovered that Tubby Brocklehurst was one of the guests that night. He came straight up to her when he saw her, looking delighted.

'Miss Sarah,' he said, 'may I have a dance

please? I was hoping you might come this evening, though I wasn't sure...'

'My brother is a friend of the host's son,' Sarah told him with a smile. 'Luke and Tom Jarratt have known each other for years. How are you, Mr Brocklehurst – and how are the horses?'

'Oh, I'm fairly, you know,' Tubby said. 'We had several winners early in the season, but Troy hasn't been around much lately. You did know he had gone for officer training in the army?'

'Someone told me,' Sarah said. 'Would that be at Sandhurst?'

'Yes, rather,' Tubby said. 'I should like to join myself, but they wouldn't take me. Apparently, I'm not fit enough for the army. I'm going to try for one of the voluntary services. We all have to do our bit you know – when the war comes.'

'When – not if?' Sarah asked, looking anxious. 'Everyone seems so certain. I know the newspapers are full of it, but I keep hoping it won't happen. I shouldn't want anything to happen to Troy...'

'No, I should think not,' Tubby agreed. 'But I shouldn't worry about Troy. He's always had a charmed life. Takes plenty of risks but comes up smelling of roses every time. Besides, they say it will only last a short time – over in a few months.'

'Luke told me it would be a short war,' Sarah said, and sighed because any talk of the war upset her. 'I suppose we shouldn't talk about it this evening. You will remember me to Troy if you see him?'

'Rather,' Tubby said, and smiled at her. 'I think he quite likes you, Miss Sarah. I mean, I like you myself, but Troy ... well, different thing...'

'Yes,' Sarah said, and accepted his arm as they walked to the dance floor. 'You are my very good friend, Tubby – but I am fond of Troy in a different way.'

'Yes, I thought so,' he said. 'You mustn't worry about this war business too much, Sarah. It may not be much of a show at all...'

Sarah entered her bedroom the next afternoon to find Rose tidying some clothes away. She realized that she had left her things all over the place and apologized for making so much work.

'It's my job to tidy and clean your room, miss. Mr Luke is far worse sometimes. Everything he takes off lands on the floor.' She smiled at Sarah. 'Did you have a lovely time last night, miss?'

'Yes, it was nice,' Sarah said. 'I danced every dance – two of them with Mr Brocklehurst. He's a friend of Troy Pelham...'

'Is he, miss?' Rose frowned at her. 'Mr Troy wasn't there?'

'No, unfortunately he is away at Sandhurst training to be an officer for the army.'

'That's better than being called up when the war starts. Jack has gone to sign up today – and I shall be leaving at the end of the week. I have

131

applied for training as a VAD. I want to do nursing if they will let me, but you don't always get what you want.'

'Oh Rose!' Sarah stared at her in dismay. 'Are you really leaving us so soon?'

'Yes, miss. I am sorry to leave you but I've had enough of being in service. My mother doesn't approve, but I want a change, and I think this is as good a time as any to make the break.'

'I shall miss you,' Sarah said. She hesitated and then impulsively kissed Rose on the cheek. 'You've been a good friend to me, Rose. I hope we shall see each other again one day.'

'So do I, Miss Sarah.' Rose smiled at her. 'Don't look so down in the mouth. You will be going away yourself soon.'

'Shall I?' Sarah wrinkled her brow. 'Mother did say she would send me to her cousin, but she hasn't said anything more to me about it.'

'Well, she will soon, you take my word for it,' Rose said. 'She was telling Mrs Marriott that you would be away for a while. I happened to overhear her this morning – so it looks as if it is all set.'

'Really?' Sarah brightened as she realized that Rose was probably right. Her mother would very likely have told her personal maid of her plans before informing her daughter. 'I've had some fun recently, because of Luke's friends, but Father will be home soon and I would rather not have to look at his reproachful face. I am not sure he will ever forgive me.'

'Oh, miss!' Rose laughed and shook her

head. 'Well, I've got to go and tell the house-keeper that I am leaving – wish me luck, please. She won't like it, because it is getting harder to find girls to take the place of those who want to leave.'

'I do wish you luck,' Sarah said. 'I don't want to lose you, because you've been such a good friend to me – but I do wish you luck. I wish that Mother would let me join the voluntary services too, but I know she would not hear of it.'

'No, I don't expect she would, miss. I'm not sure you would like it if she did. I think you would find it hard work.'

'I wouldn't mind working,' Sarah said. 'Looking after wounded soldiers would be a nice thing to do, I should think.'

'In the VADs you have to be prepared to scrub floors and empty slops,' Rose said. 'I don't think they will let us near the patients for ages. I expect it will be all the dirty jobs for us volunteers.'

'Oh...' Sarah was disconcerted, because it wasn't quite what she'd thought. 'I suppose I could do things like that if I tried.'

'Yes, you could,' Rose agreed. She thought it would come hard to her young mistress, who often just dropped her clothes on the floor expecting that they would be put away or taken for washing by the servants, but she didn't want to upset her so she smiled. 'But I am sure there are other things you could do, miss. There will be volunteer groups for all kinds of things. Your mother's cousin will be sure to be involved in something of the sort, everyone is now.'

'Yes, I daresay she will,' Sarah said, and brightened. 'I hadn't thought of that, Rose. I am certain Cousin Amelia will have something I can join…'

'It is such a nuisance,' Lady Trenwith said to her daughter later that day. 'Rose Barlow is leaving us. I am quite upset about it. It is difficult to find anyone who does their work properly these days, and we are already understaffed.'

'Rose is going to join the women's volunteer services, Mother. I think we should be proud of her for doing her duty.'

'That is as may be,' Lady Trenwith replied, with a sour twist of her mouth. 'I feel very let down, especially as your brother tells me Rose's brother has also left us to join the army. The Barlow family has been with us for years. It is disconcerting that they should both leave at this time.'

'Everyone says there is a war coming,' Sarah said. 'I daresay several servants may wish to leave and join the voluntary services if it happens.'

Lady Trenwith shuddered. 'Pray do not speak of it! I am not sure what we shall do if that happens. Standards will slip if we do not have the right servants. We may be forced to close part of the house, which will not please your father at all. It is perhaps just as well that I have decided to send you to stay with my cousin.'

'Then I am to stay with Cousin Amelia?'

'Yes, of course. I told you I should arrange it. I shall send you on the train next week. Your brother has agreed to accompany you. He has friends to see and he will go on from there once he has delivered you safely to your cousin.'

'It is good of Luke to take me,' Sarah said. 'Thank you for arranging it, Mother.'

'I see no point in you moping around here once your father gets home,' Lady Trenwith replied. 'In the event of a war it may be best to close this house, leave just a caretaker staff in charge and live in London for a while. I daresay it will not last long, and then they will all be begging for their jobs back.' She gave a nod of satisfaction as though she would be pleased when the old order was restored.

'Yes, Mother.' Sarah wondered if that would prove to be the case. She knew that Rose had been thinking of leaving anyway. And she wasn't the only young girl to think there might be a better job for her somewhere else. However, she knew better than to contradict her mother, who might be so annoyed she would cancel the trip to Hastings. 'I think I shall start to look through my clothes and see what I shall need at Cousin Amelia's...'

'Take one or two plain dresses with you just in case Amelia asks you to help her. Her house is of moderate size and I seem to remember that she does not employ many servants. She says she is capable of doing small tasks herself, and may expect the same of you. I daresay it would be a help to her if you kept your own

135

room tidy. You may have to learn to do that here once Rose has gone.'

'I shall be happy to do whatever she asks,' Sarah replied. She could hardly contain her excitement as she walked up the stairs to her own room. It would be new and exciting at Amelia's house, and she would be away from the domineering eye of her mother. For once in her life she would be free to do as she pleased.

'So you are leaving us next week?' Luke looked at the maid. She was in the kitchen yard hanging out washing. She looked very young and pretty amongst the billowing washing, and the air smelled of fresh linen. 'We will miss you, Rose – and we already miss Jack at the stables. We can manage without him, because we have a couple of good lads who are too young to join up, and the older men – but Jack was irreplaceable. I doubt Father will try. I have told him it would be best to sell some of the horses and think about buying an automobile.'

'Lady Trenwith will not like that, sir,' Rose replied. She felt the intensity of Luke's eyes, and her cheeks felt warm. Rose was aware that he looked at her often, but since he made no move to do more she did her best to ignore it. 'She takes pride in her carriage horses.'

'Yes, I know Mama will not be pleased, but we must move with the times, Rose. A lot of men are leaving service to join the army. They will learn trades and a new way of life. I think quite a few will not want to return to service after the war. We may have to think of ways to change our own lifestyles. And that might not be a bad thing. My father loves this house, but I have sometimes thought it is too big. We would do just as well in a smaller one.'

Rose looked at him oddly. 'That might do for you, sir, but Lady Trenwith and Sir James are accustomed to the old ways.'

'Yes, it will be difficult for them to adjust. I think my mother might make the attempt if she was forced, but she knows my father has standards and does not like to see any lapse in them.'

'Yes, sir,' Rose said. 'It may be difficult for them for a while.'

'Sarah told me you were going to be a VAD?'

'Yes. I hope they will let me do nursing training, but you can't choose. They decide what they want you to do.'

Luke nodded, offering his hand. 'Well, I wish you good luck for the future. We will all miss you.'

Rose hesitated and then took his hand. She flushed as he closed two hands around hers, and she glanced up to surprise a strange look in his eyes.

'May I wish you good luck, sir?'

'I haven't spoken to my father yet,' Luke said, surprising himself as well as her, 'but I may join the services myself – though I am not sure what I would be suitable for. I do not think I want to be an officer.'

'I think you would make a good officer,' Rose said, and now it was Luke's turn to colour as her eyes met his. 'You are the kind of man others like – not the sort who gives orders and expects to have it easy himself. Jack told me you often groom the horses when they are busy. He says you are a good master.'

'That was decent of him...' Luke didn't know why his throat felt so dry. He wanted to sweep Rose into his arms and kiss her. He wanted to beg her to stay – for him. Of course, he did nothing of the sort. He was a gentleman and he knew what was expected of him. It would be dishonourable to arouse expectations he could not fulfil. 'Well, take care of yourself, Rose – and if ever you need help you can come to me.'

He was still holding her hand, though unaware of it until Rose gave a little pull and he let her go. 'That is very kind of you, sir. I shan't forget your kindness – and I have promised to keep in touch with Miss Sarah.'

'Yes, good,' Luke said. He was uncomfortable, because of the feelings he was trying to suppress. Desire was raging inside him like a forest fire and he felt as if he were being wrenched in two. This was ridiculous! Nothing had changed because Rose was leaving. A relationship between them was as impossible as ever. He must put it out of his mind. 'Goodbye, then.'

Luke turned and walked back into the house. He wasn't sure why he had come in search of her. It had been impulsive, but it was foolish. The girl was nothing to him and never could be. He must simply get on with his life and forget her. Once she had gone and he did not see her every day he was sure he would forget this foolish feeling that he had lost something wonderful.

Sarah was excited by the train journey, because it was the first time she had travelled this way. Always before her mother had sent her in the carriage, which took a long time and was often uncomfortable, as the carriage tended to bump and rattle over any uneven bits in the road. The train was noisy as it blew off steam, and Sarah's white gloves collected little smears of soot as she got into the carriage. Once inside, it was comfortable enough and she enjoyed watching the scenery flash by as she looked out of the window. It was certainly a faster mode of travel than her mother's carriage. Luke had told her that they would be with Cousin Amelia by teatime. She could hardly believe it, but it was mid-afternoon when they left the train to discover their cousin's chauffeur waiting with the Phaeton to drive them back to her house.

Sarah had been in an automobile before with one of Luke's friends, but Amelia's was comfortable, which the small roadster she had been for a spin in previously had not been. She felt a flutter of butterflies in her stomach, because she wasn't sure what her mother's cousin would have been told or of her reception. However, she need not have worried, because Amelia flung her arms about Sarah, embracing her warmly.

'It is lovely to see you, Sarah darling,' Amelia cried. 'You've grown up since I last saw you, become quite a young lady – and Luke, you are a fine gentleman, but I would have known you anywhere.'

Amelia smelled gorgeous, a light, flowery perfume that suited her and floated about her like the soft gowns she wore. That afternoon she was wearing a silk tea gown of soft rose pink; her shoes were a darker rose colour and she had a long string of creamy pearls that wound twice around her throat and then fell to her waist. Her hair was a dark auburn and she had green eyes that sparkled with mischief. She looked what she was: the spoiled darling of an older man, adored, respected and entirely happy with her life.

'It is so nice of you to have me,' Sarah said, hugging her back. 'I hope I shan't be in the way. Will Sir Keith mind having me here?'

'He had better not or he will be in trouble,' Amelia said. 'My dearest Bunnykins never objects to anything I do – and he loves young company. I am certain he will adore you, Sarah, as I do. Now come and have some tea, my darlings, and then I shall take you up to your rooms.'

Sarah looked around her at the elegant and modern décor of the room. The furniture belonged to what she suspected was the new arts and crafts movement, which most people called art deco. However, the house must have been built in the previous century, and the rooms had high ceilings and beautiful long windows; the floor was covered with rich Persian-style carpets, which might have seemed at odds with the furniture, but somehow blended in well. Perhaps because here and there Amelia had retained an exquisite antique. It was probably her ability to blend old with new that gave her house its unique charm, and a feeling of warmth that Sarah immediately liked.

Amelia chattered to her throughout tea, afterwards taking them both upstairs. It was smaller than Sarah's father's house, but there were ten bedrooms besides the servants' rooms, five of them used for guests. Sarah's room was very pretty, furnished in shades of rose and cream with furniture made of a pale satinwood and clearly quite new.

Amelia looked at Sarah expectantly as she glanced round. 'Will it do for you, Sarah? I do want you to enjoy your stay with us, dearest.'

'Yes, of course it will,' Sarah assured her. 'It is lovely. I am so pleased to be here. And I shall be happy to help with anything you ask me to do, Cousin. At home some of the servants are leaving and Mama isn't too pleased. She speaks of closing a part of the house down, or going to London if there is a war.'

'Yes, that will be quite dreadful,' Amelia said. 'Bunnykins is too old to go if it happens, though he may be called to help in other ways – but he has a nephew. Justin is in the army, training as an officer. He is sure to be in the thick of it, and that will upset Bunnykins.'

Sarah laughed. 'Does Sir Keith mind you calling him that, Amelia?'

'I told you, he never minds what I do,' the adored wife said. 'He is grateful that I married him and spoils me terribly, though as I've told

141

him before I didn't marry him for his money. He is very rich, of course, and I do not object to being spoiled, but I love him for himself. You will know what I mean when you meet him.'

Sarah nodded. Her mother's cousin had not been married when they last met, and Sarah had been too young to attend the wedding. Sarah's mother, like some others, thought that Amelia had married for money, but Sarah was pleased it wasn't that way. She had liked Amelia when they met previously, but now she seemed even more confident and outgoing than before.

'I asked Mother if I could join the VADs,' Sarah told her. 'I should like to do something useful if there is a war.'

'Do not worry, my love, I shall take you to my suffragette meetings,' Amelia assured her. 'We are already raising funds to help run the cottage hospital. If the wounded are sent back home the main hospitals will not be able to cope. We have a nursing home locally for those who are in need of somewhere to live. I shall help to run it and you will be able to help me, dearest. I am quite certain we can find you a job.'

'Oh good,' Sarah said, her face lighting up. It was exactly as she had hoped. Living here with her mother's cousin was going to be far more interesting than staying at home.

Six

'You will be all right with Amelia,' Luke said, as he hugged his sister before he left to catch his train. 'She will take care of you but she won't smother you the way Mother does. I should stay here for as long as she will have you if I were you.'

'Yes, I shall,' Sarah agreed. 'I love it here already. Amelia is taking me to tea with some of her friends from the suffragettes' movement this afternoon. I am really looking forward to it.'

'I shouldn't mention that in your letter to Mother,' Luke said, and grinned. 'I don't think she would be too pleased. You don't want her telling you to come home in a couple of weeks.'

'No!' Sarah pulled a face, because it was the last thing she wanted. 'I shall be careful what I write.' She looked at him thoughtfully. 'What are you going to do, Luke? It must get dull for you at home sometimes?'

'It is better for me, because I am free to come and go as I please,' Luke told her. 'I shall stay with some friends for a week or two before I go home...' He hesitated, then, 'I am thinking of joining up. I am not sure whether I should be any good at soldiering, but I shall offer my services if it comes to a war, and it seems likely. I don't see how we could get out of it, Sarah.'

'I know. Troy told me it was all a matter of treaties,' she said. 'If you do go … well, keep safe, Luke. I should hate it if anything dreadful happened to you.'

'I shan't be a fool or a hero,' Luke told her wryly. 'But in war it is all a matter of luck. I'll do my duty if it comes to it, though I don't like the idea of killing anyone. However, I couldn't be a conscientious objector. It wouldn't be honourable.'

Sarah wrinkled her brow. 'Troy feels the same I know – but I can't help feeling that if men refused to fight wars wouldn't happen.'

'I'm not sure that is right,' Luke said, 'because it is governments and rulers who make wars, and ordinary chaps don't really get a choice – unless they want to go to prison. I don't think I fancy that much.'

Sarah pulled a face. 'I suppose you are right,' she said. 'But I hate the thought of you and … others … being hurt.'

'Poor Sarah,' her brother said. 'It wasn't fair on you, Father sending Troy away like that without a hearing – but things may turn out better than you think. Either you will meet someone else or Father may come round in time. Just be true to yourself and who knows what will happen.'

'I shan't meet anyone else,' Sarah told him. 'I love Troy. It isn't just a childish infatuation, Luke. I really do love him.'

'Well, keep your chin up and I'll write to you

when I can,' her brother said and kissed her cheek. 'I must go now or I'll miss my train.'

Sarah nodded and stood back. She waved as her brother was driven away and then went into the house. Amelia was at her writing desk, slitting open letters and glancing through them before putting them into little piles. She smiled as Sarah entered.

'Luke has gone?'

'Yes. He told me that he is going to join the army if the war happens.'

'I expect most young men will do the same if they can,' Amelia said.

'Luke might not get an active post. I hope he doesn't because he isn't suited to it. He is far too gentle and considerate to be an officer.'

'I am certain the war will come,' Amelia said. 'When Luke is assigned to a regiment, I'll ask Bunnykins to see what he can do. He has some influence in high places, you know.' She smiled at Sarah. 'You don't have to sit here with me, my love. It is a nice day – why don't you go for a walk before lunch? We are going out this afternoon, but I have a few things to do this morning.'

'Are you sure you don't mind? Is there nothing I can do for you?'

'Nothing at the moment, though another day I may find you something. Make the most of the sunshine, my love.'

'Yes, thank you, I shall,' Sarah said. 'I shall take a walk as far as the folly, if that is all right?'

'Yes, of course. I used to love the folly, but it isn't truly safe to use because the stairs are crumbling. So don't go inside, Sarah, and if you should, don't go up the tower. Your mother would never forgive me if you had an accident.'

'No, I shan't, thank you for warning me,' Sarah said. 'I'll fetch a shawl in case I need one, and I'll be back for luncheon.'

Leaving her thoughtful hostess to contemplation of her letters, Sarah fetched a paisley shawl in case the wind was chilly and then left the house. She walked through the side gardens towards an orchard, feeling a thrill of excitement to be exploring her new surroundings. She had brought the shawl but was sure she would not need it, because the sun was warm. It was a wonderful feeling to know that she was entirely free for the next couple of hours. Amelia would not question her when she returned, which meant she could do anything she liked. It wasn't that she wished to do anything more than walk and explore the countryside about her, but it was nice to feel that she could if she wished. She gave a little cry of pleasure and began to run. If she didn't dawdle she might be able to go as far as the cliffs and back before luncheon!

It was as she was returning from the cliffs, where she had stood gazing down at the water as it tumbled about jutting rocks below, that Sarah saw the two ladies coming towards her on foot. She wasn't sure for a moment, but then as they drew nearer, she was certain she knew them.

'Lady Ardingly,' she said, feeling surprised

but pleased to have met friends. 'I am not sure if you remember me – Sarah Trenwith. I met you and Miss Manley in London some months ago.'

For a moment the lady stared at her and then her face broke into smiles. 'Sarah! Of course I remember. Troy Pelham asked me to invite you to tea. How are you, my dear – and what are you doing here?'

'I am very well, thank you,' Sarah replied. 'I am staying with my mother's cousin – Lady Roberts.'

'You are staying with Amelia?' Fenella Ardingly's face wore an expression of astonishment. 'What a small world it is, to be sure. It is strange but Selina was just asking me if I had heard anything of you – were you not, dearest?'

'Yes, I was,' Selina replied. 'You seemed interested in the movement when I last spoke to you. Have you become a member?'

'I have had no opportunity,' Sarah told her truthfully. 'Amelia has promised to take me to some of her meetings. I had no idea that you lived here, Lady Ardingly.'

'Please, call me Fenella,' the lady said with a smile. 'I spend very little time down here, Sarah. I prefer London and always shall. However, I had a nasty chill a month or so ago and my husband insists that I need a change of air. He practically forced me to come and Selina kindly agreed to accompany me so that I should not be lonely. Was that not kind of her?'

'It was thoughtful,' Sarah agreed, 'but I imagine Selina enjoys visiting with you, ma'am.'

'I enjoy her company so it is to be hoped that she enjoys mine,' Fenella Ardingly said. 'We have just been for our morning constitutional, and I must say it is pleasant at the moment. The breeze keeps away the worst of the heat, and the holiday-makers have not yet invaded us. They usually come on bank holidays, of which we have one quite soon.'

'It is next week, Aunt Fenella,' Selina said, 'as you well know – but the holiday people stay nearer the town beaches and seldom visit the coves at this end.'

'Well, it is to be hoped they will,' Fenella said, and smiled. 'But sometimes they go by on boat trips and wave to one. It is embarrassing for if one does not wave back it seems unfriendly, but to do so might be thought common. What is one to do in the circumstances?'

'Wave back if they are female,' Selina said, and shook her head at her aunt. 'We are all sisters beneath the skin, Aunt. When women get the vote we shall do away with the class system altogether.'

'Well, I agree with that to some extent,' Fenella said. 'But I am not sure I want it to happen all at once, Selina. I am for change but at a reasonable pace. My life is very comfortable as it is, my love.'

'Once we have equal opportunities for all, the education standards can be raised to an acceptable level. It is education that will free the masses from poverty and ignorance, Aunt.'

'You are a radical,' Fenella said, and gave an artistic shudder. 'I just want small changes at first. It would be very nice if women had a say in things, but we must take it slowly or the men will not allow it, you know.'

'Then we will force them,' Selina said, a militant sparkle in her eyes. 'Do you not agree, Sarah?'

Sarah thought that Miss Manley had become much bolder since their previous meeting. She wasn't sure she did agree, but she smiled and nodded because it seemed best.

'I do not know much about it yet,' she said. 'But I shall look forward to learning as much as I can while I am here.'

'You must attend the meetings,' Selina said. 'We have some good speakers coming here soon. Women from America. They are more radical there, you know. I believe they will make some of our members open their eyes and realize how much needs doing here if we are to be heard by the right people.'

'They do things differently out there,' Fenella said. 'We have chained ourselves to the railings outside Buckingham Palace, and been force-fed in prison. I do not see what else we can do, except keep repeating that we have the right to vote. Eventually someone will listen. I believe certain members of parliament are beginning to come round to our way of thinking.'

'We should make them,' Selina said. 'If we did something more radical – more explosive – they might sit up and take notice.'

'Explosive? Good gracious me! I do not agree with anything like that, Selina. I must ask you not to get involved with that nonsense, my dear. In my opinion, militancy could set the cause back years.'

'Oh, do not worry, Aunt. I shan't do anything like that – at least down here. There would be no point, but I applaud those who do – where it counts, which is in London.'

'Well, as you said, the place for that kind of thing is not here. We must get on, Selina.' Lady Ardingly nodded her head to Sarah. 'You must come to dinner very soon, my dear. I shall telephone Amelia and ask her to bring you to tea tomorrow.'

'Thank you,' Sarah said. 'I hope to see you both quite soon.'

Walking on, Sarah discovered that the time had flown and increased her pace. She did not wish to be late for luncheon on her first day...

Sarah was a couple of minutes late, but she was still the first to enter the small dining room, her flustered hostess entering a few minutes after. She apologized to Sarah for keeping her waiting.

'I had a morning visitor, which is unusual,' Amelia explained. 'Some friends have come down from London and they have invited quite a few houseguests to stay with them. The Honourable Mrs William Forsythe and her daughters are old friends of my husband's. I am not sure if you know them, Sarah. The daughters are a couple of years older at least. Angela might be four years older than you. She is a pleasant girl but not in the least beautiful. I think her mother despairs of finding her a husband, but Julia already has an admirer. Nothing is announced yet, but they expect an engagement before too long.'

'That is fortunate for her, but sad for Angela,' Sarah said. 'She will feel it if her younger sister is married first, though perhaps she does not wish to marry.'

'That may be the case,' Amelia said, 'though I would not have thought it – but what have you been doing with yourself this morning, my love?'

'I walked to the cliffs and looked at the sea. It was beautiful there. On the way back I met Lady Ardingly and Miss Selina Manley. Lady Ardingly said she would telephone you.'

'Yes, she did so just now,' Amelia agreed. 'She has asked us to call for tea tomorrow and to dine next week. It will be nice for you to have some acquaintances here, Sarah. If you wish to accompany Selina anywhere you need only tell me, my dear. I shall not expect you to wait on me the whole time.'

'But I like being with you,' Sarah said. 'I shall enjoy meeting your friends, Amelia.'

'And I shall enjoy your company, my love – but if you wish to visit with friends alone it will not upset me.'

Sarah thanked her. She could not truly think that she would wish to visit anyone without her cousin, but she could not look into the future and did not know that fate was about to spring a surprise on her...

Sarah spent a pleasant afternoon with Amelia's

friends. The Misses Browning – Miss Anne and Miss Mary – were both into their late thirties, and, having been left comfortably off by their father, were content to live together. Neither of them had any interest in marriage, though they had a family of three dogs, two cats and a parrot, which swore rather rudely every time someone new was announced.

'You must forgive Polly,' Miss Anne told Sarah when they were greeted by a torrent of language more suited to the stables. 'We rescued him from a pet shop because he looked so sad and his feathers were moulting. We really had no idea of his unfortunate habits, but we love him too much to get rid of him.'

'Oh no, you mustn't get rid of him,' Sarah said, because she was fascinated by the brightly coloured Macaw. 'He would be hurt and go into a decline.'

'Knowing that rascal he would probably worm his way into some other unsuspecting person's heart,' Miss Mary said with a snort. She threw a wrathful look at her sister. 'One of these days I may wring his neck!'

'She doesn't mean it,' Miss Anne said, and shook her head at her sibling. 'She thinks I don't know she feeds him her walnut cake – but of course he is naughty. I hope you were not offended by anything he said?'

'Not in the least,' Sarah replied. After her first astonishment at hearing such language in the parlour of two very respectable ladies, she had found it amusing. She warmed to both ladies equally, enjoying their conversation and the excellent tea and cakes they served.

Sarah thought it was one of the most enjoyable afternoons she had spent visiting and told Amelia so as they were driven home.

'I am glad you liked them, because I am rather fond of them,' Amelia said. 'Mary tries to be sensible and take the lead because she is a year or so older, but she has a warm heart and would help anyone. Her threat to wring the parrot's neck was quite spurious.'

'I saw her feed him with a piece of that walnut cake,' Sarah said. 'I think she loves him as much as her sister does.'

'I am sure of it,' Amelia agreed, and smiled at her. 'They both liked you, dearest. You would not have received an invitation to call whenever you wished had they not taken to you.'

'Yes, well, I liked them too, and I may take advantage of their invitation sometimes. It is not so very far to walk.'

'It is even quicker on a bicycle,' Amelia said. 'We have one – quite a new one actually – because Justin uses it when he stays. He visits the sisters, too. He says they are good sports, whatever that may mean.' She laughed. 'Do you think you could ride a bicycle?'

'I could try,' Sarah said, and giggled. 'I think I should enjoy cycling, Amelia. Mother would not approve, of course, but she does not have to know.'

'I think it is quite acceptable in the country these days,' Amelia said. 'I would not offend your mama for the world, Sarah, but she does tend to be a little old-fashioned.'

'Yes, she does,' Sarah agreed. 'That is why I was so pleased to come to you, Amelia. Mama does not mean to – but sometimes she is a little stifling...'

'Yes, I can imagine,' Amelia said, giving her a look of sympathy. 'Well, you shall not be stifled here, my love. I want you to be happy and enjoy yourself. We have several invitations and I shall be inviting friends to dine with us often. I think we might even have a little dance for your birthday. It is your birthday quite soon, I believe?'

'Yes, next month, on the fourteenth,' Sarah told her. 'I should love a dance – if it is not too much trouble?'

'Why should it be any trouble?' Amelia asked. 'It will be a small affair, of course, but—' She broke off as she saw that a car had drawn up in front of the house. The servants were taking a trunk from the back. 'Do you know, I believe that is Justin. He must have been given leave and come down to visit us. Bunnykins will be pleased!' Amelia was clearly excited herself, though she tried to suppress it.

Sarah had heard a great deal about Sir Keith's nephew and she was curious to meet him. As she followed Amelia into the house she heard the sound of male laughter. It sounded as if there were more than two gentlemen, talking and laughing in the front parlour. A little behind Amelia, she did not see the new-comers at first, though Sir Keith was standing near the empty fireplace. He was smiling and looked very pleased with the young man

154

standing quite close to him, who was wearing an army uniform. Sarah's gaze travelled on to the third gentleman and her breath caught as he turned his head at that moment and she found herself looking at Troy Pelham. For a moment her heart raced so furiously that she thought she might faint, but as he frowned she took a deep breath to steady herself. She must not let him see that she was affected by his unexpected arrival.

'Will you introduce us, Justin?' Amelia said, as she went to kiss his cheek. 'Who is this gentleman you have brought to visit us?'

'We travelled down together, Melia,' Captain Justin Roberts replied. 'His name is Troy Pelham.'

'I know Troy's father,' Sir Keith said. 'We often use the same club in town, you know. Troy just stopped off on his way to stay with friends. I have been trying to persuade him to stay here for a couple of days.'

'Oh yes, you must, if you can,' Amelia said, and smiled at him. 'Troy Pelham – Lord Pelham's son. You know Sarah Trenwith, of course. Sarah, this must be a pleasant surprise for you?'

'Yes...' Sarah's mouth was dry and she still felt shocked but she had recovered sufficiently to come forward with a smile and offer her hand. 'It is nice to see you again, Troy.' Her expression was a little reproachful as she met his steady gaze and he arched one eyebrow, as if to question it. 'I was told you had gone for officer training at Sandhurst.'

155

'Yes, I've been there for a few weeks – since just after we last met,' Troy replied. He was frowning, as if something were on his mind, but he didn't say anything more. Sarah did not expect it since they were in company, but she would certainly have a few questions if she managed a little time alone with him. 'I should like to stay another time, but I am promised to Lady Ardingly. However, I think the house is quite near – perhaps I may be permitted to call for tea another day? I am here for the next few days.'

'Tomorrow we take tea with Lady Ardingly,' Amelia said. 'Perhaps you would dine with us the following evening? I have a small dinner party arranged, and Justin will be glad of your company, I am sure.'

'Yes, of course,' Justin said. He came towards Sarah, offering his hand. 'I am pleased to meet you, Sarah. Amelia has mentioned you once or twice. I am glad you have come to visit.'

He was tall, of a similar height and build to Troy, but his hair was blond, his eyes green. He was, Sarah realized, extremely good-looking, and his smile had a warmth and charm she had seldom seen equalled. It was hardly surprising that he was a favourite with both Sir Keith and Amelia, who had no children of their own as yet.

'Thank you,' Sarah replied. 'I am glad to meet you, because I have heard good things of you from both Sir Keith and Amelia.'

'Well, I must be on my way, because I am expected,' Troy said. His eyes moved to Sarah's

156

face, seeming to darken with intensity as he looked at her. 'I shall see you for dinner the day after tomorrow, and perhaps before then ... I am glad to see you looking so well, Sarah.'

Sarah inclined her head. She was not certain how to reply. He had no idea of the distress she had been given after his visit to her father, or of the punishment she had suffered because of it.

'Thank you,' she said in a soft voice that could hardly be heard, and then he had turned away, was leaving the room. She wanted to go after him, to explain what had happened and why she was here, but politeness held her back. Young ladies did not run after gentlemen, even if they had almost broken their hearts over them. What she had to say to him must wait for another day.

It seemed a long evening, even though Justin was charming company. He made them all laugh, including Sarah, but particularly Amelia. Amelia seemed to hang on his words and to watch him wherever he went. Watching her, Sarah suspected that her feelings for her husband's nephew might be stronger than mere friendship. He was, after all, nearer to Amelia's age than her husband was, and so attractive that most women would find him exciting to be near. Sarah wondered if they might be having an affair as she saw their eyes meet once or twice, but she dismissed the idea as ridiculous. Amelia loved her husband, and he was generous and kind. She would never do anything to hurt him.

After she had said goodnight to her friends, Sarah undressed and went to sit on a little ledge built into the slightly overhanging window. She had the window open, because the night was stuffy and warm, but she had put out her lamp because she did not wish to be seen sitting there in her nightgown.

When she heard the voices in the garden she drew back, feeling guilty because she had not meant to listen to a private conversation. She had imagined everyone had retired but Amelia and Justin must have gone down again, perhaps to meet in private.

'I've told you I can't ... I won't betray him,' Amelia's voice was low and urgent. 'I can't hurt him, Justin. He has been so good to me and I love him.'

'Not as you love me,' Justin said. 'You think of him as a father or a kind uncle. It is me you want ... me who sets you on fire with desire.'

'Yes, I want you,' Amelia admitted, and there was a note of desperation in her voice, 'but I won't lie with you, Justin. I can't do that to Bunnykins.'

'Why you use that ridiculous name I have no idea,' Justin snapped, sounding angry. 'If you had a proper relationship you wouldn't resort to using childish nicknames. You are not in love with him. You never have been.'

'I do love Keith,' Amelia said. 'No, don't look like that, please. I love him as a dear friend, and I won't hurt him. You shouldn't have come, Justin. I told you last time that I wouldn't...'

Sarah heard a gasping sound as she got up

and moved away from the window. She restrained the impulse to look out and see them kissing, because she knew it must be happening. Justin would try to persuade Amelia to give into his demands by any means at his disposal.

Sarah had thought him charming at dinner, but now she wasn't so sure. It was not the act of a decent gentleman to try and steal his uncle's much-loved wife. Amelia was also at fault, of course, because she ought never to have agreed to meet him in secret in the moonlight, but at least she was trying to resist him. Sarah did not know if Amelia would be strong enough. It depended how strong her attraction to the younger man was – and how deeply she loved her husband.

The difference between the two men was obvious. Sir Keith was twenty years older than his wife and a dear, sweet man – but Justin was young, strong and virile. Married to an older man, who treated her as if she were a goddess, it was not surprising that Amelia might be tempted, but it was a temptation she ought to fight if she could.

Retiring to her bed, Sarah thought about the strange lives people lived. Amelia was not alone in her situation; it happened often in families like hers and Sarah's. Sarah's own mother had married for position and wealth, and in the end Marianne had chosen a man she did not truly love simply to have the consequence of being a wife.

Sarah had believed that Amelia was truly

happy, but now she realized that a lot of it might be a front she put up to hide her true feelings. Discovering Amelia's secret had made Sarah even more determined that she would only marry for love. She had no intention of spending her life in useless regret. If she had the chance to experience true happiness she would take it.

In the morning Amelia chose to stay in bed later than usual. When Sarah asked if she might enter her room, she was admitted with a cheerful invitation, but she sensed that her friend's manner was a little forced.

'Are you quite well?' Sarah asked, feeling concerned as she saw the shadows beneath Amelia's eyes. She looked as if she had been weeping.

'Yes, it is just one of my little headaches, Sarah. It will soon go. I shall be better by this afternoon. Go for a little walk and I shall see you at luncheon.'

'Is there anything I can do for you before I go?'

'No, nothing at all,' Amelia said. 'As I said, it is merely a small indisposition and I shall be better presently. I shall see you at luncheon.'

'Yes, of course. I will leave you to rest.'

Sarah went downstairs. Amelia was usually so bright and happy. Sarah did not like to see her in distress, but there was little she could say to comfort her. Amelia had a problem to solve. It must be causing her some heartache. Sarah could not speak of it to her for it would be embarrassing. She ought not to have listened to those first few moments of Amelia's private conversation. Unless Amelia decided to confide in her it would be wrong to show that she knew about the secret liaison the previous night.

Sarah went out into the garden. There was no need for a shawl or wrap of any kind, because it was a very warm morning. She decided to follow the same path she had taken the previous day, and when after half an hour of walking she saw Troy coming towards her, also on foot, it had a kind of inevitability about it. He smiled a little uncertainly as they met.

'I was coming to visit you, Sarah.'

'I am walking to the cliffs. It will be cooler there – if you would care to walk with me?'

'Yes, I should enjoy that,' Troy said. 'It is a coincidence that we should both be visiting friends in Hastings, is it not?'

'Yes, though it has a connection. I should not have been sent here had you not visited my father...'

Troy frowned at her. 'Amelia seems very nice...'

'Yes, she is. It is not a punishment to stay with her – but my father is not pleased with me. I was upset and angry after you left without seeing me and I was a little hasty in what I said. Father confined me to my room until I apologized, and I did not care to for some days.'

'Ah...' Troy nodded, his expression serious. 'I see – that explains your look yesterday. I had not realized. I suppose you did not get my letter?'

'No. If you sent one it was kept from me.'

'I should have guessed it would be. Your father is not a reasonable man, Sarah.'

'I am afraid Father is very fond of Marianne. More so than of me; it has always been that way. He is angry because you did not forgive her and take her back.'

'Marianne knows that I forgave her. I thanked her, because after she jilted me I realized that we would never have suited.'

'She was sorry afterwards. I think she took Barney on the rebound.'

'Yes, perhaps...' Troy stopped walking and looked at her. 'What are we to do, Sarah? It may be some time before your parents relent.'

'My mother hinted that she might be prepared to persuade Father if we are of the same mind in a year or so...'

Troy's gaze narrowed, darkened. Sarah was aware of a lark singing somewhere above their heads and there was a heavy scent in the air that she could not identify, but would always remember when she thought of this moment.

'That is a long time, Sarah. I shall be transferred to active service as soon as war is declared. I believe that will be quite soon now ... perhaps days.'

'I would marry you now today if I could,' Sarah said. The possibility of an imminent war made her cast caution to the wind. 'I love you, Troy. I always shall ... even if we have to wait for ages to marry.'

'Are you sure?' he asked. 'I feel it would be wrong to ask you to wait. I shall be away for long periods and you may meet someone else...' Sarah shook her head, her face tight with passion. 'I may be killed...'

'No! Do not say it,' she cried. 'Please, Troy. I can't bear to think of it happening.'

'You have to accept it, if we are to be engaged...'

'Engaged?' Her head came up, her face alight with excitement. 'But Father...'

'Need not know,' Troy said. 'It will be our secret. I shall be here for a few days, Sarah. I shall give you a ring but you must wear it on a chain beneath your gown. In our hearts we shall be bound to each other, but we must wait until a few months have passed, and then I shall speak to your father again. I have asked Lord Pelham to try and mend fences and I hope he may be able to ease the way for us but...'

Sarah reached up to touch her lips to his. 'When I am one and twenty I can marry without permission,' she said, as she drew back. 'If Father still refuses us I shall run away with you then. It is not so very long, though too long for me. I wish we could be married before you have to go to war, Troy.'

'You cannot wish it more than I,' Troy said. He reached out, pulling her in close to his chest, gazing down at her with a hunger that she could not resist as his mouth came down to take possession of hers. A surging desire raced through her, because Troy had never kissed her this way. He had been gentle, restrained, but now he was kissing her as a man kisses the woman he loves – as a husband kisses his wife. In that moment Sarah understood Amelia's dilemma. She knew an urgent longing to be one with Troy and experience all the sweetness of loving.

'We have only a few days, Sarah, and we shall meet in company, but we must be alone as much as possible. Can you meet me again?'

'Yes, of course, every day,' Sarah said, and smiled up at him, all the honesty of her love in her face. 'We shall find ways to be alone wherever we are, Troy. I don't want to waste a minute...'

'We shall spend as much of this precious time together as we can,' Troy promised. 'I did not expect you to be here when I visited Lady Ardingly, but now that I have found you, my darling, I intend to be with you as much as possible.'

Sarah laughed softly as she looked up at him. She had thought they might not meet for ages; she had wondered if his anger might drive him away from her, but she had been given a short time of happiness and she was going to take it with both hands. She would make excuses to get away on her own, even if she had to lie to do it...

It seemed that fortune was determined to favour them. They met again that afternoon at Lady Ardingly's villa, which stood in a prominent position on the cliffs looking out at the sea. After tea, some of the ladies began talking of a campaign about various projects that the Women's Movement was thinking of undertaking. But Lady Ardingly asked Troy if he would show Sarah the view from the cliffs.

'Troy does not wish to hear this,' she explained with a little laugh. 'Take him away, my dear, or he will throw all sorts of spanners in the works – what a delightfully modern expression! Where does one pick these things up? Amelia will fill you in later.'

Sarah obediently followed Troy from the room and out of the house. He offered her his arm and they strolled towards the edge of the cliffs. It was perfectly proper for they were within sight of the house the whole time and there was no chance to indulge in the kisses they had exchanged earlier.

'Did you ask Lady Ardingly to send us off like that?' Sarah asked, a glimmer of amusement in her eyes as she looked up at him.

'She knows that I care for you,' Troy replied. 'She is perfectly capable of thinking of these things for herself. Would you rather have stayed?'

'No, of course not. You know that,' Sarah said, and smiled. 'What better employment than walking with you on the cliffs like this...? The sea is blue today. So often it looks grey...'

'Shall I kidnap you and carry you off to my lair?' Troy asked, a wicked sparkle in his eyes. 'If I were the rogue your father thinks me I should do it with no compunction.'

'You would not have to kidnap me,' Sarah

told him, her eyes bright. 'If you asked me to elope I should go with you...'

Troy looked at her, his eyes ablaze with passion. 'I believe you are brave enough, my love – but it would not be fair. We hope to live together for the rest of our lives and that is a long time to be estranged from your family. Your father would never forgive us – and mine wouldn't be too pleased.'

'No, I don't imagine he would.'

'I am afraid that we shall just have to wait, Sarah.'

'Yes, I suppose so,' she said. She felt suddenly as if a cold shadow had fallen over the sun, though the sky was still blue. She did not mind that they could not marry too much while she could see him and kiss him each day – but what about when he left?

The days flew by too quickly for Sarah. Each morning Troy met her as she went for her usual walk. They chose secluded spots where they could embrace and kiss without being seen, and Sarah's pleasure in his gentle lovemaking grew with every touch. Her heart, soul and mind were entirely his, and while she did her best to conceal it from her friends, Sarah knew that Troy had become her whole world, and she lived in dread of the war that all the papers were now saying was inevitable.

The announcement came as the people returned to work after the bank holiday. Amelia's husband was the first to hear and he told his wife and Sarah as they had tea together that afternoon.

'Oh no!' Amelia said, and looked quickly at Justin. 'Does that mean you must leave us immediately?'

'I shall go in a day or so,' he said. 'We shall all be recalled almost at once, but my leave is not over yet. I daresay I may receive a telegram, and if I do I may have to leave sooner.'

'According to the latest edition of the paper, it will all be over by Christmas,' Sir Keith said as his wife handed him a cup. 'No cake for me, my dear. I believe Lord Kitchener may have a different opinion...'

Sarah was on thorns. They were due to spend the evening at home and she had no idea when she would see Troy again. Would he choose to stay until the end of his leave or rejoin his regiment at once?

It was difficult to make small talk and Sarah was glad to escape to her room. She had changed for the evening and was walking downstairs when she heard voices in the hall. As she reached the bottom she saw that Troy was talking to Amelia and Justin. He turned his head, his eyes meeting hers urgently.

'I wanted to see you, because I must leave in the morning.'

'Must you...?' Sarah said, her throat tight with emotion. 'I thought another day or so...'

'Things have changed,' Troy said. 'Amelia has asked me to dinner but I should like to spend the time with you if...' He left the question open.

'Yes, of course.' Sarah turned to her cousin.

'Will you excuse me, please? I am not hungry and I should like to go for a last walk with Troy...'

'Of course,' Amelia said. 'I understand completely. I shall tell the others that you did not feel like coming into dinner.' She smiled at them. 'Run along, my dears. Make the most of your evening.'

'Thank you!' Sarah said, and kissed her cheek.

'Will you need a coat?' Troy asked but Sarah shook her head. She did not want to waste a second of their last evening together.

'I left a shawl in the hall,' Sarah said. 'I can pick it up as we go...'

Troy held his hand out to her as they went out of the house. She clung to it, saying nothing as they walked away from the house. For the moment they would be in full view of the front windows and must therefore behave with discretion. However, they chose to walk in the direction of the lake and the folly, which Amelia had warned might be unsafe to use. However, when they reached it, the door was open. Without speaking, they went inside. It had been furnished with cane furniture and a chaise longue, piled with cushions. For somewhere that was thought unsafe it was in excellent repair. Sarah wondered briefly if Amelia had reasons of her own for setting it off limits. However, she had little time to ponder for Troy pulled at her hand. They sat down on the sofa together, their eyes meeting.

'I wanted to say goodbye in private,' Troy

said. He reached inside his jacket and brought out a small velvet box. 'This isn't what I planned to buy for your engagement ring, but please accept it for the moment. When I am next in London I shall buy something more fitting.' Sarah took the box and opened it to find a beautiful cluster ring of assorted precious stones. She knew that the first letters of each gem spelled 'regard' and smiled as Troy slipped it on her finger. 'It is not an engagement ring but it is the promise of one – the promise that when all this sorry business is over I shall come back and claim you for my wife.'

'Troy, it's beautiful,' Sarah said. 'I love it and shall treasure it always.' She moved towards him, her eyes bright and her breath coming faster as her lips parted on a lingering sigh. 'I love you. I hardly know how I shall bear it when you leave...'

'I wish that I didn't have to leave you,' Troy said, pulling her towards him. 'I hate it that nothing can be settled between us...' He bent his head, kissing her hungrily, with a passion that set little flames of desire racing through her. He cradled her face with his hands, gazing into her eyes. 'You are all I love ... all I want. I want you so much, my darling Sarah.' He leaned towards her, his thumb moving over her bottom lip.

'Troy...' Sarah swayed towards him, her body aching with desire. 'I love you so much. Couldn't we...?' The words would not come because she was a little frightened of this overwhelming feeling sweeping through her.

Troy smiled and kissed her softly on the lips. 'I know,' he whispered close to her ear. 'It is what I want too, my darling, but we must wait. I shall get leave. I shall come back to you and then we'll ask your father together for his permission.'

'If Father doesn't give it I'll elope with you to Scotland and be married over the anvil,' Sarah declared, her face filled with blind passion. 'I swear I will, Troy!'

He laughed, some of the tension going out of him as he began to kiss her. 'We shall be patient for a little longer, my darling. I will come to you as soon as I can get a pass...'

'And we still have tonight,' Sarah whispered. 'I don't want to sleep tonight, Troy. I want to sit here with you and watch the dawn break...'

He drew her to him and they kissed. Sarah sighed with longing. She wanted more than kisses and she knew Troy did too, but because he was a man of honour he was being patient. And perhaps what people said was true. This horrid war would be over in a few weeks and Troy would come back to her.

A little voice at the back of her mind was asking a question she could not bear to face. For the moment at least she would ignore it. She was in Troy's arms and she would not think about her life if he did not return...

Seven

Sarah slipped into the house by a side door at just after five in the morning. Troy had left her reluctantly, because he had to get ready for the journey he planned to make later that morning. Sarah had smiled, kissed him one last time, and then run from him before she gave way to the tears that were pressing hard behind her eyes. She went upstairs and was in time to see Amelia disappear into her own room. Had she been up all night too? Had she been saying goodbye to her lover?

Sarah dismissed the thought, because she had no right to question her cousin's actions. Amelia was a married woman but her husband was much older. Sarah could not condemn her if, faced with the prospect of war, she had given in to Justin and made love to him. If she had been just a little braver Sarah might have persuaded Troy to forget his principles and make love to her.

She sighed as she slipped into bed, knowing that she needed to sleep for a while. Her throat was tight and a few tears slid down her cheeks as she buried her face in soft pillows, but mercifully sleep claimed her.

It was almost noon before Sarah finally went

downstairs. Amelia came down a little later as she was sitting in the parlour, looking out at a dull morning and trying not to feel sorry for herself.

'There you are, my love,' Amelia said. Her face was pale and there were suspicious red blotches on her nose, which she had attempted to cover with face powder. 'Justin decided that perhaps he ought to rejoin sooner rather than wait for the summons. He left early this morning. I saw him off.'

'Yes, I see,' Sarah said, and forced a smile. 'I hate this war, Amelia. It is horrible to think of people killing each other.'

'Yes, it is,' Amelia agreed. 'But we can't sit about and mope, Sarah. We shall be needed. There are all kinds of volunteer jobs that need doing. We were talking of it the other day. Soldiers will need extra socks and scarves, things like that, of course. We are setting up a group to knit and sew, because we shall send parcels out to them, food as well. And we are setting up a committee to deal with the wounded when they are sent home. In past wars many disabled soldiers have been treated disgracefully, left to beg on the streets or seek help in an infirmary where only rudimentary treatment is given. Our committee has decided to take over a small nursing home and run it for the benefit of badly wounded soldiers. Similar schemes will be set up all over the country and in that way we shall make a contribution to the war effort.'

'I should like to help with that,' Sarah said,

the shadows banished from her eyes, at least for the moment. 'I asked Mother to let me become a VAD some weeks ago but she wouldn't agree, but I could help with your convalescent home, couldn't I?'

'Yes, of course, once the men start to come home,' Amelia said with a smile. 'At the moment crowds are cheering on the streets and waving flags. It is good to be patriotic, Sarah. However, the truth is that the war will be nasty. Sir Keith is very worried about Justin and he has agreed to help fund our home. We shall need to raise more money, of course. You can help with that for the time being, and then we shall find you something to do at the home.'

'You are a brick,' Sarah said, and smiled at her. 'I want to help in any way I can. Besides, it will give me something to do, make me stop worrying about Troy, at least for a while.'

'Exactly.' Amelia's smile was more natural now. 'We both have someone we love involved in the fighting – or we shall have when it starts,' she said. 'We'll help and support each other, Sarah. And we will help others.'

'When do we start?'

'We are having a bring-and-buy sale at the church hall next week,' Amelia said. 'I should like you to help out on the cake stall if you will. And in the meantime you can help me go through my wardrobe. I am going to sort out some things for the second-hand clothes stall...'

'You have such lovely things. I am sure there

will be a queue to buy anything you decide to give.'

'We'll see,' Amelia said, and looked happier than she had for a couple of days. 'Shall we have a look together? You can help me decide what I should give and what I should keep...'

Sarah got up at once. She would have done anything to keep herself busy, because her heart ached and she knew that if she sat still she would not be able to think of anything but Troy and the feel of his lips on hers. Already she was regretting that she had not been braver. If she had asked Troy to make love to her she would at least have had that to remember.

Sarah worked hard for the next few weeks. Everyone had ideas about how to raise funds for the convalescent home. Amelia was always being asked to sit on a new committee and she never refused. Sarah suspected that she needed to keep busy too, because otherwise she would be thinking of Justin.

They held tombolas, jumble sales, fêtes and a concert in the church hall, all in aid of the convalescent home. Sarah was kept busy running errands, knitting, sewing and helping out at the various events. In the third week of August the committee took over the home and the nursing staff arrived. Cleaners had been in there first and scrubbed the floors and walls so that the whole place smelled of carbolic when Amelia and Sarah joined the inspection party.

Some of the ladies wrinkled their noses at the

smell, but Amelia was more practical. She had organized proper beds and the bedding that would be needed, also chests, a chair and cupboard for each bedroom. New curtains were being made and all the other little things that were needed to make it feel more like a home than a small hospital. The common room was furnished with comfortable chairs and tables, and there was a games room where the men who were able could play billiards or darts.

'What we need now are books and puzzles, something for the men who can't move very far,' Amelia said, and Sarah added it to the list she was making for the committee. And we need vases, lots of them. I think we kept a few back from the bring-and-buy sale, but we shall need more. I think flowers brighten a home and make it look more cheerful.'

Sarah scribbled busily as the tour continued. She was introduced to the nursing staff, and talked to Sister Norton for more than twenty minutes when the committee went off to drink tea and talk some more in the committee room at the end of the tour.

'I should like to help out when the men start coming in,' Sarah confided. 'I'm not trained like you, but if there is anything I can do...'

'We can always find work for willing helpers,' Sister Norton told her. 'I'll speak to Matron, but I know she will agree. The men who can't leave their beds need help and we don't always have the time. If you were willing to come in for a few hours each day you could do errands. The flowers Lady Roberts wants need the water changing and the dead ones taken away. Books will get left in the wrong place, and some of the men will like to be read to – often letters from home. Some of them might need help with writing letters. Fetching a drink or perhaps bringing something in from the village is always helpful...'

'Oh yes,' Sarah said eagerly. 'I should enjoy doing all that kind of thing, but I don't mind doing some of the dirty work if you need help.'

'I think we have volunteers more suited to that,' Sister Norton told her kindly. 'A lot of the time just seeing your pretty face will be enough to lift the spirits of a man feeling ill. Make yourself useful and that is all we ask.'

Sarah felt she was being let off lightly, but she was happy to do everything that was asked of her. It took her mind off her loneliness, stopped her worrying for a few hours. Troy had written to her once, telling her that they were all up to their eyes in training exercises.

It isn't so bad for the officers, because we knew what to expect, but some of the volunteers are finding it hard. Most of them don't have uniforms yet and they look a raggle-taggle lot: some of them need new boots and I think they can never have had a decent pair in their lives. It makes me realize how privileged I have been, Sarah. I am glad to hear of all your fund-raising. Some of these poor devils won't know what has hit them when they get over there. They laugh and jest and seem to think it is all a great lark. I don't suppose they have any idea of what is coming. One of them brought his dog on

176

parade until the sergeant sent it packing. But the discipline is coming slowly. I doubt any of them realized they would spend hours learning how to dig a trench when they rushed to sign up!

The food is tolerable for the officers but I am not sure the men feel the same way. I sent out for fish and chips for my own men the other night. The cheers echoed round the camp and the next morning I noticed I was getting rather more enthusiastic salutes as I passed.

Everyone speaks of it being a short war – except Lord Kitchener and a few of us who think that the German Army may turn out to be more formidable than the government seems to imagine. They are so damned slow. One would have thought there had been ample time to get ready because the signs have been there for months, but the supplies are woefully short. I only hope that by the time we actually get over there we shall have real guns!

Try not to worry too much, my love. I daresay it will all turn out to be a storm in a teacup, as some of the papers seem to think, and I shall be back with you before you know it. I love you and think of you all the time, Sarah. Please keep loving me. I am not sure if I shall get leave before they ship us over. Take care of yourself.

Your loving friend and husband to be one day, Troy

Sarah wasn't sure whether his letter, which she read over and over again, made her want to laugh or cry. His stories about the men in camp were amusing, but underneath she knew there was a more serious side. England was under-prepared for war, and she sensed that Troy felt they ought to wake up and take things more seriously. There had been so much euphoria in the papers. Everyone seemed to imagine it was going to be easy to teach the Hun a lesson, but Troy's letter gave Sarah serious misgivings.

At night when she lay in bed her thoughts were of him in the army camp and sometimes she felt close to tears. She hated to think that he might be hurt or killed and she longed for him to be here with her. She knew that it was the same for hundreds and thousands of other wives, mothers, sisters and girlfriends. They were all left at home with time on their hands to think about what might happen. No matter how much they threw themselves into the war work they could not forget that the men they loved would soon be putting their lives at risk.

'There's a letter for you,' Amelia said, as she came into the parlour that morning. 'I think it is from your home...'

Sarah took the letter without enthusiasm. Her mother's letters were more a duty than a pleasure, but as she looked at the writing she saw it was from her sister. Marianne must have been staying with her parents because Sir James had franked it for her.

I daresay you are having fun with Cousin Amelia. I am stuck at home with Mother and Father because Barney has deserted me. He has joined up! I begged him not to but he wouldn't listen. I wept but he simply ignored me and said it was his duty to join. He is so selfish I can't tell you. He knows that I am in delicate health at the moment because ... I am with child. It is all too horrid and I feel miserable. Mother says the sickness will pass but she doesn't understand. I do not wish to have a child yet. It is much too soon and Barney is so inconsiderate. No one cares how I feel...

Sarah scanned the remainder of the letter. It was all in the same vein. Marianne had no thought for anyone but herself. She did not care that Barney felt it his duty to sign up. All that mattered to Marianne was that she felt ill and wanted her husband at home to run after her.

'Something wrong?' Amelia asked, as Sarah laid the letter to one side.

'Marianne is with child and feeling sorry for herself,' Sarah said. 'Her husband has joined up and she thinks he should have stayed at home to look after her.'

'Ah, I see,' Amelia said, and frowned. 'Marianne always was a little self-centred, but I believe that having a child is a difficult time. She will feel better when the child is born.'

'Perhaps,' Sarah agreed. 'I know she hates to feel unwell.'

'You don't wish to go home to be with her?'

'No, she would be impossible,' Sarah cried, and pulled a face. 'It is best if she feels that she is the centre of attention for the moment. If Mama wanted me home she would say.'

'I am glad. I should hate to lose you, Sarah.'

'I should hate to leave,' Sarah said. The idea

179

of being at home while Marianne was staying with their parents was enough to make Sarah shudder. Her sister's temper had always been uncertain but she would be almost unbearable now, because Sarah knew Marianne would find reasons to find fault with her. She would never forgive her for taking Troy from her, even though it had happened after she had told him their engagement was over.

Sarah knew that Marianne was unhappy. She didn't love her husband as she ought, and she resented the fact that she was now carrying his child. Sarah felt some sympathy for her, but it did not make her want to return home. She was much happier staying with Amelia than she had ever been.

The news of the bloodbath at Mons came with the papers the next morning. After all the euphoria it was shocking reality to learn that so many soldiers had died. Despite the efforts of the British forces, the enemy had been too strong for them and they had been forced to retreat.

Sir Keith had ordered all the papers and they all sat together reading the dreadful news.

'It says that civilians were caught in the cross-fire as they attended church,' Amelia exclaimed. 'How terrifying that must have been for them.'

'The casualties were high,' Sir Keith said with a frown. He looked at his wife. 'Are you ready to take wounded in, Amelia? I think you may be getting them very soon now.'

180

Sarah was reading another paper. The report said that there were many bloody battles along the line that ran from Belgium in the north to Alsace and Lorraine in the south. The British had been forced to retreat to the Somme, which was the last barrier before France.'

'Do you imagine the Russians will fare any better than our men?' Sarah asked, looking up from her paper.

'They have already suffered a heavy defeat,' Sir Keith told her, looking grim. 'We will exchange...' He passed his paper over and Sarah read the report he had indicated. 'Does this mean it is over? Have the Germans won?'

'Good grief no,' Sir Keith said gruffly. 'We shall fight on, do whatever is necessary to hold on. It isn't the first time we've had setbacks in a war, Sarah. I admit that it looks bad now, but we'll come about, never you fear.'

Sarah nodded but couldn't trust herself to speak. She was much affected by the gloomy news and couldn't help thinking of Troy. She knew her host and hostess would have fears for Justin. No one was saying too much, but they were all thinking a great deal.

'I think I shall go down to the home,' Amelia said. 'We must be ready for our first batch of patients and I want to be sure we have all we need.'

'May I come with you?' Sarah asked. She couldn't bear to be at home. She was restless, her fear for Troy so strong that she felt sick.

'Of course you can,' Amelia replied, giving her a look filled with sympathy. 'If nothing else we can fill some vases with flowers and take in the books and magazines I bought this week...'

The news had continued to be gloomy for the past weeks but Sarah no longer read the papers. She found them too depressing, and it only made her feel anxious when she read of more casualties. She had received one letter from Troy, much of which had been crossed out so that she could only guess at what it said, but he had been alive after the defeat at Mons and that was all she needed to know. At the end he spoke of loving her and missing her. She pressed his signature to her lips and put the letter away in her writing box.

Sarah had been sending letters to the last address Troy had given her and she hoped they were sent on to him in Belgium. However, they now had twenty convalescing soldiers filling their rooms at the home and she found most of her time was spent there. Several of the men had minor injuries, which was why they had been sent to a home rather than a hospital. A couple had lost limbs and were still very ill. Sarah was not allowed to visit them for the first few weeks of their stay. However, the men who had lesser injuries were always pleased to see her.

She changed flowers in the mornings and she kept the books and papers tidy, which was a thankless job because the men were always leaving them about. For those who were still confined to bed she fetched drinks. She also smuggled cigarettes in for some of them, though Sister Norton did not like the men to smoke in their rooms. Sarah bought sweets, magazines and cakes from her own money to supplement what the committee had allocated for such things, because she enjoyed seeing the pleasure it gave her patients. They called her their angel and greeted her with cheers and jokes, some of them bringing a blush to her cheeks. A few of the men were officers, but Amelia had made it plain from the start that the home was open to all wounded soldiers and some of the privates were rather loud and cheeky. But none of them would have dreamed of being coarse or rude to the young woman who gave up so much of her time to entertain and help them.

September was halfway through when Sarah saw the young officer who had been blinded by an enemy bombardment on their lines. His face was badly burned on one side, but she had heard from the nurses that his right side was unblemished. When you looked at him from that side he appeared attractive, normal, but when he turned his head the extent of his injury was evident.

He had been off limits except to the nurses who cared for him until that morning, when one of them came to the common room to ask Sarah if she could spare a few minutes.

'Captain Tom Shaw has been asking if some-one will write a letter for him,' Nurse Ellen Browne told her. 'I would do it but Sister has been after me all morning. We have two new cases and they are pretty bad. Captain Shaw is over the critical stage now. He was still in a lot of pain and we kept him drugged until yesterday. Now he is awake and beginning to realize that he is going to live he has started to ask questions. We had to tell him that he will be permanently blind, because he insisted on knowing.'

'How sad,' Sarah said, feeling her eyes prick with tears. 'Yes, of course I will write his letter. I would have visited before but they wouldn't let me.'

'He can have visitors now if he wants.' Nurse Ellen frowned. 'I don't know if he realizes what his face looks like yet. Don't tell him it is awful if he asks. We don't want him to know, because he has to get used to the blindness first.'

Sarah promised she wouldn't. She felt a bit nervous as she collected her writing materials. Most of the wounds she had seen were not too serious. Even those who had missing limbs, had empty sleeves or trouser legs, hiding their fearful injuries. A lot of the men joked about being crippled, though she knew it was often bravado and that in private they shed a few tears, but she hadn't yet seen anyone with a mutilated face. She steeled herself not to show emotion in any way. Captain Shaw might not be able to see her face, but if she made a sound of alarm or hesitated he would notice it, and she would hate to add to his problems.

She knocked at his door, which was closed, and was bidden to enter. Peering round the door, Sarah saw the damaged side of his face first. It was red and angry-looking, though it had begun to yellow at the edges, which was a sign that it had begun to heal. The doctors had allowed him to come off some of the drugs, which must mean they thought he was healing and that the pain was less than it had been. Sarah was shocked at what had happened to him, but thankfully the sight didn't make her shudder or feel sick; she just felt very sad that he had been hurt so terribly.

'Who is it?' he asked.

'My name is Sarah Trenwith. I've come to write a letter for you if you want me to?'

'Sarah ... are you the one they call the angel?'

'Yes, some of the men call me that,' Sarah said, as she advanced into the room. 'I suppose it is because I try to help them if I can.'

'Do you have a cigarette?'

'I am sorry. I don't smoke, but I can get some for you.'

'I don't know if I have any money. I'm not sure of anything much.'

'You don't need money,' Sarah said. 'We have a fund for that sort of thing. I can get some for you but Sister Norton may confiscate them. She doesn't like the men to smoke in their rooms.'

'She'd be the one with a voice like a steel grater,' Captain Shaw said. 'You have a soft voice, Sarah. Are you pretty?'

'Some people think so. If you saw my sister you wouldn't think so. She was the beautiful one in our family—' Sarah broke off as she realized what she had said. 'That was thought-less of me. I am sorry.'

185

'You don't have to be. I'm blind. You can't pretend I'm not, but you don't have to tiptoe around me.'

'No, but I shouldn't let my tongue run away with me, should I? My hair is fair but Marianne's is like spun silk.'

'What does my face look like?' He put his fingers up to his cheek and she saw him wince. 'It must be a bloody mess.'

'It isn't too bad,' Sarah told him. 'You know you were burned. The pain must be awful. I think all of you are so brave.'

'It doesn't hurt as much now,' he said. 'I want you to write a letter to my girlfriend. We were engaged but I want to break it off...'

'Why?' Sarah exclaimed, without thinking. 'Surely you don't mean that? She will be hurt. I am sure she wants to come and see you as soon as they say she can.'

'You don't know April. She can't stand anything ugly. She won't want to be tied to a man who looks the way I do – and there's the blindness. I shall need everything done for me until I get used to it. I can't expect her to spend her life looking after me. She is bright and beautiful and she deserves better than I can give her now.'

'Why don't you think about it for a little longer?' Sarah asked. 'You might feel differently when—'

'Damn you!' he said. 'Either write what I tell you or go away!'

'If you are sure, I shall write the letter,' Sarah said. 'I am sorry if I spoke out of turn. I just

186

thought – but it isn't my place to think. I will write exactly what you tell me.'

Sarah sat down on the chair near his bed, her pencil at the ready. She would write it out now and then copy it in ink later.

'How would you like me to begin?'

'Say "My dearest April ... "' he said, and then stopped and shook his head. 'No, I can't. Just say that in the circumstances I feel it best that our engagement is ended. Her name is Miss April Thompson and her address is in the letter in my cupboard. Can you find it and write it for me please? I thought I could but I can't. I just want her to know it isn't any use.'

'Shall I write as myself and tell her the facts?' Sarah suggested. 'If she feels she can't face it she will write or come and tell you herself.'

'April won't come when she knows,' he said, a note of bitterness in his voice. 'Why should she? She is beautiful and she could have had anybody. She still could. Why should she give up her life to take care of me?'

'I'll tell her the facts,' Sarah said. She got up and found the letter, tucking it into her writing case. 'Is there anything I can do for you? Would you like sweets or ... anything?' She had been going to ask about magazines but obviously they were no good unless someone read to him. 'I could visit again. I read to some of the men. What books do you like?'

'Please do not bother,' he said. 'I don't need your pity, Miss Trenwith.'

'I wasn't offering because I pity you,' Sarah said. 'I will send your letter. I hope you are wrong about April. Goodbye...' She was on her way out when he called her. She glanced back and saw that he was crying silently.

'I'm sorry,' he said in a muffled voice. 'I like poetry...'

'I'll come tomorrow,' Sarah promised. 'And I will send your letter when I go home.'

Sarah wrote the letter. She made it clear that Captain Shaw would not recover his sight and that one half of his face was badly burned. She said that he would need a lot of help for the next few months and might never be able to live independently. She made no mention of his wanting to break off the engagement. If April wished to break it off she must do it herself.

Sarah posted the letter and walked home. Her heart ached for Captain Shaw and all the others like him, men who had gone to war filled with hope and the wish to help their country, returning to a life that would never be the same. Sarah found it terribly hard to accept the suffering some of the men were forced to endure. Captain Shaw was facing it in the only way he could. She prayed that his girlfriend was brave enough, in love enough, to stand by him, but she wasn't sure Captain Shaw would let her even if she wanted to.

Sarah was in the parlour the next morning when Amelia's maid brought in the telegram. She offered it to Sarah, a scared, anxious look in her eyes.

'Do you think it is bad news, miss?' she asked. 'I was afraid to take it up to her.'

'This is addressed to Sir Keith,' Sarah said, 'but he ought not to open it if it is bad news. I shall take it up to my cousin now.'

'Yes, miss. I hope it isn't bad...'

Sarah nodded. She ran upstairs to Amelia and knocked. Amelia was dressed, apparently ready to come down. She looked at Sarah, turning pale as she saw the envelope in her hand.

'Is it for me?'

'For Sir Keith,' Sarah said. 'I thought I should bring it to you.'

Amelia's hand was shaking as she reached for it, then she drew back swiftly. 'I can't,' she whispered. 'Open it for me please, Sarah.'

Sarah did as she asked and read it through quickly. She felt shocked, stunned as she read it again to make certain. It was the worst news possible.

'I am sorry,' she said. 'Justin is dead. He was killed three days ago...'

'I knew it...' Amelia swayed, her face deathly white. 'I felt it...' She stumbled towards a chair, sinking down into it. For a few moments she stared in front of her as if it were too hard to take in, and then she turned to look at Sarah. 'My husband will be devastated. I must go to him...'

'Would you like me to tell him?' Sarah asked. She saw the agony in Amelia's eyes. 'You are shocked, upset...'

Amelia looked at her. 'You know that I spent

that night with him, don't you? He begged me to let him … and I did…' She blinked hard, refusing to cry even though the pain she was feeling was there in her eyes. 'I am glad I had that and I'm not sorry. I betrayed my husband but I loved Justin in another way…'

'I am so sorry,' Sarah said, but Amelia shook her head. She stood up, lifting her head.

'The telegram, please. I must go to my husband. The servants will be guessing. I don't want him to hear anything before I speak to him. Justin was his heir, because we do not have a child. It will be a huge blow for him.'

Sarah gave her the letter. 'Is there anything I can do for you?'

'No…' Amelia's face was pale but her manner showed determination. 'You must go to the home. You will be expected.'

'But you—' Sarah stopped as Amelia shook her head. 'I shall be all right. Please do not make a fuss. I know you want to comfort me, but I must do this in my own way.'

'Yes, of course,' Sarah said. 'I am here should you need me – if you wish to talk.'

'You are a sweet girl and will be a comfort to me,' Amelia said, lifting her head proudly. 'I must think of Sir Keith now. Excuse me, Sarah. I must go to my husband.'

Sarah watched as she walked from the room. She was holding her grief back because she knew her husband would need her, but at sometime it would need to come out. Amelia loved her husband. If she had given in to her lover's persuasion she must have loved Justin

190

very much.

Sarah went down to the library to fetch a book of Wordsworth's poetry. She would be there for her cousin when Amelia was ready, but for the moment Captain Shaw would be expecting her to visit him.

Sarah saw a young woman in tears coming from the direction of Captain Shaw's room. She called to her, asking if she could help, but the very attractive woman shook her head and broke into a run, clearly not wanting sympathy or contact from anyone.

Sarah hesitated outside the captain's door. If the young woman had been April he might not be in the mood for a visit. However, he might need someone to talk to. She knocked and then went in because there was no answer. He was lying with his head turned away, his hands clenched on top of the sheets. He turned his head, looking at her with one sightless eye: the empty socket covered by a patch.

'Come in, Sarah,' he said in a voice filled with bitterness. 'Why didn't you tell her to stay away? I don't want her here. I don't want her pity.'

'She looked upset to me. Had you been horrible to her?'

'I told her to go away and forget me – if that is being horrible in your estimation then yes, I was.'

'Perhaps she doesn't want to forget you. Have you thought that you might be being selfish by refusing to let her into your life?'

'The sight of my face made her feel sick. She was disgusted. You lied to me, Sarah. You told me it wasn't too bad.'

'I don't think it is,' Sarah said, and went closer. 'Stop feeling sorry for yourself, Captain Shaw. There are worse cases than yours. You still have both legs and arms. Sister Norton told me about a patient who has lost both arms and legs and has burns on his face too. Compared to him you are lucky.'

'So I should shout hurrah and jump up and down thanking the Lord?' he demanded angrily. 'I can do without your sort, thank you. Get out of here and don't come back.'

'I would but I borrowed this book just for you,' she said. 'I am going to read some of it aloud so you can damn well listen to me!'

Sarah sat down and began to read. She didn't look at the man in the bed but she knew he was angry. He didn't say much but he snorted a few times. After she had been reading for some minutes she glanced at him and saw the tears trickling down his cheeks. She kept on reading. To offer sympathy would make him angry again.

The tears dried after another ten minutes. She read a bit longer and then closed the book. 'Is there anything I could get for you?'

'Have you got a cigarette?'

'Yes. Do you want me to light it for you?' He nodded. Sarah put one of the slim tubes between her lips, struck a match and sucked. She coughed as the smoke stung the back of her throat and Captain Shaw laughed.

'Serves you right,' he said. 'You told me you don't smoke. Give it here.'

Sarah took it to him. She put the end close to his mouth and he took it with his lips, bringing his hand up to hold it with his fingers. He drew deeply and then blew a smoke ring at her. She moved back.

'If Sister Norton catches us she will have my guts for garters.'

'Language, Sarah,' he said, and smiled oddly. 'I'll bet your mother didn't teach you to say things like that?'

'She would be horrified at some of the things I've learned since I've been visiting here,' Sarah said. 'Are you all right now?'

'I'll live,' he said. 'You can go now if you want.'

'I'll stay until you've finished that cigarette.'

'Afraid I'll set the bed on fire? I wouldn't be much loss.'

'I wasn't thinking of you. I don't want all our hard work to go up in smoke.'

Captain Shaw laughed. 'Good! You are a breath of fresh air, do you know that, Sarah Trenwith? April wept all over me. She wanted to devote her life to me and she assured me that my family were anxious to have me home.'

'They probably are...'

'Yeah,' he said, and drew on the cigarette. 'I would rather stay here. At least I shan't be that freak upstairs in his room.'

'Well, you can stay if you wish,' Sarah said. 'But what makes you think your family would see you as a freak?'

'I know them. You don't,' he said, and handed her the cigarette. 'Put it out and go. You can come again if you want.'

'Thank you for nothing,' Sarah said. 'I'm not sure why I should want to – but if I have nothing better to do I'll come tomorrow morning.'

Captain Shaw laughed. 'You'll do, Sarah. Get out of here and let a man have some sleep, will you?'

'Of course.'

Sarah left his room. She saw a convenient plant pot and stubbed out the cigarette, discovering that she wasn't the only one to have used it as an ashtray. She felt sad for his hurt and sad for the young woman who had run from him in floods of tears. Sarah didn't mind his rudeness but it would be hard for April to take rejection. Perhaps she would write to her again and ask her to be patient. It was going to take a while but Captain Shaw might adjust in time.

Sarah was just about to leave the grounds when she heard someone call her name.

Sarah spun around looking for the source of the voice. She saw a man in uniform coming towards her and her heart took a flying leap. She ran to him, laughter and tears mingling as he caught her in his arms.

'Troy,' she cried. 'Oh, Troy! I've missed you so much. I've wondered if you were all right...' She looked up at him, searching for some kind of injury but he looked the same as always. 'How did you get home?'

'I think my father must have wangled it

somehow,' Troy said. 'I got sent back with dispatches, some nonsense of getting a medal or something. All a load of rubbish if you ask me, but it means I've got five days' leave...'

'Five days!' Sarah said, her face lighting up in sheer delight. 'Can you spend it all with me?'

'Well, it's four now actually,' he admitted. 'I went home first. But I intend to spend the rest of it with you – if you want me to?'

'You know I do,' Sarah said. 'I love you, Troy. I would spend all my time with you if I could.'

He looked down at her face, touching her cheek with his fingertips. 'I asked my father if yours had relented but he said there was no change yet. I had hoped but it seems we shall just have to go on waiting...'

'We could elope,' Sarah told him. 'We could get married in Scotland.'

'We would need to be there for three weeks. I have four days, my love,' Troy said, and kissed her. 'But we could spend them together. You could pack a few things and we could go some-where quiet where no one knows us – separate rooms, of course...'

'Amelia has had some bad news,' Sarah said. 'Had you heard about Justin?' She saw that he hadn't, saw the way the excitement died from his eyes as she told him. 'I am so sorry...'

'It is happening all the time,' Troy said, a nerve flicking in his cheek. He was hiding his shock and grief, but she knew he felt Justin's death deeply. 'You have a patient here I need to see ... Captain Tom Shaw?'

'I've just left him,' Sarah said. 'I've been reading poetry to him but he wanted to rest. Come up to the house, Troy. You can walk down later and visit. I am sure Amelia and Sir Keith will want to see you.'

'Yes, I must pay my respects in the circumstances,' he said. 'It is a pity that we couldn't just go off together, though I suppose your cousin would not have approved.'

'Amelia wouldn't tell my mother,' Sarah said. 'We might have a daytrip somewhere, Troy, but I couldn't leave her at a time like this...'

'No, of course not,' he said. 'There will be other times and perhaps your father will have seen sense by then...'

'Yes, perhaps,' Sarah said. She offered her hand. He took it, his strong fingers curling about hers. Sarah smiled, feeling as if she were walking on air. Troy was here with her and for the moment everything was right with her world. 'We shall be together as much as possible. It is so lovely to be with you again, Troy.'

'I've thought of you all the time,' Troy said, and there was hunger in his eyes as he looked at her. 'You can't imagine how good it is to know that you are here waiting for me when I come back...'

Eight

'There cannot be a funeral,' Sir Keith said that evening when they had gathered in the drawing room before dinner. Amelia had invited Troy to stay so that he and Sarah could make the most of their time together. Troy had gratefully accepted. 'I am told he was buried where he fell with others who died. I find that incredibly painful. It would have been better if he could have been brought home to lie with his family in the chapel here.'

'Please, my dearest,' Amelia said, her face strained. 'You mustn't upset yourself because of it.'

'I have accepted his death. We knew it could happen. I just wish he could have come home.' Sir Keith sounded calm but his hands shook, though his face showed no expression. 'However, we shall have a memorial service instead. I have asked for it to be soon. You were his friend, Pelham. Perhaps you would say a few words?'

'Yes, of course, if you wish it,' Troy said. 'I am very sorry for your loss, sir. Justin was very popular with the men. He will be much missed.'

'It is harder to bear since he was my heir.' Sir

Keith looked at his wife, who was very pale. 'We shall miss him, my dear. He brought some life to the place. I fear it will be very lonely in the years ahead for you.'

Amelia raised her head, looking him in the eyes. 'This may not be the right time to tell you, Sir Keith, but perhaps it will help. I am ... I have discovered that I am with child...' Her words fell into a stunned silence. 'I know this must be a shock to you, as it was to me.'

For a moment her husband stared at her in stunned disbelief and then a smile broke over his face. He got up, walked towards her as she stood, looking a little nervous, uncertain. He opened his arms, embracing her.

'Such happiness, Amelia. You could not have given me a better gift – and at such a time. I felt that there would be no light in our darkness, but you have provided it, as you always do. I am fortunate indeed to have such a treasure.'

A pulse twitched at the corner of Amelia's eye but otherwise she gave no sign of her distress. Looking at her, Sarah suspected her guilt, guessed her secret, and sensed the pain it had given her to allow her husband to believe the child was his. She had announced it in public because she could not bear his incredulity and his delight.

'You are so good...' Amelia choked. The tears were very close but she held them back, raising her head as the housekeeper came to announce that dinner was served. 'Thank you...'

Sarah glanced at Sir Keith. He looked genuinely pleased. Obviously he was happy that his wife was to have a child, suspecting nothing. She felt a little uncomfortable because she was certain that Amelia's child was not her husband's, but she smothered her doubts. She could not judge. It was not her place. If Sir Keith wished to believe the child was his, it was best for all that he was allowed to keep his dream.

'Nonsense, my dear,' Sir Keith said. 'We must not keep Cook waiting.' He glanced at Troy. 'Will you do me the honour of taking a glass of port later, sir? I should like to know how it really was out there for our men.'

'Yes, of course, sir,' Troy said, and offered Sarah his arm. 'I am at your service...'

Amelia looked at Sarah when they were alone in the drawing room later. She poured tea for them both and handed Sarah her cup.

'Do you despise me?'

'No, of course not.'

'It isn't as bad as you think. Keith knows the truth, he told me himself that he could not have children, but I wanted to make it easier for him. If I had told him privately he might have broken down. He would never do so in public.' She smiled oddly. 'A gentleman's honour comes in handy at times.'

'He knows ... but he looked genuinely pleased?'

'I believe he is in a way. It must hurt of course to know that Justin was my lover, but he will be glad of the child – and he will accept the babe as his heir, in his nephew's stead. That is what matters naturally, an heir, someone to carry on the family name...'

'Sit Keith loves you, but does he know Justin was your lover rather than someone else?'

'Yes, I am sure he does. I think he knew long ago that we felt something for each other, but I was faithful to him. I might still have been had it not been for the war.'

'The war...' Sarah sighed. 'I hate it for what it does to people's lives. You, Justin ... all the men who have been killed or wounded, and the women left at home to grieve.'

'Yes, it is a terrible thing.' Amelia sipped her tea and then smiled at Sarah. 'It is a relief to have that off my mind. Once I was certain, I knew I must tell Sir Keith, but I am glad it is over. I was not sure how he would take the news. Now he has accepted the fact I can be easy again.'

'Did you love Justin?' Sarah asked because Amelia seemed too calm, too emotionless.

'Yes, of course,' Amelia said, and her eyes glittered. 'He has gone from us, Sarah. Life moves on. I must think of my husband now – and the child. Sir Keith will be much happier now he has a child to look forward to...'

Sarah wondered how she could contain her grief. Amelia had always seemed such a light-hearted person, but she was showing another side now that made Sarah wonder who she really was inside.

'The old man is broken over this,' Troy said. 'Put a brave face on it of course, but the cracks showed once or twice when we were alone. He wanted to know if Justin would have suffered. I told him it would have been quick. It isn't always, but I couldn't tell him that sometimes the men wounded during a sortie lie untended in no man's land; they scream for hours and we can't get to them. We can't bring them back until the shelling stops...'

'Oh Troy,' Sarah said, a catch in her voice. 'I am glad you didn't tell him that; it would have been too much for him.'

'Yes, I know.'

She turned to him as they walked in the moonlight. He pulled her close to him, bending his head to kiss her hungrily. 'I love you so much, Sarah. I want you, my darling...' He stopped abruptly, his voice breaking. She knew that he had seen too much suffering since they last met. 'If I shouldn't come back...'

'Troy don't...' Sarah turned to him, putting her arms about him, pulling his head down to kiss him passionately. His hands moved down her body, holding her pressed against him so that she was aware of his need. 'I love you ... want you ... tonight...'

Sarah shivered at his touch. Her body was tingling with a need she barely recognized as desire. All she knew was that Troy was about to leave her. It might be weeks or months before she saw him again. If he were killed in action this might be their last night together. She ought to be his wife! Her father had denied them the happiness of being man and wife. As Troy's kisses grew more and more demanding,

201

Sarah knew that he too felt the need to seal their love and her doubts fled as love made her reckless.

'Sarah, my love...'

'Make me yours,' she whispered against his ear as he held her pressed in an agonized embrace. 'Take me now, Troy...'

'You do not know what you are saying, my love,' Troy said, drawing back to look at her, his expression half shocked, half eager. 'It is like your sweet self to offer but I should be selfish to take advantage of your innocent—'

Sarah touched her fingers to his lips, gazing up at him, eyes intent on his face. 'No, that is not true, because it is what I want too...'

'But if I should not come back?' His eyes begged the question. She understood all that he did not say, because there was no need to spell out the dangers.

She took his hand, tugging at him, drawing him towards the folly. The moon filtered through the windows, giving them sufficient light to find the daybed. Sarah sat down, pulling him down beside her. She let go of his hands, reaching up to stroke his face, her eyes pleading with him.

'I would have known the happiness of being yours at least for one night. Troy, please do not deny us both, my love. I know you think it dishonourable to take advantage but it is what I want. I love you so much. Please ... please love me tonight ... don't leave me to regret what might have been.'

Troy's eyes were dark with need as he gazed

down at her, his voice husky as he said, 'You know I love you, Sarah. I swear that we shall always be together...' He kissed her, his hand moving over the softness of her breast, pulling back the opening of her gown to reveal the silky perfection of her flesh, his fingers caressing her. He bent his head, his tongue licking at her delicately. Her nipples peaked beneath his touch, her body arching towards him as she lay back on the elegant daybed, drawing him down to her. 'God, forgive me, but I want you so much...'

'I want you,' Sarah said, her hands reaching up the back of his neck, into his hair as his mouth covered hers, 'so very much...' Her back arched as his hand moved down her body, caressing her through the thin material of her gown, making her gasp and cry out as she welcomed his touch. His hand slid beneath the gown, stroking her thigh. Sarah moaned softly, her head going back as she gave herself up to the pleasure his caress gave her. 'Troy...'

'My darling...' Troy held back, gazing down at her face once more. 'You are quite sure?' She was so beautiful, her face caught with passion, her mouth soft and loose with desire. 'Oh, my darling...'

Troy's hand sought and found her moist centre. He stroked her softly at first and then firmly, making her moan with pleasure as he brought her to a state of whimpering need. She could feel the heat of his manhood as he moved against her. When at last he thrust up into her, she cried out at the sudden sharp pain, but his mouth covered hers in a kiss and the pain was nothing. Her fingers dug into his shoulder and she writhed beneath him as his hard length filled her, penetrating deeper and deeper. The passion mounted between them and then, quite suddenly, Troy shuddered and clung to her.

'I'm sorry ... it was too soon. I wanted you too much...'

Sarah kissed the top of his head, laughing softly as she ran her fingers through his hair, stroking the back of his neck. 'You never have to say sorry to me,' she whispered. 'I wanted you to love me. I am not sorry and I think it was lovely...'

'Sarah, you wanton little minx,' Troy growled, as he heard the husky tones of her laughter. 'If you keep doing that to my ear I shall retaliate much sooner than you think!'

'Good,' she murmured softly. 'I wish I could stay here like this for ever and never leave you again.'

'Witch,' Troy growled, as he nuzzled at her neck. He had known he wanted her, loved her, but until this moment he had not fully understood that Sarah was his soulmate. She had given herself to him with such sweet abandon and now she was ready to do it all over again. Only a few months ago he had thought her little more than a child, but this evening she had proved that she was a warm, passionate woman. He felt the growing desire, the need to possess her again, to make love to her once more, but slowly this time, relishing every last second. They had only a few hours but he would take every second and make it special for them both. If this night was all they had they would both remember it until their dying breath...

'If I shouldn't come back to you, Sarah, do not forget that I loved you. From this night you are my wife in everything but name and I shall never betray you. I swear it by all I hold sacred.'

Sarah lifted her head, kissing him once more. 'You will come back,' she said fiercely. 'You will come back to me, because my life is nothing to me without you.'

Sarah and Troy spent as much time together as they could during the next few days. They walked, read poetry together, visited Captain Shaw and rode out on a fine sunny morning. At night they went to the folly and Troy made love to her, sweetly, tenderly with an intense passion that left her in no doubt of his feelings for her.

The memorial service was held on the morning of Troy's last day with them. He stood up in church and gave a moving tribute to Justin and all the other men who had given their lives or suffered grievous wounds in the service of their country. Everyone left the church looking sober, clearly shocked by the death of a much admired young man, and saddened to see Sir Keith looking so ill and aged. His hand trembled as he held his wife's arm when they walked from the church, and people whispered that the shock might be too much for him to bear.

A small reception was held at the house, but people came to pay their respects and soon left. An atmosphere of sadness hung over the house and Sarah sensed a little distance between Sir Keith and his wife.

Amelia spoke to her when they were alone. 'I thought Sir Keith had accepted the child, and he has,' she told Sarah that afternoon when Sir Keith was in his library and Troy had walked down to the home to pay a last visit to Captain Shaw. 'However, he told me that any intimate relations between us are over. I am to remain here as his wife, unless I choose to spend most of my time at the London house, which he is prepared for me to do – but he has expressed his hurt. He did not reproach me. Indeed, it was his very kindness that was my undoing, Sarah. He understands that our marriage was a mistake. The age difference is too great...' Amelia held back a sob. 'I did try to be faithful, Sarah. I never wanted to hurt Bunnykins ... but he has asked that I do not use that name in future...'

'Amelia, I am so sorry. I know you love him.'

'We were very happy until Justin began to pursue me,' Amelia said. 'I do love Sir Keith but Justin...' She shook her head. 'It wasn't worth it. One night of passion and I have lost so much.'

'Sir Keith may forgive you in time.'

'He has forgiven me, Sarah. I hurt him and he forgave me – but the closeness, the trust we had, has gone.'

Sarah looked at her sadly but there was not

very much she could say, because nothing would change what had happened. It wasn't possible to turn back time.

Time was passing too quickly for Sarah. She welcomed Troy when he returned from his visit, and instead of taking tea in the parlour they went walking in the gardens. In the seclusion of the shrubbery, they stopped to kiss. Troy held her close, his gaze intent as he looked down at her face.

'Tom was telling me how much the men like you, my love,' he said. 'A part of me is jealous. I want to lock you away and keep you all for myself, but you are needed at the home. Besides, I want you to promise that if I should be killed you will not shut yourself away and mourn for too long. You are young, Sarah. I want you to be happy and enjoy your life.'

'Please do not talk of dying,' Sarah said. 'I love you. You have no need to be jealous of anyone. The patients are my friends; I like helping them, but you are the only one I love. I shall be waiting for you when you come home, Troy.'

'I love you,' Troy said, and kissed her. 'Let me take you out this evening. We could go to a hotel ... somewhere there is dancing...'

'Yes, please.' Sarah agreed. Her mother would not agree with such an outing for she would think it improper for Sarah to dine out alone with a man, but Sarah was a modern girl with modern ideas. Young women were breaking free of the bonds of convention, reaching for a new way of life. Many of them were finding war work, taking the chance to be independent in a way their mothers never could have been. 'I should like that very much.'

When they returned to the house, Sarah told Amelia that they were going out to dinner at a hotel that evening. She saw doubt in her cousin's eyes, for Amelia knew that Lady Trenwith would never have allowed it, but she was too wrapped up in her own cares to try and stop Sarah. Perhaps she knew that Sarah had gone beyond the bounds of such restraints. She was no longer a child. She was a woman, and as such she would make her own choices.

The evening had been as near perfect as it was possible to be for Sarah. Only the knowledge that Troy was leaving the next morning cast a shadow over her happiness. When they made love in the folly before saying goodnight, Troy told her that they would have many lovely evenings just like this one once they were married.

'We shall live in London for part of the year,' he told her. 'My father will not expect us to stay in the country, though we'll visit him for the shooting and at Christmas. He will give the London house over to us after the wedding, because he prefers the country these days.'

'I can't wait for the day you take me home as your bride,' Sarah told him, kissing him on the mouth. 'Do you think your father will approve of me?'

'I am sure he will,' Troy told her. 'I've made a will naming you as my main heir, though of course Andrew would inherit the family property. I have my own money and that will be yours if I should die.'

'Please, do not,' Sarah begged, pressing her fingers to his lips. 'I refuse to think of what might happen ... I want you back, Troy.'

'I shall come back if I can,' he promised. 'But after the things I've seen ... this isn't the easy war they promised us, Sarah. I was lucky to get back for a few days. When it starts again...' He stopped, shook his head. 'Now I shall have this time to remember. It will sustain me in the trenches. Thank you for giving me so much, my darling.'

Sarah pressed herself against him. The tears were close. She wanted to weep, to scream and shout, but she knew it would only make him feel worse than he did now.

'You are my love, my life,' Sarah said. 'Make love to me one more time, Troy, and then we must part...'

She thrilled to his touch as he drew her to him once more and she felt the throb of his need against her thigh. Floating away on the crest of a gentle wave, she allowed herself to enjoy the pleasure their loving gave her, to forget that this was the last time, perhaps for many months. She would save her tears for later when she was alone in her bed.

Sarah wept a few times in the days following Troy's departure, but only when she was alone. She tried to keep a smile in place in public, because Amelia was feeling low. A serious matron who seemed now to think of nothing but helping the war effort had replaced the confident, happy young woman Sarah had liked so much when she first came to stay.

Missing Troy was like having a constant ache in her chest, but Sarah continued to help out at all the fêtes and events the committee organized to raise funds for the convalescent home. She continued to visit Captain Shaw every morning until the end of October. Then one morning she went in to find his bed empty. Her heart stopped beating for a moment and the room started to spin. She caught at the back of a chair, feeling peculiar, and was still staring fixedly at the bed when Sister Norton entered.

'Is something the matter, Sarah?' she asked. 'You look unwell.'

'Captain Shaw...' Sarah gasped. 'Has something happened to him?'

'Good gracious, no,' Sister Norton said. 'Sit down, my dear. You have had a shock. Someone should have told you, he was transferred to a convalescent centre nearer his own home last evening.'

Sarah breathed deeply. 'I see ... I am glad to hear it. I thought for a moment that he might have...' She felt very sick of a sudden. 'Excuse me...' Making a dash into the toilet just along the hall, Sarah vomited three times. She was still feeling unwell when she came out to discover Sister Norton standing outside the door. 'I am sorry. I don't know what happened.'

'It may have been the shock,' the sister said.

'However, you do not look as well as usual, Sarah. I think you should go home and rest. You may be sickening for something and I do not want you infecting my patients. A tummy bug could be fatal to some of them.'

'Yes, of course. I was feeling perfectly well until a few moments ago, though I have been feeling a little tired lately.'

'You may have been doing too much,' Sister Norton told her. 'If you are no better in a day or so I should see a doctor.'

'Yes, I shall, thank you,' Sarah said. 'I will go home now in case I have something that might affect others.'

Sarah was thoughtful as she walked home. Amelia had been sick once or twice lately and she had also complained of feeling tired. Perhaps they had both picked up some kind of infection. She would mention it to her friend and ask if she had spoken to her doctor about it.

Amelia stared at Sarah in silence as Sarah explained why she had returned home early. She sat down in one of the comfortable chairs by the fire and indicated that Sarah should do the same.

'I do not have a sickness,' Amelia said after a moment. 'My symptoms are exactly what is to be expected for a woman in my condition – it is called morning sickness, Sarah, and the tiredness is something that some women experience, though not all...'

'Oh...' Sarah sat in silence for a moment. She

saw the way Amelia was staring at her and suddenly she understood what she was saying. 'You mean ... are you asking me if I could be...?'

'Well, could you?' Amelia looked troubled. 'You stayed out late with Troy several times. I said nothing to you, because I understood that you wanted to be with him as much as possible. I thought he was too much the gentleman to ... Sarah, did you do anything that could have led to a difficult situation?'

'Yes, we did,' Sarah admitted. 'I shall not lie to you, Amelia. Troy was against it at first. He is very honourable but he knew he might not come back next time and I wanted...' She saw the shock in Amelia's eyes and lifted her head proudly. 'I love him and he loves me. We did nothing wrong.'

'Oh Sarah,' Amelia said. 'I am not condemning you for what you did – how could I? I behaved no better – but you are so young and unmarried. The scandal will be awful. Lady Trenwith will be so angry, with you and with me. It was my duty to look after you, to protect you...'

'Mother must not blame you,' Sarah said at once. 'I am not sure that I am having Troy's child, but if it is so I am not ashamed. I love him. We are married in all but name. It is my father's fault for not allowing us to marry sooner.'

'Your parents will not see it that way,' Amelia told her. 'I know you love him, dearest, but have you thought what would happen if...?'

She broke off as she saw the look on Sarah's face. 'You do not wish to think of it. Oh, my love, what have I done? I should have set you a better example. You knew that I … and it made you reckless…' Tears had begun to trickle down Amelia's face. 'I am so sorry…'

'You mustn't cry,' Sarah said. She got up and went over to Amelia's chair, kneeling down by her and putting her arms about her. They embraced as Amelia wept the tears she had held back for so long. 'It was not your fault. I made my own choice, Amelia, and I am not sorry.'

'But what will you do?' Amelia looked at her anxiously. 'I would keep you here, try to hide the truth from your mother – but she has written asking that you go home. Marianne has gone to live with her husband's family for a while. It appears that her husband is not fit for active duty and has been given an administrative position at the War Office and your sister is to live in London to be near him.'

Sarah went back to her own seat. 'I could not lie to her for ever,' she said. 'The truth will have to come out one day.'

'Perhaps if you were to give the child to a good woman to bring up—'

'No! I shall never give my child up,' Sarah declared. 'Mama may disown me if she pleases, but I intend to keep my child. If she has asked for me I think I must go – and I shall tell her as soon as I can summon enough courage.'

'My poor Sarah,' Amelia said. 'Lady Trenwith is bound to be very angry. If she throws you out

213

you may return to us. I should have been glad of your company in the coming months, but I fear she will forbid it. I shall not be thought a suitable person for you to know. She will be within her rights to blame me. I should have prevented this happening.'

'Of course you are suitable for me to know. You are one of the dearest, nicest people I know,' Sarah told her. 'I have loved staying here and I wish Mama had not written, but since she has I must go home. I should like to return one day if I may?'

'Of course you may. You will always be welcome here,' Amelia said, and took out a scrap of lace to wipe away the tears. 'I shall miss you very much, Sarah. I hope that Lady Trenwith deals fairly with you.'

'I am not a child any longer,' Sarah said. 'Had I been allowed to marry the man I love this would not have happened. I shall tell my mother quite soon, but I shall never give up my child...'

The train journey home had been less pleasant than the one going in the opposite direction. Sarah had been looking forward to the visit but she was not enjoying the prospect of being at home again. Even had she not had a guilty secret she must eventually share with her mother, she would have felt a loss of spirits on leaving Amelia. The one bright spot in the situation was that Amelia seemed to have become a little more cheerful. She had hugged Sarah as she saw her off, telling her that she would always be welcome in her house.

Sarah almost wished that her mother might turn her off. At least then she would be free to make her own way in life. However, she had not forgotten the weeks she had spent locked in her room for speaking to her father in a rude manner. Her punishment for getting into the kind of trouble that Lady Trenwith associated with the servants and lower orders would doubtless be more severe. However, Sarah's mind was made up. She would not give her child away, whatever her mother threatened.

It was when she was leaving the train that Sarah saw someone she recognized. Rose Barlow was walking away from her and had not seen her. Sarah ran after her, catching her arm. Rose was startled but her face broke into smiles as she saw her.

'Miss Sarah,' she cried. 'Well, I never! I thought you were away staying with Lady Trenwith's cousin?'

'I have been,' Sarah told her. 'If I'm honest, I wish I was still there, but Mama wrote and asked for me and I had to come home. How are you, Rose? You look well. Do you enjoy what you're doing?'

Rose looked thoughtful. 'It's a lot of hard work at the moment,' she admitted. 'Even harder than working up at the house, but once the training is over I think I shall like it. At the moment all I've done is scrub floors and clean up; they don't let us near the patients, but I've met some of them in the pub after they leave hospital, and I enjoy going out with my friends.'

'Your mother would be shocked if she heard you say that,' Sarah said. 'But then, I've been doing things that my mother would not approve of either.' She told Rose about helping out at the convalescent home as they walked from the station.

'You've done more than me then,' Rose said. 'It sounds a lot more fun than the VADs.'

'Yes, I suppose it was,' Sarah agreed, 'but it was sad too. One of them was blinded and his face was burned too.'

'That was awful for him,' Rose said. 'Jack told me about some of the injuries the men get. He's kept safe so far, though he says it's a wonder he has with the officers they've got! He reckons most of them are wet behind the ears and have no more idea of soldiering than a ninny! He says the captains are cannon fodder and the army think of them as dispensable. They lead the men and get cut down like lambs to the slaughter.'

'As long as Jack is safe, and all the men we love,' Sarah said. 'That is all we can hope for, Rose. We can't stop what is happening, no matter how much we hate it.'

A wagon had drawn up outside the station. One of the farm workers was driving it and Rose waved to him. She looked about but there was no sign of Lady Trenwith's carriage.

'Would you like a lift with us, Miss Sarah?' she asked. 'Or shall you wait for the carriage?'

'Would Jim mind me coming with you?'

'Of course not. He'll fetch your trunk and put it on for you. I only brought a small bag. I've got two days off and I spend what time I can with my mother...'

'That must please her,' Sarah said. 'She didn't want you to leave us, did she?'

'I think she expects me to change my mind and ask for my job back,' Rose said. 'But I shan't do that if I can help it. There are plenty of jobs about if you're willing to work.'

'Are there?' Sarah nodded. 'We must keep in touch, Rose. Can I write to you sometimes?'

Rose looked doubtful, then nodded. 'Yes, why not? There's no reason we can't be friends – as long as Lady Trenwith doesn't know about it...'

'I choose my own friends,' Sarah said, a hint of pride in her face. She accepted Jim's hand to help her climb into the wagon, feeling happier than she had on the way home. It was good to feel that she had at least one friend she could turn to should she need her. 'You are my friend, Rose. Please don't forget that, will you?'

'No, Sarah, I shan't,' Rose told her. 'Your mother and mine would tell us that the divide is too great, but things are changing, and I don't see why we have to cling to the old ways.'

Sarah smiled in agreement. She was glad that she had bumped into Rose again, and she enjoyed talking to her about the things she had seen and done in London.

'The carriage would have brought you had you

waited,' Lady Trenwith said, giving her daughter a hard look as she came downstairs having changed for tea. 'There was absolutely no need to arrive on a wagon like one of the servants.'

'I met Rose Barlow at the station,' Sarah said. 'She offered me a lift and since the carriage had not arrived I accepted. There was nothing improper about it, Mother.'

'That is a matter of opinion,' her mother said. 'You seem to imagine you can carry on as if you were a common village girl, Sarah. I would ask you to remember that you are my daughter and behave as you have been taught to behave.'

'I am sorry if my behaviour offends you, Mother,' Sarah said, 'but the carriage was not waiting for me. I did not know if it would come and I see nothing wrong in riding on a wagon with Rose.'

'I see no point in discussing this further with you, Sarah. I shall only say that you disappoint me. I do hope you have not learned to behave badly during your time with Amelia. I should feel that my decision to send you there has been at fault.'

'Whatever I have learned or done is through no fault of Amelia's,' Sarah said, instantly defending her friend. 'I am not a child, Mama. I have opinions and a mind of my own.'

'Indeed?' Lady Trenwith's expression and tone were slightly below freezing. 'Well, I have no time to listen to your opinions or interest in them. While you are living beneath my roof you will behave as I expect.'

It was on the tip of Sarah's tongue to tell her

mother that she would prefer to live with her cousin. She would have to wait for a favourable moment to inform her of her condition, for she had consulted Amelia's doctor before she left and he had confirmed that she was indeed carrying a child.

'Yes, Mother, of course,' Sarah said, keeping her voice flat and emotionless. 'I am sorry I did not wait for the carriage.'

'Very well, we shall say no more about it.' Lady Trenwith's eyes went over her. 'You are looking very well, Sarah, which is more than I can say for your sister. She is taking her condition very badly. Even your father remarked on her ill humour.'

'I am sorry to hear that, Mama,' said Sarah, avoiding her mother's eyes. 'I daresay she does not like to feel sick in the mornings.'

'Oh, it is more than that,' Lady Trenwith said. 'She was forever grumbling about something. I was quite relieved when she took herself off to stay with Lady Hale. I did not make such a fuss when I was carrying my children.'

'Marianne will be happier now that her husband is not to be sent overseas,' Sarah said, hoping to appease.

'You would think so,' Lady Trenwith agreed, 'but she gave me no sign that she was relieved. I am not at all sure that your sister is as satisfied in her marriage as she ought to be.'

'Marianne may have married in haste, Mama. It is a pity if she is not as happy as she might be.'

'She made her choice and she must live with

219

it,' Lady Trenwith said, and glanced about her. 'I have forgotten my knitting. Will you go upstairs and fetch it from my room please, Sarah? I must make an effort to get something finished. We should all do our bit for the war effort.'

'Yes, Mama,' Sarah said, hiding her smile. She had never known her mother to knit anything and could not imagine her doing anything of the kind. 'Amelia's friends are all busy sewing and knitting socks for the troops.'

'I daresay,' Lady Trenwith said with a sigh. 'However, I am making a scarf. I do not find it pleasant employment, but I was asked to make some contribution.'

'Perhaps I could finish it for you, Mama? I have been making scarves, gloves and socks.'

'Very industrious of you, Sarah. I shall finish what I started, but perhaps you will make some items of your own? I have been foolish enough to say that we will help with a village fête. Your father said we must be seen to make an effort, but I do not find it comfortable. I may very well let you represent me and send something for the white elephant stall as my own contribution.'

Sarah left the room to fetch her mother's work. The scarf Lady Trenwith had been making was no more than a few inches long and would take many hours to finish. Sarah gathered it up and took it with her back to the parlour. When she arrived her father was there and tea had been brought in.

'Pass this tea to your father,' Lady Trenwith

said, giving Sarah an odd look as she handed her a cup.

'Good afternoon, Father,' Sarah said, as she passed the cup. 'I hope you are feeling well?'

'Thank you, Sarah. I am very well,' Sir James said. 'I am glad to see you home.'

'Thank you,' Sarah said. She took a cup from her mother and sat down, a lump in her throat. Her father had welcomed her kindly, which showed he had at last forgiven her, and she was dreading the moment when he discovered that she had disgraced him.

Glancing at her mother, Sarah saw that she was looking at her, her eyes narrowed. Her heart missed a beat. Surely Lady Trenwith could not have guessed her condition already? She had been hoping for a few days' grace before she needed to make her confession. She turned her head, gazing out of the window.

The afternoon had turned cold and the skies were grey. It would be dark soon. She tried not to dread the dark evenings sitting with her mother in the parlour. Transferring her gaze in her mother's direction, Sarah saw her look of disapproval. She knew that it would be very hard to confess her secret to Lady Trenwith. She had never felt less comfortable in her mother's company.

If only Troy could be here to stand by her! Sarah felt her chest tighten with emotion. She loved Troy so very much, and the knowledge that he was somewhere on the Somme, perhaps in danger, at the least cold and damp, made her eyes sting with tears.

'Pelham told me his eldest son had been recommended in dispatches,' Sir James said suddenly. 'Showed great bravery under fire. I must say that I approve of a man who risks his life for the sake of others.'

Sarah caught her breath. Was her father beginning to change his mind? In that moment she wished that she did not have to confess that she had shamed her family. If Troy had been here now her father might have allowed them to marry, but she knew he was unlikely to return before she was forced to reveal her secret. After that, her father would either disown her or forbid her to see Troy ever again...

Nine

Sarah finished vomiting into the toilet adjoining her bedroom. She walked out of it wiping her mouth on a cloth. She halted as she saw her mother waiting for her. Lady Trenwith frowned at her and Sarah's heart caught, because she knew that her mother had been giving her odd looks for the past two weeks and was already suspicious.

'You are unwell, Sarah?'

'Just a little stomach upset, Mother.'

'Please do not insult my intelligence,' Lady Trenwith replied coldly. 'I have noticed that your waist has thickened and something in your face aroused my suspicions ... Now I find you being sick. Were you intending to tell me the truth or did you hope that I would not notice?'

'I had hoped that I might keep it from you for a while,' Sarah replied, lifting her head proudly. 'I know you will be angry, but if Father had allowed me to marry Troy this would not have happened.'

'Please do not try to excuse yourself. You have behaved shamefully, Sarah. I do not know how to express the extent of my disappointment. I had expected you to remember you are a lady, Sarah. Please do not try to blame your father. Had you waited, he might have given his permission in a few months' time. However, you cannot expect it now. Troy Pelham has not behaved in a gentlemanly way. I am disgusted with the pair of you. This is beyond anything I could have expected from a daughter of mine.'

'I am sorry you feel that way, Mama. Troy was leaving. I did not know if I would ever see him again...' Sarah swallowed hard as she felt her mother's cold eyes on her. 'I am not ashamed of what I did. I love Troy. We are engaged and we shall marry as soon as possible.'

'If you are not ashamed, you should be,' Lady Trenwith said coldly. 'A marriage at some distant date is not acceptable. The scandal would be terrible. You will go away somewhere and have the child and it will be given away to a family that will care for it properly. We shall naturally pay for its keep. I will not have you disgrace us! If this got out it would kill your father!'

'I am sorry for any distress I have caused you or my father, but I shall not give up my child, Mama. I shall leave this house today. I will try to keep my secret until I can be married but I shall not give up my child.' Sarah faced her mother defiantly, though she was trembling inside.

'If you refuse to obey me I shall wash my hands of you,' Lady Trenwith told her coldly. 'You will no longer be my daughter.'

'If that is your wish, Mama,' Sarah said, 'I shall bear the breech between us as best I can...' She gasped as Lady Trenwith moved towards her swiftly. Her hand snaked out as she slapped Sarah across the face.

'You will be given no opportunity to disobey me. You will stay in your room until the carriage is ready. I shall put you on a train for the north. My aunt Agatha will take you in. You will not behave badly in her care, Sarah. She would lock you in your room before she allowed you to shame us further.'

Sarah made no answer as her mother left the room. Another outburst of defiance would avail her nothing. She would make a show of obedience but she would not take the train north to Aunt Agatha. She still had a little money left of her own; she would use it to take her to London. She knew that she could not go to her cousin Lucy or Amelia for help, because both of them would feel disloyal to Lady Trenwith if they took her in, but there was someone who might help her.

Sarah blessed the chance that had brought her into contact with Rose. She had the address in London that Rose had given her and she would go to her and ask her to give her a bed for the night. After that, she would find herself a job of some kind. Somehow, she would manage until Troy came home.

Sarah did not see her mother again before she left the house. Had Luke been at home he would no doubt have been ordered to escort her to Aunt Agatha, but he had joined the army and was away serving with his unit somewhere. For some reason he had not yet been sent abroad, though his last letter had told Sarah that he expected to be sent overseas at any time. However, she would not approach him for help, because she knew that her brother would also feel obliged to take Lady Trenwith's side.

At the station the servant hesitated as he helped Sarah down from the carriage. He was about to summon a porter to take charge of her trunk when Sarah touched his arm.

'Please leave this to me,' she said. 'Did Lady Trenwith give you money for my fare?'

'She told me to buy your ticket and see the trunk placed in the guard's cabin, miss.'

'Would you let me purchase my own ticket, please?' Sarah asked, giving him a melting look. 'I have very little money of my own and I prefer to travel second class and keep the change.'

'Lady Trenwith would be angry if I bought a second-class ticket, Miss Sarah.'

'If you give the money to me I shall buy it. You may simply tell her that you saw me on my way, Bennett.'

He hesitated and then took a white five-pound note from his pocket. 'I was to give you the change, miss. Take it – and I wish you well.'

'Thank you,' Sarah said. She would have hugged him but he would have found it embarrassing. She hailed a porter and asked him to wait with her trunk and bags while she purchased her ticket. The fare to London was very much less than it would have been to Yorkshire and she had some guineas left in her pocket when she directed the porter to put her trunk on the London train. Bennett had already left. She knew that he had guessed she was running away. She hoped that he would not be dismissed when her mother discovered that she had not gone to Aunt Agatha. However, seeing her on to a train did not mean that she would arrive at the planned destination, because she could have disembarked at one of several stations, so perhaps he would retain his place.

Sarah had no doubt that Lady Trenwith would be furious. She had meant it when she said that if Sarah disobeyed her she would cut her off without a penny. Sarah's allowance was not large but without it she would find it difficult to live alone for very long. It was imperative that she found work quickly. Had she not been carrying a child she would have applied for the VADs, but in that case it would not have been necessary to run away.

Perhaps she could find a job in a shop of some kind? Sarah really had no idea of what she might be able to do. She had been gently reared and, at Amelia's, spoiled. She glanced down at her hands, knowing that beneath her gloves her skin was soft and white. Anyone looking at her hands would know instantly that she was not used to hard work.

Sarah raised her head as she boarded the train and found a seat. She was not used to hard work, but she would persuade someone to give her a chance. Surely there must be something she could do?

Rose might know of a job that would suit her. Sarah knew that she was relying on her former maid's goodwill heavily. If Rose refused to let her stay for a day or so she really did not know where to turn.

It was teatime when Sarah found the street that matched the address Rose had given her. Her heart beat very fast as she went up to the door of number 15, Green Street. She took a deep breath and then knocked twice. Nothing happened for a moment and then a small girl came to the door and stared up at her, her thumb in her mouth.

Sarah smiled at her. The child smiled back and then stuck her tongue out. 'That is a very pink tongue,' Sarah said, amused. 'Is Rose in, please?'

A woman with dark hair came to the door

and pulled the girl back. She studied Sarah for a moment without smiling.

'What can I do for you, miss?'

'Is this where Rose Barlow lives? I was hoping to see her.'

'She is still at work. Can I give her a message?'

'I was hoping I might be able to stay, just for a day or two,' Sarah told her. 'I need to talk to Rose. May I come in and wait for her?'

'Who is it, Milly?' An older woman, plump and short, came to the door and looked Sarah up and down. 'You had best come in,' she said. 'I don't know who you are but I know a girl in trouble. Is it just the one bag you have, dearie?'

'I have a trunk at the station,' Sarah said. 'I left it in storage because I wasn't sure where I would be staying.'

'You can stay here for tonight,' the woman said and smiled. 'I am Mrs Hall and this is my daughter Milly and her daughter Susan. Girls run in our family. I am a widow and Milly's husband is away fighting. She's staying with me and so is Rose. You'll have to share a bed with Rose, but I daresay she won't mind for a night. You can look for a room tomorrow.'

'You are very kind, Mrs Hall,' Sarah said. 'I thought Rose might be living alone...'

Mrs Hall cackled with laughter, her double chins wagging. 'She's with the VADs. They find respectable lodgings for all their girls, which is why I can't keep you here – unless you've got a husband away fighting?'

'Yes, he is,' Sarah said and took off her left

228

glove. She was wearing the gold wedding ring left her by her maternal grandmother. 'My name is Mrs Peel...'

'Well, as long as you're married, I might let you stay a bit longer if Rose doesn't mind,' Mrs Hall told her with a wink. 'My Milly never had the benefit of a church service, but she has a ring on her finger and I'd challenge them snooty lot to prove she ain't got a husband.'

Sarah smiled as she was drawn into the front parlour. It was furnished with what looked like an overstuffed Victorian sofa and chairs; a tall dresser stood against one wall with an attractive display of blue and white china and there was a table with twisted gate legs and flaps that could be put up when not in use. However, the room did not look used and Sarah was not surprised when she was led into the back kitchen. This was much larger than the parlour and extended into the backyard. It was clean, furnished in dark oak, and again there was a dresser with a collection of blue and white earthenware, but this set was obviously well worn. A couple of rocking chairs stood by the fireplace, which had both an open fire and a closed grate for cooking. The room smelled of baking. It was very much like the kitchen at Rose's home, and Sarah understood why Rose would be happy here with this family.

'This is very nice,' Sarah said, and made to sit at the table, but Mrs Hall gestured to one of the rocking chairs. 'But they are for you and Milly...'

'I know a lady when I see one,' Mrs Hall said,

and gave her an appraising look. 'Run away from home, have you? Why didn't that man of yours make sure you were safe before he went?'

'He ... it wasn't his fault,' Sarah said. 'My father wouldn't...' She blushed as the older woman nodded. 'We are very much in love...'

'And you are not the only young woman to find yourself in a pickle. This war has a lot to answer for,' Mrs Hall said, with a glance at her daughter. 'Not that Milly can use that as an excuse. She got caught the first time and she wouldn't marry Ned, though he's a good lad. Regretted it now though, haven't you, love? Expecting her second in six months. How long are you advanced, dearie?'

'Oh, I'm not sure,' Sarah said, and blushed. 'I have longer to go than Milly, I think...'

'About a couple of months gone,' Mrs Hall said with a practised eye. 'You don't show yet, dearie, but there's always something in the eyes. I should know. I've been helping babies into the world since I was your age, and my mother before me. What did your mother say when you told her?'

'She wanted me to give up the child...' Sarah blushed but Milly smiled at her and sat down in the chair opposite. 'I ran away. I have a little money and I'm willing to work.'

'You'll find it hard with those hands,' Milly said, looking at them. 'Unless you can sew? There's work going for a seamstress up at the shop...'

'Don't talk daft,' Mrs Hall said. 'She would not last five minutes in a place like that, now would she?' Milly shook her head. 'She should know, dearie. Milly worked there before she had the first one. They work you like slaves. Milly called it a shop – I call it a sweatshop. The girls hardly ever see the light of day. No, we'll have to think of somethin' else, dearie.'

'My name is Sarah...' Sarah looked at her uncertainly. 'I thought perhaps a teashop ... something like that if I could find it?'

'There's a canteen at the factory,' Milly said. 'I do a few hours at nights, or I did until last week. They threw me out because the manager's wife found out I was having a kid.'

'Not likely to take Sarah then, are they?' her mother said. 'We'll have to put our thinking caps on...' She looked up as they heard the front door open. 'That will be Rose...'

The child ran shrieking with glee into the next room, leaving the kitchen door wide open. She met Rose in the parlour and was swung round off her feet, making her squeal with laughter. Rose put the child down, felt in her pocket for a twist of sweets and gave them to her. She looked at Sarah in surprise and walked forward, taking off the coat she wore over her uniform.

'What happened?'

'I ran away,' Sarah told her. 'I'm having Troy's baby and Mother wanted to send me to Aunt Agatha in the north. She said I had to give the baby away and that I would never be allowed to marry Troy.'

Rose stared at her for a moment and then nodded. 'Good thing you had my address then,

Sarah. You can sleep with me for a while – if Mrs Hall agrees.'

'I've told her she can stay for a bit,' Mrs Hall said. 'I'll need a an extra couple of shillings for food and washing...'

'Have you any money?' Rose asked.

'A little. I shall find a job if I can...'

Rose was thoughtful. 'I'll pay for the food for a while, though there is a job going – if you are prepared to take it?'

'I will try anything within reason,' Sarah said.

'It's at the Mission,' Rose said, and Sarah saw understanding in Mrs Hall's eyes. 'I sometimes help out at night but they've given me longer hours at the hospital because of all the new intakes. We've got so many wounded coming in that they are letting us do more now. The Mission is for fallen women, Sarah, and orphans too sometimes, no men. They need someone to help get the food, do a bit of scrubbing sometimes...' She shook her head. 'I shouldn't have suggested it. Your mother would have a fit if she thought you were working at a place like that...'

'She doesn't have to know,' Sarah said. 'I can give it a try, see how I get on...'

'It is hard work, not very nice work sometimes. Some of the girls are vulgar, and others ... well, they are dying...' Rose pulled a face. 'No, it isn't for you, Sarah. We'll manage until something better comes up.'

'What would they pay me?'

'About five shillings a week. They aren't too fussy about who they take – well, most won't work there...'

'I will,' Sarah said. 'At least for a while. I may have to stop in a few months.'

'Mr Troy will be back on leave before then,' Rose said. 'When he discovers you're not at Lady Amelia's he is bound to go to your home. I'll leave word with a couple of the men next time I go home. They will tell him where to find you.'

'Thank you,' Sarah said, feeling overwhelmed by the kindness she had been shown. Tears showed in her eyes. 'I wasn't sure what to do, but I thought you would help me.'

'Of course I will,' Rose said, and smiled at her. 'If you find it too hard at the Mission, don't stay there. We'll manage somehow...'

Sarah was nervous when she approached the Mission for a job the next morning. Rose had declared all her clothes too good and lent her a serviceable dress of her own.

'If you go looking like you own the street they won't take you on,' Rose told her, and gave her one of the uniforms she had worn when she worked at Trenwith Hall. 'I brought this with me in case I needed it, and it is easy enough to alter it to fit you, Sarah. If they ask where you've worked before say you were in service but wanted something different. They may not believe you but they will be glad to get some- one. They can't keep people long as a rule.'

Sarah had wondered if the Mission would take her on, but after a few brief questions she was given an apron and told to help the kitchen staff prepare a meal. Her first task was to peel potatoes. Fortunately, she had been a regular visitor to the kitchen at home as a child, and she found the task easy enough. After the potatoes were done, she was sent to scrub the pine tables in the dining hall. The soda and hot water stung her hands, but she made a thorough job of it, and Mrs Smithers, her supervisor, nodded her head in approval.

'You'll do,' she said. 'Now dry your hands and help me set the tables. You will help serve the meal, and then there's the washing-up. The girls are supposed to keep their own rooms clean, but we go through them once a week – and the kitchen will be cleaned once we've finished. After that there's the supper to prepare and then you can get off home.'

'What time do I come in, in the mornings?' Sarah asked.

'Seven sharp,' Mrs Smithers told her. 'Breakfast is at half past and you'll have to clean the tables and serve, then help with the washing-up. You may be asked to scrub the dining hall floor and then help with the chores as you have today. Do you think you are up to it?'

'I'll do my best,' Sarah said, head up and eyes proud. It was going to be a very long day, and she wasn't used to doing so much hard work, but she was determined to stick it out for as long as she could.

She finished her work that afternoon and was given her supper before she left. She had the same as the other girls, which was cheese on toasted bread and some soup. Sarah was hungry after all the work and she ate it without

234

complaint.

When she got back to Mrs Hall's house the woman looked at her with sympathy and told her to sit down by the fire.

'Found it hard did you, love?'

Sarah couldn't help yawning. Her back ached and her fingers felt stiff and sore, but she was proud of herself and she smiled as her kind hostess brought her a cup of tea.

'Yes, it wasn't easy, and I am tired,' she said. 'But I enjoyed it. I liked talking to the staff there and the girls. Some of them use language that would shock Mama, and some of them are not very nice – but others are lovely. The supervisors let them keep the babies with them until they decide what to do. Some of the girls give them up for adoption, but others want to keep them. If they decide to keep the children they have a month to find themselves employment. There is a nursery for the children of the mothers who work. I met one who works in the sweatshop as a seamstress. She doesn't see much of her child, but she says she will set up for herself one day, and I think she will.'

'That must be Nancy,' Milly said, coming in from the yard with a basket of washing. 'I've found a job ironing for a few hours a week, Sarah. I could ask around for something like that for you, if you like?'

'I think I shall stay at the Mission until it gets too hard for me,' Sarah said. 'Do you think I could send for my trunk, Mrs Hall? It has most of my clothes in it and I thought I might sell one or two of my dresses. I shan't need half of them. When I'm married I shall buy new...'

'You mean when your husband comes home, dearie,' Mrs Hall reminded her. 'You want to be careful, don't want anyone guessing you ain't Mrs Peel, do we? Rose would have to leave us then and I'd have to find a new lodger. But you go ahead and send for your things.'

'I forgot,' Sarah said, a faint blush in her cheeks. 'I'll be more careful in future.' She finished her tea and put her cup on the table.

Rose came in a moment later, taking her coat off to hang it on the peg on the yard door. 'How did you get on?' she asked Sarah. 'Your hands look red. I've got some cream you can rub in. You will need to use something or they will get sore.' Rose sat down and accepted a cup of strong tea from Mrs Hall. 'I'm going to a meeting this evening at the Corn Exchange hall. It's a talk by a member of the Women's Movement. I was going to ask if you would like to come, Sarah, but you may feel too tired?'

Sarah's back was aching. All she really wanted was to lie in a bath of hot water and soak, but Mrs Hall didn't have a bathroom and she couldn't ask them to vacate the kitchen to let her bathe in the tin tub they kept in the shed outside. Everyone got to use it once a week and washed upstairs in their rooms in between.

'I should like to come,' she said, and looked down at herself. 'I have a dress that might be suitable upstairs – if I've got time to change?'

'Yes, of course you have,' Rose told her. 'I'm going to change myself in five minutes so you can go first if you like.'

Sarah thanked her and went up. She found cool water in the jug left from the morning and had a quick wash. She changed into the plainest dress she had and brushed her hair back into a knot at the back of her head. The only hat she'd brought was too smart, and she decided to keep it for another occasion. She had other clothes in her trunk, but most were not suitable for her new life. She thought she might try to sell some of them and buy something she could wear to go out with her friend.

Rose had brought a can of hot water up with her. She looked Sarah over and gave a nod of approval. 'You look nice,' she said. 'I've decided to go home this weekend. I'll tell Ma to look out for Mr Troy, and I'll speak to a few of the men. I could give them a letter for him if you like?'

'Yes, I'll write a few words,' Sarah said. 'I am going to send a letter to Amelia's house for him. I shall ask her to give it to him, but I shan't tell her where I am. She wouldn't open Troy's letter, but if I gave her my address it would make her feel uncomfortable, because Mama is sure to ask if she knows where I am.'

'You could write to his home,' Rose suggested, and Sarah looked thoughtful.

'I had thought about it but I wasn't sure...'

'Why not? His father would be sure to give it to him. Mr Troy will be worried when he hears you've run off.'

'Yes, he will,' Sarah agreed. 'I shall write to him at his London house then. I don't know where he is at the moment. I think he will send letters to me at Amelia's home but I can't ask her to send them on.'

'Something will turn up before long,' Rose told her. 'You look a bit tired. Are you sure you want to come with me?'

'Yes, I do,' Sarah said. 'I feel better since I had a wash. It is tiring, Rose, but I like working at the Mission. I am doing something worthwhile, even if Mama wouldn't approve. I expect I shall get used to the hard work after a while.'

'It will come easier in time,' Rose agreed. 'We might go to a music hall at the weekend if you like – or we could go dancing with some friends at the Pally...'

Sarah stared at her for a moment. She had never been to a music hall or a public dance hall, and Lady Trenwith would be horrified at the idea, but her mother need never know.

'I should like to go to a music hall,' Sarah said. 'Thank you, Rose. It is good of you to take me in like this and help me. I am not sure what I would have done without you.'

'You would have managed,' Rose said, and laughed. 'I'm proud of you for taking that job at the Mission. You didn't have to. I would have helped you and you could have sold something to keep you going until Mr Troy turns up.'

'If he doesn't I may need whatever I have to live on when I am forced to stop working,' Sarah said. 'I don't want to think about it, Rose, but I know it is possible that he won't come back...'

Rose nodded. 'With the news we've been

getting recently it's best you do face it, Sarah. I worry about Jack a lot of the time, but we have to believe they will both come home when this is all over.'

'When will it be over?' Sarah asked, and sighed. 'No one thought it would be like this, Rose. All that talk of it being over by Christmas and now ... so many men hurt and dying...' Her throat caught with emotion.

'Jack always said it would be a long war,' Rose said. 'And Mr Troy did too. It was all that daft stuff in the papers that had people thinking it would be easy.' She shook her head. 'I see the men every day, Sarah, and it breaks my heart – but we can't do anything. All we can do is keep praying and join all the societies to help the men out.'

'Yes,' Sarah agreed. 'I was helping with all kinds of things at Amelia's. I shall not have much time now I am working, but I could knit or sew something in the evenings.'

'There are plenty of other things we can do,' Rose said. 'We'll hear about some of them this evening. The Women's Movement is running all kinds of events – fund-raising, and flag days, social evenings. I am sure there will be something more interesting than knitting socks...'

The meeting was noisy because of some hecklers who tried to shout down the speakers until they were ejected, but Sarah enjoyed listening to the main speaker, who was an American lady and told them all about what was going on in the movement in her own country. Besides the speakers, there was general conversation about various groups that had been set up. People were being asked to contribute scrap metal for the war effort, and they were asking for volunteers to help collect if from the houses. All kinds of fund-raising was suggested, and volunteers were asked for. Sarah knew that she was not expected to work on Saturday and only from seven to half past twelve on Sunday. Before she knew it, she found herself offering to help with one of the fund-raising efforts.

Rose had offered to help serve teas at one of the clubs for servicemen and when it came to her turn to be allocated work, Sarah was given the job of standing outside a busy store in the West End with a tin and a box of paper flags.

Rose pulled a face at her. 'You should have asked to help out at the social evenings,' she said. 'It will be cold standing on the street. Besides, people think you're asking for charity when you rattle tins at them.'

'I don't mind,' Sarah said. 'I think they were finding it difficult to get anyone to do the flag day, and it is for charity but very worthwhile.'

'Well, I still think you're mad,' Rose said, 'but it's up to you. What did you think of the speaker?'

'She was interesting,' Sarah said. 'It sounds as if they are ahead of us over there. Perhaps they are more militant. Someone I know was saying we should be more like that here.'

'Well, I wouldn't throw myself in front of the King or chain myself to the railings at the

240

palace,' Rose said. 'I wouldn't have gone at all if I hadn't wanted to help with the social evenings.' She smiled naughtily. 'It's a good chance to meet soldiers and the flyboys too. They all go to these meetings and there's dancing, everything...'

'It sounds fun,' Sarah said. 'Maybe I'll ask next time, but I really don't mind doing the flag day.'

Over the next two weeks, Sarah settled into her new routine. At first she had to be woken and found it hard to get up early, but she soon found herself waking at the right time, and was sometimes the first downstairs, because Rose didn't always have to go in early. Rose's shifts varied and now that she was being allowed to help on the wards she didn't have to do so much of the menial work. She was talking of putting in for nursing training, because she really enjoyed that side of things and thought she would like to go further.

Sarah was getting used to an aching back and sore hands. She used the cream Rose got from the hospital and it helped, but the softness that had marked her out as a lady was fast disappearing. She found the work she was doing hard but had made friends with some of the girls at the Mission. Some had young babies or were expecting their first. Sarah took one or two pretty things from her trunk into work and gave them to her friends, including a paisley shawl for a girl who hadn't got one for her baby. She had taken two of her least favourite gowns to the second-hand shop. The woman had haggled hard over the price and Sarah almost went away without selling them, but in the end she got five pounds for them, which she decided to keep for the future in case she needed it.

She had bought herself two cheap dresses from the shops that Rose and Milly used when they bought clothes for themselves. It was the first time Sarah had ever bought a readymade dress, and she was a little shocked at how badly they fitted. However, she did a few alterations herself and was pleased with the result. She had one extra dress for working, and another for going out with Rose.

They went to a music hall a couple of times at the weekends, and Sarah loved the atmosphere and the way everyone called out from the audience and joined in the songs they all knew. It was very different from the few times she had visited a theatre with her mother, and she enjoyed the freedom of her new life. Afterwards, they bought hot pies from a stall and ate them as they walked home.

Rose did not have a steady boyfriend. She sometimes went out with a group of friends to a dance hall and she told Sarah about various young men she had danced with, but she didn't date any of them.

'I haven't got time,' she told Sarah. 'I'm studying hard. I've asked to be transferred to nursing training but they haven't told me if I can yet. I'll have to work hard if I want to pass the exams. Besides, I'm not ready to get married yet. I am not sure I really want to be. I might prefer to be independent.'

Sarah didn't accompany Rose to the dances. She didn't want to meet young men, because she already knew who she wanted to marry. Rose tried to persuade her, saying she needn't get involved with anyone, but Sarah felt it would be wrong. She enjoyed going to the music hall and the suffragette meetings. She had helped out with one flag day and promised that she would do teas for an afternoon bring-and-buy sale.

Sarah had written to Amelia, telling her she was well and enclosing a letter for Troy if he should enquire after her. She had also written to Troy at his father's London home. As yet there had been no reply, but she didn't really expect it. Troy had been lucky to get home leave the first time. It was unlikely he would be given more time off for a while.

Sometimes, Sarah couldn't help being anxious. If she got a letter from Troy it would at least set her mind at rest. She knew that if he wrote he would send it to her at Amelia's house, but she didn't want to put her friend in an awkward position by asking her to send letters on. She would have to be patient and wait for Troy to get leave. Sarah was confident that he would try to find her as soon as he came home. All she could do was to wait and hope that it would not be too long before he was given home leave.

The shops were busy, because there were only

three weeks to Christmas. People were well wrapped up with scarves and gloves, hats pulled down well over their ears to keep out the bitter wind. Sarah was feeling cold. She had been standing outside a department store for a couple of hours, shaking her tin at the shoppers as they hurried by. It felt quite heavy. Most people were generous and put a few coppers in when they saw it was for the troops. Some stopped to chat for a minute, remarking how cold and uncomfortable it must be for the men out there in the trenches. One man in a smart coat with an astrakhan collar had given a five-pound note, though he hadn't smiled or said anything, just folded it and slipped it into her tin.

Sarah wondered if she had done enough for the day. She was just thinking about going to have a cup of tea and a sticky bun when she saw two ladies walking towards her. Her heart raced as she recognized them: Lady Ardingly and Miss Manley! Sarah wasn't certain whether to turn away and she hesitated, and then it was too late. Selina Manley had seen her and was drawing Lady Ardingly's attention to her. Sarah lifted her head, feeling glad that she had dressed smartly for the flag day, and determined to face her friends bravely.

'Sarah,' Lady Ardingly said as she came up to her, 'how brave of you to face the weather on such a cold day. I am afraid I said no when they asked me. I do other things...' She hesitated and then looked at her companion. 'This is rather awkward. I am not sure how things stand ... but I think I should say...'

Sarah waited, feeling embarrassed. If they had noticed the bulge beneath her coat they would be thinking that the rumours were true.

'I am sure you ought to be told. Troy Pelham was sent home from the front line two weeks ago badly injured...' Sarah swayed as the faintness swept over her and Selina caught her arm, helping to support her. 'My poor child, perhaps I shouldn't have told you...'

Sarah fought against the sickness rising in her throat. 'I want to know. Where is he? What happened to him?'

'He was caught by the blast from a mortar shell during a night attack as I understand it. A truck exploded next to him. There were some bad injuries ... particularly to his face ... burning I believe. Also a wound to his thigh.'

'Where is he?' Sarah asked. The faintness had passed, replaced by an ache in her chest. 'Please, I have to know.'

'I believe he is in a private hospital,' Lady Ardingly said. She took a little notepad in a silver case from her bag and wrote something down. 'This is the address. I went to visit as soon as I heard, but he refused to see me. I was told he did not wish to see anyone for the moment.'

Sarah looked at the address, which was in Hampshire quite close to Lord Pelham's country seat. She tucked the paper into her pocket. Tears were burning behind her eyes but she held them back.

'I must go...'

'You poor child,' Lady Ardingly said. 'If you need help at any time, Sarah, you can come to me. I am not sure ... there have been rumours. Marianne said ... but she always was a little harsh where you were concerned...'

'The stories you may have heard are quite possibly true,' Sarah said, lifting her head proudly. She was feeling ill, her chest so tight that she could scarcely breathe. 'I thank you for your offer of help, Lady Ardingly, but I am staying with friends. Thank you for telling me about Troy. I have been expecting a letter. I shall go down to Hampshire tomorrow and visit him.'

'If he will see you,' Selina said. 'No one but his father has been allowed to see him so far, but you can always try.'

'Yes, thank you.' Sarah swallowed hard. She was finding it very hard to continue the conversation. Her eyes were filled with the tears she had not yet allowed to fall, and her mind was reeling from the shock. All she could think about was Troy. How ill he must feel and how very alone...

'Are you sure you should go?' Rose asked the next morning as Sarah got ready to catch the train. She was taking just a small bag, the rest of her things to remain where they were for the moment. 'If he doesn't want to see anyone it will be a wasted journey. You know how it is for some of the men when they've been burned or badly disfigured—' She broke off as she saw the look in Sarah's eyes. 'I am so sorry, love,

246

but you have to face it. He may not want to see even you. A lot of the men feel that way.'

'He has to see me,' Sarah said fiercely. 'I am not going to run away in tears like Captain Shaw's fiancée did. I love Troy and I am going to marry him no matter what.'

'Maybe you should wait for a while – until he is ready?'

'I can't wait,' Sarah said, a note of desperation in her voice. 'While I thought he was still out there I could wait, but now I have to see him. He may not want to see me at first, but I shan't give up.'

'What about your job at the Mission?'

'I called in on my way back last night and told them I wouldn't be in for a while. They knew I would not continue much longer, because it is obvious that I am having a child. When I told them my husband had been wounded, they said I could go back if I needed to, but I shan't. Troy will marry me as soon as he is able. We love each other. I know he will marry me.'

'I am sure he will,' Rose said, and kissed her cheek. 'Good luck, Sarah. You can come back here if you need to.'

'Thank you. I've paid my rent for the next week, and I'll send for my things. You can have the blue dress I've left on the bed, Rose. It is to say thank you for all you've done for me. I know you like that one.'

'I don't want anything,' Rose told her. 'We've enjoyed having you here, Sarah. You've paid your share.'

'Take it as a present then,' Sarah said. 'It is too tight for me now and I shall have to buy new ones soon anyway.'

Sarah took her leave of the others and then went out into the street. She carried her case and then took the tram to the station. The next train for Hampshire was due in another ten minutes, and she sat on a wooden bench to wait. When it arrived, a soldier offered to help her with the case, lifting it on to the rack above her head.

'Going away for Christmas?' he asked in a friendly way.

'My husband is in hospital,' Sarah told him. 'I am going to visit him.'

'Ah ... bad is he?'

'It was a mortar attack I think. He got caught in the blast as a truck exploded nearby...'

'He'll likely be burned then, poor bugger,' the soldier said. 'And you with a little 'un on the way. I'm sorry, missus. It's hard when something like that happens to your man.'

'Yes...' Sarah swallowed the sob that rose to her throat. She wasn't going to break down and weep on a train. She had cried until her eyes ached. There was no point in crying anymore. She had to be brave for Troy's sake.

She remembered Captain Shaw's ugly scars and her heart ached for Troy. He had been so very handsome! One of the favoured. It would be difficult for him to adjust and accept scarring like that, but as far as she knew he wasn't blind. Lady Ardingly had been a bit vague about his other injuries. Sarah's throat felt tight as she wondered what they might be. How would Troy feel when she went to visit him? She would make him understand that her love remained as constant as ever. She would do whatever it took to convince him that she would not take no for an answer. He would probably try to set her free from her promise. It was the kind of thing Troy would do, what he would consider the honourable thing – but she wouldn't accept it as April had. She would fight for her happiness and for his.

Whatever he felt now, in time he would want to be with her. He would know that their love was more important than anything else.

Sarah stared out of the window at the passing countryside, her mind racing as she tried to think of everything she must say to Troy. She was prepared to be turned back by the nurses at first, but if she had to haunt the hospital day and night she would make Troy see her.

Somehow she would break down the barrier he had erected against his friends, because she couldn't bear it if she never saw him again. But it wasn't going to be like that, she refused to contemplate a life that did not include Troy. He loved her, and he had promised to marry her. She would remind him of his promise if she had to, use anything in her power to overcome his doubts and scruples.

Ten

Sarah booked into a small guesthouse. She had chosen to dress plainly and took her left-hand glove off so that her wedding ring was in full view. The man behind the desk gave her a cursory glance. He didn't seem very interested and Sarah was pleased that he sent a boy with her to carry her case. The room she was shown into was small but clean and, as it was also cheap, Sarah was satisfied. She sighed and sat down on the bed, feeling tired for a moment. She was in no mood to unpack, and yet if she didn't her clothes would crease. At least there was a bathroom down the hall and she could have a warm bath before she went to the hospital.

An hour later she was dressed and feeling much better. She left her key at the reception desk, as she had been asked, and caught a bus to the hospital from a stop just across the road. Once she left the bus she still had a short walk, because it was a small private cottage hospital and set in grounds of its own. She went up to the desk and asked where she could find Captain Troy Pelham. The man looked at her and frowned.

'I am not sure if Captain Pelham is receiving

250

visitors yet, madam.'

'I think he will see me,' Sarah said, and smiled at him. 'I am Mrs Pelham.'

'Oh ... well, in that case, his room is number five. You go down that hall to your right, madam.'

'Thank you so much,' Sarah said. She was glad that she had put on one of her prettiest hats and her best coat. She wanted to look her best for Troy, and her appearance had obviously impressed the receptionist enough for him to believe her story. She hesitated outside the door of room number five and then knocked. No one answered. She hesitated and then opened the door carefully and went in. Troy was lying with his eyes closed. She approached the bed, her heart racing. Her heart caught with pain as she saw the red puckering on his left cheek. The burn stretched from the corner of his eye to his jaw and was still raw and swollen; the damaged flesh had not yet begun to turn yellow but his mouth and eyes were not affected. She knew that the injury must be very painful and she wanted to weep for the pity of it, but she held back her tears.

The last thing Troy would want from her was tears! She had to show him that she didn't find him repulsive, but for the moment she could look at him without fear, because he wasn't aware of her. She sat down in the chair by his bed, watching as he slept. Her heart ached for him, a wave of love surrounding him, as she wished she could surround him with her arms

251

and her body, taking away the hurt. Perhaps twenty minutes or so passed before his eyelids flickered and then he opened his eyes and looked at her. He moaned and shut them again, his face working with distress.

'Troy,' she said softly. 'I came as soon as I heard.'

'You shouldn't be here,' he said. He opened his eyes and looked at her. 'Who told you I was here? I told you not to come ... I had them write you a letter.'

'I didn't get your letter,' Sarah said, and smiled as he cursed. 'It wouldn't have mattered if I had, Troy. I should still have come.'

'I didn't want you to see me like this.'

'Why? Did you think I would scream and run away in floods of tears? I'm not disgusted by what I see, Troy. You know I've seen it before. At least you still have your sight. Captain Shaw wasn't so lucky.'

'Lucky?' Troy made a harsh sound in his throat. 'I have a wound in my thigh that hurts like hell and my hands are burned...' He lifted them from under the sheet to show her the thick bandages that covered them. I may not recover the full use of my fingers ... what kind of a man am I now? I told you not to come because it is over between us, Sarah. I shan't keep you to the promise I had from you before I left last time. You are free to love and marry elsewhere. It will be better for you. Your parents don't like me...'

'I don't care what they think,' Sarah said. 'I love you and that will never change, whether you can use your hands or not. You promised me marriage, Troy, and I think you should keep that promise. You swore that you loved me.'

'You know I love you, Sarah,' Troy said in an anguished tone. 'That is why I want you to leave now and never come back. I am sending you away for your own sake.'

'And I am refusing to go,' Sarah said. 'Whatever you say, I can't stop loving you. I'm not made that way.'

'I can tell them not to admit you, Sarah. I won't have you waste your life on me—'

'I think you may change your mind...' Sarah said. She stood up and took off her coat. Without the coat her condition was obvious. 'You are the father of my child, Troy, as I am certain you will accept. I have not betrayed you.'

'Sarah...' his tone was horrified. 'Oh Sarah, what did your mother say to you?'

'She told me that I would never be allowed to marry you and that I must give the child away. She was going to send me to my aunt in Yorkshire, who would probably have kept me locked up in my room until the baby was born, but I ran away to London. I have been living in a house with Rose Barlow. She used to work for us. I have been working at a Mission for fallen girls.' She took off her gloves and showed him her hands, which were red and sore. A pulse twitched at his temple and he reached out to her with his hand. She sat on the edge of the bed, taking his bandaged right hand carefully and laying it on her stomach. 'I would go back and work there again if I had to, but I do not think you are going to force me to do that, are you, Troy?'

Tears had started to trickle down his cheek. 'You shouldn't have let me. I shouldn't have taken advantage of you. I've ruined your life.'

'I wanted you to make love to me,' Sarah said. She bent forward and kissed him gently on the mouth. He closed his eyes but did not respond to her. 'My life isn't ruined – at least, only if you refuse me.'

'You know I can't do that, don't you?' Troy said, and there was a harsh, slightly bitter note in his voice. 'I couldn't desert you now. I'll marry you as soon as I can, but –' he turned his face from her – 'don't expect it to be the way it was. You will have a home and a wedding ring on your finger, but that's all. I can't be a husband to you, Sarah. I am not even sure if I'm still capable. They haven't told me how bad all the injuries are.'

Sarah felt her throat tighten with grief. She knew how much it was hurting him to say these things, and a wave of despair swept over her, because she longed to be in his arms again, for him to be whole and beautiful as he had been before the explosion that had mutilated him.

'I shall be your wife as soon as we can marry,' she said. 'The rest of it is something we have to be patient about and wait to see what happens. Please don't withdraw from me, Troy. I love you so much. I want to be with you ... whether you can be a proper husband or not.'

'I don't think I can bear this,' Troy told her. 'Please go away, Sarah. You can come back tomorrow. Father will visit later. Where are you staying? He will want to see you, talk to you.'

Sarah wrote the name of the hotel on a piece of paper from her bag. She put it down on the top of the locker beside his bed and stood up. He stared at her as she put her coat on.

'Are you all right for money?'

'Yes, thank you. I have enough.'

'Father will look after you ... make the arrangements...'

'Yes,' she said, accepting it, though inside she was hurting. 'I love you, Troy. I always shall.'

'Please go now,' he said. 'I'm feeling ill. The nurse will bring me something soon.'

Sarah wanted to kiss him, to lie down beside him and hold him, but she knew she couldn't. He was in too much pain, and she had caused a part of it. She had gained access much more easily than she had expected, and she had forced Troy to accept that they must marry ... but he was denying her. He was trying to shut her out, to shut out the memory of their loving, because it hurt too much to remember.

Back at the hotel, Sarah had tea and sand-wiches. She didn't feel much like eating any-thing, but she knew she must keep her strength up for the sake of the baby. She was sitting in the front parlour staring out of the window when she sensed something. Turning, she look-ed up and saw Troy's father. She got to her feet, aware of the shock in his eyes as he took in the fact that she was carrying his son's child. He recovered quickly, but she knew he must think less of her.

'Miss Trenwith ... Sarah,' he said, his voice caught with emotion. 'Troy told me. I am so sorry, my dear. I think you have had an uncomfortable time. I wish you had come to me at the start.'

'Thank you,' Sarah said, her eyes stinging with unshed tears. 'You are very kind, but I was with friends. I did not mind working. You have spoken to Troy of course?'

'He says you are to be married. He said a lot of other foolish things. I think you should know that the doctors say he will make a pretty good recovery in time. His hands may be scarred and he may not be able to do all he could before. He was, as you know, an excellent sportsman, and that may be beyond him, but otherwise he should be able to live a normal life – in time. His face will always bear the marks of...' His voice faltered and he broke down, tears starting to his eyes. 'It is hard for him to accept, Sarah. He was always the golden boy of the family. Everything came easily to Troy – he was adored, lionized, perhaps too much was given him on a plate. He cannot accept that he is no longer the favoured of the gods.'

Sarah took the hand he held out to her. 'Yes, I understand that, but he is still Troy – still the man I love. He doesn't want to accept that yet. He would have sent me away if it hadn't been for...' She placed her hand to her stomach. 'You must think I am no better than I should be but I do love Troy. I am sorry if you feel I

256

have let your family down.'

'Good grief, I couldn't be happier,' Lord Pelham told her. She looked at him, hardly believing at first and then seeing the truth in his eyes. 'It is exactly what Troy needs, my dear. His honour will make him take responsibility for you and the child. I had begun to wonder if we should ever get through to him, but I saw a difference in him instantly this afternoon. He asked me to fetch you home, Sarah – and that is what I have come to do. If you are living under my roof I shall be able to take care of you until Troy can do it himself.'

'He says it will be nothing more than a marriage to give me a name and a home,' Sarah said, her grief in her eyes. 'It will be more than that one day. I shall make him love me again.'

'I doubt if he has stopped loving you,' Lord Pelham said. 'He has simply stopped loving himself. He hates what he has become, and that is what you have to fight, my dear. Until Troy recovers his self-esteem he will think he is unworthy of you.'

'That is so foolish,' Sarah said. 'I didn't fall in love with him just because he was handsome and clever.'

'Didn't you? A lot of women did; they ran after him shamelessly. He was a spoiled darling of society, and used to having his own way. He will find it hard to accept the way people will look at him now and to know that he is no longer beautiful to look at.'

'Are you saying Troy was vain?' Sarah stared at him in surprise.

'Aren't we all a little if we are fortunate enough to be thought of as attractive? I love my son, Sarah, but I know his faults. All I am saying is that you must be patient with him. It will take a while before he is confident enough to accept your love for what it is and not think of it as pity.'

'Yes, I do understand,' Sarah said. 'His friend – Captain Shaw – he couldn't bear to think that his fiancée would pity him. She ran away in tears when she visited. I think he must have said something to upset her, because she knew about the burns. I wrote to her and told her.'

'But you didn't run away, Sarah.'

'I told Troy that I want to be with him whatever happens, and I do.'

'Then I hope he can learn to accept that,' Lord Pelham said, and smiled at her. 'So – will you come home with me?'

'Yes, thank you, I will,' Sarah said. 'I shall need to be near the hospital until Troy is able to leave. And I can't go home to have the child, because my mother would not allow me to keep it.'

'I shall have to see what can be done to mend fences,' Lord Pelham told her. 'Obviously, the sooner you are married the better. Troy should be able to come home in three weeks or so. He will not be completely well, of course, but I shall employ a nurse to take care of him and I think he will be better at home. He had refused, told me he wanted to go to a convalescent home with the other wrecks, but he has changed his mind now. He says that the

258

wedding should take place in a month.'

'Do you think my father will agree?'

'I shall write to Trenwith, ask him to come down,' Lord Pelham said. 'I daresay I could do a spot of arm-twisting if it comes to that...'

'Thank you,' Sarah said. 'I do not think he will forgive me, but all I need is his signature agreeing to the marriage.'

'Leave it to me for the moment,' Lord Pelham said. 'I asked for a maid to pack your things, Sarah. Your suitcases should be waiting in the hall. If you are ready, my dear?'

'You were certain I would agree?' Sarah said, and laughed. 'You are rather like your son, sir.'

'Perhaps that is why I understand him,' he replied. 'Shall we go?'

Sarah knew that she had been given the very best guest bedchamber. She was being thoroughly spoiled by her future father-in-law, and felt very pampered as she lay in bed and smiled at the maid who had brought up her breakfast on a tray.

'Will you have it in bed, miss – or over on the table by the window?'

'Oh, I think I shall get up and eat it by the window,' Sarah said. She threw back the covers and got out, walking over to the occasional table where the maid had set out the various dishes. 'Thank you, Janet. I can pour for myself. I am sure you have lots of other things to do.'

'Yes, miss, but it is a pleasure to serve you.'

Sarah smiled but said nothing as the girl went

out. She had been careful to put her things away the previous night. Sharing a room with Rose had taught her to keep her own things tidy. After getting up at six every morning to work at the Mission it was a luxury to lie in bed until eight, but she did not wish to waste her time. She would visit Troy later that morning, but in the meantime she intended to write some letters to Rose, and also to Mrs Hall and Milly, thanking them for their kindness and asking them to have her trunk sent on here.

She must also write a letter to her mother, telling her that she wished to be married as soon as possible. She knew that Lord Pelham had promised to deal with her father, but she owed it to her mother to tell her that she was safe and that she was to be Troy's wife.

Lord Pelham had told her that her home was with them, here at Pelham Place, and all the other houses they owned. Even if she had to wait until she was twenty-one to be wed she would live here. It would be difficult for her parents to resist in the circumstances. Lord Pelham would use all the influence he had and she could only hope that it would be enough.

Sarah ate the soft rolls and honey the maid had brought for her, relishing the luxury of things she had once taken for granted, like good linen and pretty porcelain. Even though her life would be easy again, Sarah was determined not to forget the people she had met at the Mission. She had asked Lord Pelham the previous evening if there was some charity work she could do in the district, and he had promised to enquire. She knew that he was a charitable man himself, and he could probably find her some committee work but she had made it clear she wanted more and he had told her that he had something in mind himself and would explain later.

He was in the garden as she looked out, talking to someone. She thought it was his agent, for they had been introduced the previous evening. She did not tap the window or make herself known to them for they seemed to be deep in conversation. However, by the time she had dressed and put up her hair, the maid returned to ask if she would join Lord Pelham in his library when she was ready.

'Yes, of course,' Sarah said. 'I know where it is. Lord Pelham showed me last evening.'

She went down to the hall and turned towards the back of the house. The library was a long room with mahogany shelves lining three walls. Sofas were set at intervals about the room and small tables provided for books or a glass of wine. Placed on each side of the fire were two large wing chairs in the Georgian style, and Lord Pelham sat in one with a book in his hand. He put it down and got to his feet as Sarah entered.

'Good morning, my dear. I trust you slept well?'

'Yes, very well. I have such a lovely room. Thank you so much, sir.'

'I am glad you were comfortable,' he said. 'Would you be so good as to sit with me, Sarah? I have something I should like to dis-

261

cuss with you if I may?'

'Yes, of course,' she said. 'I have been writing some letters. I left them in the hall, if they could be sent with your own?'

'Certainly. I have written to your father, asking him to come and see me. I have explained the situation and we must wait for his answer. In the meantime I have a little proposition. I understand from Troy that you were concerned in the setting-up of a convalescent home run by Lady Roberts and some friends of hers?'

'Yes, that is true,' Sarah said. 'I did very little really except make notes of everything they considered necessary. However, I helped once it was set up. I used to do things like reading to the men and writing letters for them. You know the kind of thing.'

'Yes, I remember Troy telling me, Sarah. You asked me if there was something you could do – well, I have decided to set up a home here in the grounds of Pelham. I was speaking to my agent this morning. We have the dower house, which is a large, good solid building. It was let to a tenant until recently and I have had some repairs done. I think we shall need more bathrooms and certain other changes, but Bernard thinks it can be achieved easily in a short time. I wondered if you might like to help me set it up, Sarah? I do not really have the time to do more than sign the bills. It is rather a lot to ask of you, of course...'

'Oh no,' Sarah exclaimed, her face lighting with excitement. 'I should love to do that for you. I have all the notes of what was done at

Amelia's home, and I am sure it would be much the same here.'

'Then that is settled,' Lord Pelham said, and looked relieved. 'We shall employ all the necessary staff to run it, but you may wish to visit and help out as you did before when it is ready? I think it helps the nurses, for they cannot do everything, especially with so many patients coming in.'

'Yes, I should,' Sarah said. 'And to oversee the running once it is open if necessary. You are very good to offer me the chance, sir.'

'After what you told me of your life in London I believe you to be a girl of good sense,' he said with a smile. 'I look forward to consulting you on other charitable projects that may come along in the future, my dear.' He glanced at his gold pocket watch. 'Do we have time for coffee before you go to the hospital?'

'Oh yes,' Sarah assured him. 'It would not be a good thing to arrive just when the doctors are making their rounds. I shall walk down to the village and catch the bus in half an hour.'

'No need for that,' Lord Pelham said. 'We have two cars, Sarah. One of them is always at your disposal.'

'I shall feel very important,' Sarah declared, and laughed. 'Two cars, sir? How very extravagant!'

'One was to be my gift to Troy this Christmas,' he replied. 'It remains to be seen whether he will ever drive it, but it is there and may as well be used for your benefit.'

'I shall learn to drive if someone will teach

me,' Sarah said. 'I shall be able to drive Troy out then if he cannot drive himself.'

'One of the men will teach you. Bernard is a good driver. I shall ask him to give you lessons, if you really wish it?'

'Oh yes, certainly I do,' Sarah said. 'If you do not think me too forward or modern, sir?'

'I take great pleasure in contemplating the modern world with all its benefits,' he replied. 'Ring for coffee, Sarah. I think we should make this little time in the morning a regular habit. It is very enjoyable to talk to a young woman of spirit.'

Sarah found Troy sitting propped up against the pillows when she went into his room a little more than an hour later. He looked up as she entered the room but did not smile.

'I thought you weren't coming.'

'I couldn't come too soon because the doctors would have been making their rounds,' she said. 'Would you like something to read? I brought a book of poetry and also a newspaper. I could read to you if you wish?'

'Later, perhaps,' he said. 'Did my father come to the hotel?'

'Yes. I am staying with him at the house. We get on well, Troy. Lord Pelham is very kind.'

His face showed no expression. 'I have been thinking about the wedding. If your father will not agree we could go to Scotland as soon as I am able to travel.'

'Your father is writing to him. Lord Pelham believes that my father will be forced to agree in the circumstances.'

'The wedding ought to be soon,' Troy said, sounding angry. 'This is a damned mess, Sarah. It is all my fault. I should have been more responsible. You must have been frightened when you realized about the child. God knows what might have happened to you if you had not had Rose Barlow to help you!'

'I was a little,' she admitted. 'I knew my parents would be angry. Mother was furious. I don't think she told my father. He would have been disappointed and shocked but also angry. I think Father's disappointment will be harder to bear than Mother's anger. He was upset with Marianne for jilting you, but this...' Sarah shook her head. 'I hope that Lord Pelham will make him see sense, but I fear he may still refuse us.'

Troy said nothing. He was staring across the room rather than at her. 'Did Father tell you about the convalescent home?'

'Yes. I am going to help him set it up.'

Troy nodded. 'When it is ready I shall go there. You will live at the house with Father. You can visit me sometimes.'

'But when you are better you will come to the house,' Sarah said. 'Surely you would rather be at home?'

'Like this?' Troy asked, putting a bandaged hand up to his face. 'Do you think I want everyone staring, tiptoeing around me because they are afraid of upsetting me? I can't stand pity!'

'It doesn't have to be that way. Besides, only

ignorant people behave like that,' Sarah said. 'I know you aren't quite as beautiful as you were, but it doesn't matter to me. I love you just as you are.'

'You say it but you don't feel it,' Troy said, glaring at her. 'You can't – not in your heart.'

'I wish it hadn't happened for your sake. I know it hurts and I'm sorry, but it will gradually get less painful. The doctors say it will look better in time; the scarring will fade.'

'I've seen the way people react to burns,' Troy said. 'They can't look at you. I'll marry you, because it would be unfair not to in the circumstances, but I won't live with you, Sarah. In time you will find a lover and forget me.'

'Damn you, Troy Pelham. If it wouldn't do you too much damage I would slap you,' Sarah said angrily. 'You don't deserve that I should love you but I do. You can behave like a spoiled child if you like, but you aren't getting rid of me so easily. If you won't come to the house I'll move in with you at the home.'

'Now you are being bloody ridiculous! You can't live in a place like that with all those men ... some of them will be common soldiers—'

'And you are a damned snob! Those men are getting killed out there every day so what difference is there from you and me? They are flesh and blood just like us.'

They glared at each other and then Troy laughed. 'Stubborn little thing, aren't you? I didn't know what I was getting into when I fell for you, Sarah Trenwith.'

'No? Well, that's too bad, because you've got

me whether you like it or not, Troy Pelham. You made me a promise and I'm going to hold you to it whether you like it or not.' She glared at him furiously.

'I'm not going to live at the house.'

'We'll see how you feel when I move into the home with you.'

'I believe you would do it too.' Troy glared back at her but she didn't flinch. 'Think you've got me just where you want me, don't you?'

'It isn't like that,' Sarah said. 'But I am not going to let you throw your life away and ruin mine. I'll make you love me again if I have to—' She gave a sigh of exasperation. 'You are an impossible man!'

'And you are beautiful,' he said. 'I'm trying to stop you wasting your life, Sarah.'

'Well, you can stop wasting your breath, because I am not listening.'

'All right, I'll come to the house if you insist. It makes no difference. You'll get fed up with being tied to a freak and when you do I'll move on somewhere.'

'If that happens you can go,' Sarah said, giving him a furious look, 'but I can't see it happening. I might be tempted to murder you when you're in one of your moods, but I shan't give up on you.'

'You're losing your temper,' Troy said. 'And I'm not supposed to get upset. You had better read me some poetry to calm us both down.'

Sarah picked up the book. She could have thrown it at him but refrained as she saw the smile in his eyes. Their argument had cleared the air. She knew then that he still loved her deep down. It was just too hard for him to accept the way he was. He would need time and proof of her love before he came to terms with the changes to his face and body. She began to read.

'That is supposed to be a love poem,' Troy objected. 'Stop scowling, Sarah. You've got your own way.'

She looked up and then she laughed. 'You're the one who was scowling, Troy. But you're right; I should put more feeling into the poem. Perhaps the paper might be better.'

'Not if it is all about the war,' he said. 'Continue reading the poem. I like it – I like the sound of your voice.'

'Really?' She smiled as she saw he looked relaxed, perhaps for the first time since she'd come to the hospital. 'I enjoy this one...'

She continued to read for a while, and then she saw that Troy had closed his eyes. He tired easily, because he was still very ill. He needed rest and time to heal, and she would need to be patient because he resented what had happened to him. However, she felt that they had turned a corner. Troy was fighting with his back to the wall. He had to learn to trust her and realize that she was on his side.

Returning from the hospital one afternoon some days later, Sarah heard the sound of voices as she walked towards the sitting room where she normally took tea with Lord Pelham. Her heart caught as she recognized her father's tones and her first reaction was one of fright. She couldn't go in there! She couldn't face him! After a minute or two she fought down the feelings of panic. She wasn't alone. Lord Pelham was there. He at least was firmly on her side.

She opened the door and walked in. Both men turned to look at her. Her father's expression sent icy tingles down her spine. He was so cold, so disdainful. She swallowed hard, lifting her head as she moved towards him, holding on to her nerve and her dignity as best she could.

'Father...'

'Sarah,' Sir James said, and glared at her. 'I see it is true that you have disgraced me. When I had Pelham's letter I could hardly credit that you would so far forget yourself and what was due to your family, and your mother refused to discuss the situation. She wishes you to know that she has no daughter. She will not see you again, Sarah. I need hardly say that I am extremely disappointed in you.'

'I am sorry I have disappointed you, Father,' Sarah said. 'As far as I am concerned I love Troy. Had we been able to marry when we wished this would not have happened. However, I know that you must be angry with me – and that in your mind I have let you down.'

'Well, there is no use in crying over spilt milk,' Sir James said, surprising her. 'Your mother was of the opinion that we should disown you, but Pelham is willing to stand by you and I believe the scandal will be minimized if the wedding goes ahead as soon as possible. There will still be gossip, of course, and some hostesses will not receive you—'

'If they wish to retain my good opinion they will not slight my daughter-in-law,' Lord Pelham said forcefully. 'Come now, Trenwith. This is an unfortunate affair but not the end of the world. There is a war on and Sarah is not the only young woman in this situation, I'll swear.'

'We are speaking of my daughter,' Trenwith said, and frowned. 'But I will allow that if I had permitted Troy to speak this disgrace might have been averted and I am therefore prepared to give my permission. Unfortunately, Sarah's mother is not as forgiving. She will not see Sarah again. I shall come down for the wedding, which will be quiet because of Troy's illness, naturally. We shall tell everyone that Lady Trenwith is unwell. Sarah's sister is also unwell but her cousin Lucy and her aunt may attend if they are invited, I daresay.'

'Thank you, Father,' Sarah said. She lifted her head, her expression one of pride as she looked at him. 'That is generous of you.'

'I may visit you occasionally when the child is born. It is best that the estrangement is not generally known,' he said. 'However, Lady Trenwith has requested that you do not visit us.'

'Yes, I understand,' Sarah replied. Her throat was tight and she could feel the heat in her cheeks but she would not give any sign that his words had hurt her. 'Thank you for making the journey here to tell us of your decision.'

'Well, I shall not stay, but if you inform me of the date I shall attend the wedding.'

Sarah inclined her head. Her father stared at her for a moment, a mixture of frustration and anger in his eyes, before turning away. After his departure there was silence until Lord Pelham spoke.

'I am sorry that you had to suffer that interview,' he said. 'I was unable to spare you, but at least we can now plan your wedding. As Trenwith said, it must be a small wedding for Troy's sake, but if there is anyone you wish to invite you must do so, Sarah.'

'My aunt and Cousin Lucy,' Sarah said. 'Perhaps Rose Barlow if she can get time off. I do not think Lady Roberts would be willing to travel at the moment, though I should like to invite her.'

'Is that all? I did not mean that you could not have some of your friends, Sarah.'

'Troy will not wish for a lot of people he hardly knows to be staring at him,' Sarah said. 'I am quite content to have just a few witnesses, thank you, sir.'

'And you are quite sure that you want to be married, Sarah? I know it must distress you to look at Troy's face and remember what he once was.'

'I am quite sure, and it does not distress me, except that I know he feels it badly,' Sarah told him. 'I love him and the scar will fade a little in time.'

'A little perhaps,' he agreed, his eyes thoughtful. 'You are a remarkable young woman,

271

Sarah. Your father should be proud of you. At the moment he cannot see further than the end of his nose, but we shall hope that one day he will see you for what you are.'

'My father is very proud. He has always been strict and we were instructed to be mindful of what we did lest we cause a scandal,' Sarah said. 'I shall not easily be forgiven, sir, but I do not mind if I have Troy – and your friendship, Lord Pelham.'

'I can find no fault in you, Sarah,' he told her with a warm smile. 'Trenwith was at fault denying you hope, and my son played his part. Had he behaved as a gentleman ought this would not have happened. However, I have not censured him for something that lies between the two of you. I am happy to welcome you to my family, and I shall delight in my grandchild. Indeed, had this not happened, Troy would almost certainly never have married. His honour is forcing him to marry you and I am heartily glad of it.'

'Thank you, sir.' Sarah was warmed by his generosity and his kindness. She knew that she owed the happy solution to her situation to his advocacy and was determined that she would do all she could to please him. 'When do you think Troy will be well enough to hold the wedding?'

'I imagine another month at most, though if we had the ceremony at the house it might be sooner. I shall see about a licence and all that needs to be done, and then we'll see.'

'I shall write to Lady Roberts, and to my aunt

272

and Cousin Lucy,' Sarah said. She smiled at him. 'In the meantime we have the convalescent home to set up. I have prepared a list of all the things I believe you will need, though of course I am not qualified on the medical side.'

'I would not expect you to be. I have taken advice on that side of things,' Lord Pelham said. 'I have an hour or two to spare. Why don't you fetch your list and we will talk about it over tea?'

Sarah agreed and left him to fetch her lists. It was as well to keep busy. If she allowed herself to think of her mother's refusal to forgive her and her father's disapproval she would be miserable. No doubt Lady Trenwith had sent the message in order to punish her, but Sarah refused to dwell on the breach with her family. She was to be married as soon as possible and nothing else could possibly matter.

Sarah wrote her letters and received a very kind reply from her aunt. Lucy wrote to say that she loved her and would always do so whatever Marianne or anyone else said concerning her behaviour.

You are always my dearest friend and I do not care what anyone says of you, Sarah. Mama says it is a pity but she is glad you are to be married and she blames your father for not allowing you to become engaged. She is coming down for the wedding and I am too. I should like to come a little sooner if I may so that we can be together. Mama has told me about Troy's poor face and I am very sorry for it but as long as you love him I do not see that it matters. Do please write and say I may come down sooner. Mama will follow in time for the wedding.

Sarah took the letter to Lord Pelham and was cordially told that she was free to invite anyone she pleased to stay, because his house was her home. Sarah wrote back and said that she would love to see Lucy whenever she wished to visit.

The next day she received a letter from Amelia.

I was delighted to learn of your wedding, Sarah my dear. I understand your unfortunate circumstances and I do not censure you – how could I? I would have loved to attend your wedding but I am not as well as I might be. The doctor was concerned that I might lose the child at one time and I was ordered to rest. Sir Keith was worried about me. He has been very kind and I believe he may truly have forgiven me, though it is not quite as it was between us. I am aware of the grievous hurt I inflicted but I think that once the child is born he may be happier. I pray that he will live to see the child, because sometimes he is very frail. However, no more of my problems. You have enough of your own. Your mother is unkind to refuse to see you, for once you are wed the scandal will soon be forgotten. And of course Troy is ill. I am devastated at what happened to him. He is a beautiful young man and this must be devastating for all of you. I wish you the very best and shall pray for your happiness.

Amelia

PS, what would you like as a wedding gift? I think something personal as your father-in-law has a wonderful house full of treasures.

Sarah wrote back to say she was sorry that Amelia had been feeling unwell. She thanked her for her kindness and said that she would be happy with any gift Amelia cared to send.

After reading some of the symptoms Amelia was suffering, Sarah decided that she was lucky to feel so well. Indeed, she was full of energy and she divided her time between visiting Troy at the hospital and overseeing the alterations that were being made to the dower house in order to turn it into a convalescent home. She knew that many such houses were being made available in various parts of the country. The numbers of severely injured men grew daily and the news from the war continued to be cause for concern. Any hope that it would be finished by Christmas was dashed as the festive season was upon them.

Troy's condition had not improved as quickly as it might, and it was decided that they would wait until a week after Christmas for the wedding. He was to remain in the hospital, and Sarah visited him there on Christmas Eve. The hospital staff gave a carol service, going from ward to ward to sing their Christmas songs. On Christmas Day there was a special meal for the patients, and a lot of the visitors took in treats that were shared around. Troy was in his own room away from the larger wards, but there were visitors in and out all the time Sarah was

275

with him – mostly other patients, men who were now fit enough to hobble about under their own speed or in a bath chair. The mood was generally cheerful, and quite a few practical jokes were played on the nurses, by men who had begun to feel better.

Many of them would be moving on in the New Year. Some were going home, others into convalescent homes as near to their loved ones as possible. The hospital had arranged for Christmas Day to be as pleasant as the staff could make it, and there was a decorated tree in the common room with presents for the men and the nurses, brought in by relatives and visitors.

Sarah had brought pretty parcels down for several nurses who had been kind to Troy and to her, and she brought flowers and some chocolate truffles for Troy. He thanked her but gave her nothing in return. Sarah had not expected anything, because he could hardly go shopping stuck in a hospital bed. She had also brought a new book of poetry from which she read to him for half an hour.

'It is dull for you here,' Troy told her, after jelly and ice cream had been served to the patients. 'You should have been at home having fun with your family.'

'You are my family,' Sarah said, and ignored his scowl. 'Next year we shall have a child and I shall make Christmas special for us all then. Besides, Lucy is coming tomorrow and I shall celebrate with her.'

Troy frowned. 'Don't bother coming in

276

tomorrow. I'll be home in a few days. You don't have to come every day. I'm not a child. I don't need you to look after me.'

'I like to come,' Sarah said. 'I don't think of you as a child. I come because I want to. If I didn't wish to see you I shouldn't come.'

Troy glared at her. 'They are taking the bandages off my hands tomorrow. I would rather you didn't come until later...'

'I'll come in the evening then,' Sarah said. 'If that is what you want.'

'It is. I need time to see how it feels.'

'Yes, if that is how you feel I shall spend some time down at the home. It is almost ready. I think we've made a good job of it. Your father is very pleased. We have a couple of rooms for relatives to come and stay as well as the patients' rooms.'

'I hope you aren't doing too much, Sarah. You should take care of yourself and the child.'

Sarah smiled. 'Thank you for worrying about me, Troy, but I am very well. Amelia isn't well – I did tell you that she is having a baby, didn't I?'

'I thought Sir Keith was past it,' Troy said. 'I daresay he is pleased.'

'Yes, he is,' Sarah said. She had not revealed Amelia's secret even to Troy, because it was not hers.

'My father is excited about your child,' Troy said suddenly. 'I wouldn't want anything to happen to disappoint him. It isn't likely that we shall have another.'

'It is fortunate that I am carrying this one

277

well then, isn't it?' Sarah turned away. He had never told her what the doctors had had to say about his health in general and she had not liked to ask. 'The doctor says he is pleased with me, though I am beginning to get very fat now. I didn't at first, but it must be the way everyone is spoiling me up at the house. I eat far too much.'

'You are eating for two,' Troy said, and smiled at her. 'I like it – you are even more beautiful than before, Sarah.'

'Thank you, sir.' Sarah did a mock curtsey. They both heard a bell ring. 'That means I have to leave, visiting is over for today.' She bent down to kiss his cheek. Troy turned his head and their lips met briefly. 'Happy Christmas, my darling. Next year it will be much better, I promise.'

'Perhaps,' he said. 'I asked Father to buy a gift for you from me. He will give it to you after dinner this evening – that is when we always exchanged gifts. I hope you like it.'

Tears caught at her throat, but she smiled, refusing to let them fall. 'Thank you, Troy. I shall look forward to opening it.'

'Wear it when you come tomorrow evening,' he said. 'Happy Christmas, Sarah...'

Eleven

Troy's gift proved to be a beautiful diamond and sapphire three-stone ring. Sarah felt tears prick her eyes when she saw it, because she knew it was the engagement ring Troy had promised to buy her when he gave her the ring she wore on a chain about her neck. She slipped it on the third finger of her left hand, and then, after a moment's hesitation, she took the love token that he had given her before he left for that last fatal trip to France from the chain and slid in on to her right hand.

'I hope you approve of my choice?' Lord Pelham asked. 'Troy would have wished to buy it for you himself, but in the circumstances he had no choice.'

'It is lovely,' Sarah said. 'I am very glad to have it.'

'Troy wanted you to have a ring before your aunt and cousin arrived.' He picked up a long, narrow box from beside his own plate and handed it to her. 'I thought this would go with the ring well. It is my own gift to you this Christmas, Sarah. I hope you approve.'

Opening it, she found a gold bangle with diamonds and sapphires set into the band at the top, the underneath plain gold. It looked a good match for her ring and she smiled at him across the table.

'This is very kind of you, sir, thank you so much.'

Lord Pelham nodded. He was disappointed that nothing had come for her from her family except a small plain card from her father, though he believed her cousin might bring something the next day from her aunt. However, it was clear that neither Sarah's father or mother considered she deserved a gift. Wedding gifts had been arriving from Pelham relatives all week, and Sarah's friend Lady Roberts had sent her a beautiful silver-gilt brush, comb and mirror set for her dressing table, but he considered it disgraceful that Sarah's family should be so neglectful. However, it might have made her feel it all the more had he mentioned the discrepancy and he had been scrupulous not to say a word.

'Troy has an estate of his own in Huntingdonshire, as I daresay you know,' he said, as Sarah slipped her bracelet on and admired it. 'However, I wished to mark the occasion of your wedding with something special, my dear – I am therefore giving you both the house in London and the income to run it. Troy may not wish to visit for a while, though in time I daresay he will become accustomed to the changes in his appearance. You may wish to go up yourself sometimes to meet friends and buy clothes, and I have very little use for it these days, though I shall visit if you invite me.'

'Of course you are invited,' Sarah said. 'You

are very generous to give up the house to us, but we should wish you to stay whenever you felt able.'

'Troy may not feel the same,' his father said, 'but thank you, Sarah. I am of course hoping that you will want to spend a lot of your time here in the country with me, but I am not sure how my son will feel once he is more himself again.'

'They are taking the bandages off his hands tomorrow,' Sarah said. 'A lot may depend on how badly injured they are. You know he loves to ride and play sport. If he can still ride to hounds and play cricket and shoot he may settle but if...' She shook her head not wanting to think about what would happen if Troy could not do simple things for himself. 'Well, he will make up his own mind.'

'Yes, I expect he will,' Lord Pelham said. 'He usually does...' He looked at her across the table. 'Your cousin will be here tomorrow, and then it will soon be your wedding day. I shall miss our little talks, but you mustn't feel you have to spend time with me when Lucy comes, my dear.'

'I enjoy them too,' Sarah told him. 'I certainly shall not be too busy for you, Father.'

'Father...' He smiled. 'How nice that sounds, Sarah. Shall we go into the drawing room now? I thought perhaps you might play the piano-forte for me for a while before we go up?'

'It's so lovely to see you again.' Lucy said, and hugged Sarah. 'I've got lots of presents for you in my bags. Mama said you should have Christmas presents as well as your wedding gift. Tubby Brocklehurst told me Lord Pelham had sent him an invitation to the wedding and he is coming down tomorrow. He asked me what he should buy you and I said a silver tea and coffee service – I hope that was all right?'

'It will be very expensive,' Sarah said. 'Perhaps you should have suggested something smaller, Lucy?'

'Oh no,' Lucy said airily. 'He said he wanted to give you both something good, and he was pleased with the idea. I like Tubby. He is such good fun and he often comes over to take me for a drive or stay to tea. We have become very firm friends.'

'Yes, he is very pleasant,' Sarah said, and smiled as she led the way inside. Lucy was pretty and full of life and it was nice to have her company again. 'Do you remember when we fed the horses, Lucy?'

'I remember you might have been hurt,' Lucy said, and shuddered. 'Tubby is hoping that Troy will be well enough to advise him about his horses soon. He says he hasn't had a winner since Troy left to join his regiment and he has been wondering about letting the brood mares go.'

'That would be a pity,' Sarah said. 'I believe he and Troy had built quite a reputation before the war came and spoiled everything.'

'Tubby would like to be in the army too, but he has flat feet.' Lucy went into a fit of giggles. 'He was most indignant because they wouldn't take him, but they said his feet – and the fact that he is a little overweight...' Sarah's eyebrows rose and Lucy smiled. 'Yes, I know he is a lot overweight but he is trying hard to lose some of it. He was very upset when they gave him a civilian job at the War Office sitting behind a desk. He says people will start giving him white feathers soon if he doesn't get a uniform, but of course they won't. He has a letter excusing him from active service. His father is quite pleased about it, but Tubby hates being left out.'

'It isn't a game, Lucy,' Sarah said. 'So many men have been hurt and killed. I am glad for his sake that Tubby has been given something at the War Office.'

'Yes, I know, poor Troy; it must be awful for him,' Lucy said. 'Is it very bad, Sarah – his face?'

'His face is burned on one side,' Sarah told her. 'At first it looked very raw and red, but it is turning purple and yellow now.' She saw the look in Lucy's eyes. 'No, you mustn't feel like that, Lucy. I hardly notice it these days. I am more worried about his hands; they were burned too and he isn't sure how much damage was done because they have been wrapped up until now. They are taking the bandages off today. We are hoping he will be able to regain at least some of the use of his fingers after a while.'

'That is awful, Sarah. What will he do if...?'

'We won't think about that,' Sarah said firmly. 'I am praying that he may be able to do most things for himself when the mobility returns. If he could ride a horse again that would be wonderful.'

'You are so brave,' Lucy said. 'I am not sure how I would feel if someone I loved was badly burned. Marianne said—' She stopped and shook her head. 'No, I shall not tell you what she said when I met her in London. She is selfish and unkind and I think her cruel.'

'What did she say, Lucy?' Sarah saw the anxiety in her face. 'I may as well know.'

Lucy hesitated, then, 'She said that she was glad she had had the good sense to throw Troy over, because she could not have stood being married to a man with half a face. I told her she was horrid and we had words. I do not regret a thing I said to her!'Lucy cried. 'She was gloating, Sarah – as if she were clever and you were a fool...'

'Is that all?' Sarah said, and laughed. 'I am surprised she didn't have much more to say, Lucy. Marianne has resented the way Troy fell in love with me after she jilted him. She will never forgive him for not taking her back – or me for attracting his attention. She may say whatever she likes, providing she does not say it to Troy.'

'She says she is too ill to come for the wedding, and I told her it was a good thing because you would not want a mean cat like her. She was very angry with me and told Mama that I was an ill-mannered child.' Lucy giggled. 'Mama did not say anything then, but when I told her later what had passed between us she said that if she had heard Marianne's spite she would have told her something of a similar nature herself.'

Sarah laughed. 'It is as well that I did not count on my sister as a wedding guest then, is it not?'

'Barney is coming, though,' Lucy said. 'He called on us before we left London and apologized for Marianne. He said that Troy was his friend and he would come for the wedding, though Marianne was not well enough to attempt the journey.'

'Yes, well, she has had a bad time,' Sarah said, with more understanding than she might have had had she not experienced morning sickness for herself. 'And I think she must be near her time now. I am sure she will be very glad when it is all over.'

'You look wonderful, Sarah,' Lucy told her, and giggled. 'I mean, I can see you are increasing but you don't look bloated the way Marianne is – her face is almost twice it's normal size and she can hardly waddle when she walks. Not that I mean to be cruel, but it is true.'

'My poor sister,' Sarah said. 'She must be suffering. I am not surprised Barney has decided to come to the wedding. I think he must be anxious to get away for a while. She will not be in the best of tempers.'

'Oh no, she certainly isn't,' Lucy said. 'But you look so well, Sarah. I can hardly believe it. I thought you might be ill like Marianne.'

'At the moment I am very well, though I have started to put on a lot of weight, but I suppose that is to be expected.'

'Well, you could hardly stay the size you were, could you?'

'No, of course not,' Sarah said. 'Come upstairs and take off your things, Lucy. Would you like to see the wedding gifts first or the nursery?'

'Oh ... the nursery, I think,' Lucy said, a dreamy look in her eyes. 'Mama sent you some baby things as well as all the rest. She has loads of things she kept and she says your mother gave all the christening robes and shawls to Marianne, so she sent you some of our family things.'

'How kind,' Sarah said. Lord Pelham had instructed Nanny to show her the Pelham family christening robe, which had been used for four generations and was exquisite, but she knew her aunt Louisa was intending to be kind and she would make use of whatever had been sent her. 'Lord Pelham will be back for tea. I usually spend the afternoon with Troy, but because the bandages are coming off I shall not go down until this evening...'

Sarah felt nervous as she approached Troy's room, because she knew that a great deal depended upon what had happened that afternoon. He might learn to accept the scars on his face if he could lead something approaching a normal life once he was fully recovered. However, she knew that he would feel it dreadfully if he could not manage to fasten his clothes or do any of the things that gave him pleasure. She knocked and went in, stopping

286

abruptly as she saw that he was sitting up against the pillows reading one of the books she had brought in for him. His hands showed signs of scarring and two fingers on his left hand were still bandaged together but it was obvious that he was holding the book with the left and could manage to turn a page with his right hand.

'Troy...' Sarah smiled as he looked up. 'Is everything ... what did the doctors say?'

'They seem to think I shall eventually have ninety per cent mobility in my right hand and perhaps fifty to sixty in the left, though I need to use creams to stop the skin drying out and do exercises to regain the dexterity I had.'

'That is good news, isn't it?' Sarah asked, approaching the bed. 'How do your hands feel now?'

'The right one is itching a lot,' Troy said with a wry smile. 'The left is still sore, that is why they have bound two fingers up. They are not healing as they should and ... at worst they might have to come off, but for the moment they are being monitored.'

'Perhaps it is just a matter of time before they heal too.'

'Yes, perhaps,' he said. 'Even at the worst it is better than I feared Sarah. I wasn't sure what would happen when they took the bandages off. I have one hand that will do some of what I tell it, and the other ... I shan't be able to do everything I could but I shan't be completely helpless.'

'That must be a relief to you.'

'Yes, it is. I would have hated to be a burden to everyone.'

'You wouldn't have been, Troy, but I do understand.'

'Do you?' He studied her face. 'Yes, remarkable as it is, I believe you do. I was extremely lucky to find you, wasn't I, Sarah?'

Smiling, she moved towards the bed and perched on the edge. 'I think I am the lucky one. I am loved for the first time in my life. Your father cares for me and I think you truly love me, don't you?'

'Yes, I do,' he said. He reached out to her with his right hand. Sarah took it very carefully, conscious that she might still hurt him. Some of the scars felt rough beneath her fingers and she knew it was difficult for him to move his fingers; it would take a lot of time to make damaged skin pliable again. 'I tried to send you away for your sake, Sarah, but I thank God that you refused to go.'

She bent her head and kissed his hand, holding it to her cheek for a moment. 'We can be happy, Troy. I know we can. You just have to believe in our love and make the most of each day as it comes.'

'I can do that if I have you,' he said. 'Now tell me about Lucy. Has she arrived and what does she have to say?'

'You know Lucy, she talks all the time. Tubby is coming for the wedding and so is Barney Hale. Marianne isn't well enough. My father will be there but Mama does not feel up to the journey.'

288

'She refuses to forgive you?' Troy's eyes were intent on her face. 'It is my fault—'

'No,' Sarah stopped him from saying more. 'Mother never showed any of us real love. Of all her children she favoured Luke the most, but even he felt her displeasure when he did something she didn't approve of. Father always favoured Marianne, of course. Luke is closer to me than he is to Marianne. I know he would come to my wedding if he could, but I believe he is overseas. He hasn't written to me for ages, though I am not sure his letters would be passed on. He wrote to me once at Amelia's but since then I have heard nothing.'

'It isn't easy to write or send letters out there,' Troy told her. 'Try not to worry, Sarah. If there was any official news you would have heard.'

'Yes, that is what I thought,' Sarah said. 'I am sure Luke will be in touch when he can.'

'And you are quite, quite sure you can bear being married to me?' Troy asked, gazing into her eyes.

'I couldn't bear not to be.'

Her answer was honest and direct enough to make Troy smile. 'Well, the good news is that I should be home tomorrow. I have had a practise on crutches, because my leg isn't quite right yet. I may have to sit for the wedding, but as it is at home I daresay that won't matter. I'll need to be pushed in a chair for a while, but they tell me I shall walk if I persevere.'

'And ride too,' Sarah said. 'I believe Tubby needs your advice about the horses, Troy.'

'Yes, I may be able to ride in time, and I still have an eye for a decent horse. You were right, Sarah. I am luckier than Tom Shaw.'

'You came home, a lot of men haven't,' Sarah said. 'That makes me feel lucky.'

Troy nodded. Sarah noticed him flexing his fingers. She knew that he was still in some pain, and his body needed more time to heal properly, but his mind and spirit were recovering. He had recovered the will to live and that was a huge step forward. Courage would carry him through the months to come.

Troy came home the following afternoon. A bedroom and sitting room had been prepared downstairs at the back of the house. Troy's sitting room had French windows, which opened out on to a terrace and lawns; a ramp had been fitted so that his chair could be wheeled outside.

Troy asked for his chair to be placed near to the windows so that he could look out, and Sarah had a comfortable armchair brought close to it so that his visitors could sit and talk to him. Tubby had arrived that morning and he spent an hour after tea talking to Troy alone. After that, Sarah took Lucy in to say hello.

'I am looking forward to the wedding,' Lucy told him in her normal cheerful way. 'Sarah is letting me be her bridesmaid. Tubby says he is to be the best man and that I am to make sure he doesn't forget the rings. He has been practising his speech for afterwards. I know it isn't to be a large wedding, but there will at least twenty of us, because some of your relatives have insisted on coming.'

'They may as well,' Troy said. 'We might as well get the horror show over in one go, give them all nightmares.'

'Troy Pelham!' Lucy exclaimed. 'You may have a scar on your face but that doesn't make you a monster. You are not half as ugly as a picture I saw of Frankenstein's monster!'

Troy stared at her hard for a moment. Lucy gasped and looked at Sarah in stunned dismay as she realized what she had said, and then, suddenly, Troy threw back his head and laughed. His laughter was deep, amused and without restraint.

'Thank you very much, Lucy,' he said after a moment or two. 'I take that as a compliment ... I think...'

'I didn't mean to ... I mean I was trying to say...' Lucy floundered and Troy looked amused.

'I know what you meant. Thank you, Lucy. It was the best thing you could say. I shall console myself with the knowledge that I am not as ugly as that unfortunate creature Frankenstein brought back to life.'

'You ... you're not upset or angry with me?'

'Not at all,' Troy replied. 'I am glad that Sarah has such a good friend.'

Lucy nodded and smiled. Troy wasn't much different from when she had first met him if you discounted the scars, and it was the person that mattered. She felt relieved that the air had cleared and she need not feel awkward with him any longer.

As Lord Pelham came in at that moment, the two girls excused themselves and went up to change. Lucy looked thoughtful as they paused at the top of the stairs.

'Troy is just the same really, isn't he?' she said. 'I mean inside ... the bit that really matters.'

'He is deep down,' Sarah said. 'It has taken a while for him to come this far. I am not sure how long it will be before he feels able to face the world at large, but he is adjusting to his new life. At least he is not helpless, which is I know what he feared.'

'You were right,' Lucy told her, and kissed her cheek. 'You don't see the scar after a while; you only see Troy.'

'There will be some people who can only see the scar,' Sarah said, 'but we must hope they have the good sense to keep their disgust to themselves.'

More guests arrived the following day, including Lucy's mother. Lord Pelham had invited relatives and close friends, and most had accepted. Sarah realized that the wedding reception would be bigger than she had expected and she wondered how Troy would feel about it. However, since all his friends and relatives went to see him in his room they were unlikely to be shocked when he appeared for the wedding. Sarah heard one young woman telling her mother that she was shocked by the changes in Troy, but most seemed to accept them without comment. Troy was seldom without a visitor and the men in particular made a habit of congregating there in the mornings.

Pausing outside his door the morning before the wedding, Sarah heard laughter and left them to it, deciding to return later when Troy's visitors had gone. It was best that he should have male company for he needed to feel comfortable with his contemporaries if he were to go into society again.

Barney Hale arrived that afternoon. He seemed a little embarrassed at first, apologizing three times for the fact that Marianne was not with him. In the end Sarah laughed and kissed his cheek.

'I know my sister is feeling ill,' she said. 'Please do not worry, Barney. We are just delighted to have you.'

'Well, I couldn't stay away – best friend, you know,' Barney said, his neck red from his discomfort. 'Brought you some presents. There's a full set of crystal from Marianne and some decanters in a silver stand from me. Hope that is all right? Didn't have a clue what to get, you know what an idiot I am about these things.'

'I don't think you are an idiot,' Sarah said. 'Whatever you chose will be lovely. I am just glad you came and I know Troy will be pleased to see you. Would you like to visit him? I daresay Lucy and Tubby may be there; they spend hours with him everyday but he will enjoy a visit from you I am sure.'

Barney stared at her. 'Troy is a lucky fellow,' he said. 'Good thing he had the sense to fall in love with you and not—' He broke off and coughed as if aware that he had said too much. 'Like to see him now if that's all right?'

'Yes, of course it is,' Sarah said. 'I'll take you in...' She led the way to Troy's sitting room. The sound of voices told her that he already had at least two visitors. When they went in they found Tubby, Lucy and Troy's elderly uncle Matthew ensconced in the chairs grouped near the windows. 'Troy darling, you have another visitor...'

Troy turned his head and looked at Barney. He frowned for a moment and then held out his hand. 'Glad you could come, Barney.'

Barney went forward and clasped his hand, shaking it several times. Lucy got up and offered her chair. Barney shook his head but Lucy insisted.

'I'm going to talk to Sarah now,' she said. 'I shall leave you gentlemen to talk together. Sarah, I want you to look at something and tell me what you think. It's a feminine thing...'

They went out together. The gentlemen were laughing as they closed the door. Lucy put an arm about Sarah's waist.

'What did you want to show me?'

'Nothing. Barney looked so awkward. I thought I would give him my chair. He needs to stay with the others for a while and become comfortable. I think Marianne made him feel that Troy was some kind of a monster and it will take him a little time to accustom himself to the fact that it isn't so.'

'Bless you,' Sarah said, and kissed her cheek.

'Poor Barney was embarrassed because Marianne wouldn't come for the wedding, but I don't mind.'

'Is your father here yet?'

'Not yet,' Sarah said. 'I daresay he will leave it until the last moment, but he gave his word and he will not break it. My father's honour is everything to him.'

Lucy nodded. 'I think your mama is unkind, Sarah. It isn't as if you've done anything terrible.'

'I have in Mother's eyes,' Sarah said. 'Don't be upset for me, Lucy. I really don't mind. Look, here is your mama.' She smiled at her aunt, who had shown her real affection, making it clear that she did not censure her in any way. 'Why don't we all go and have some tea in the parlour?'

'Oh, Sarah!' Lucy said as she looked at her cousin in her wedding dress. 'You do look so lovely. I've never seen you so beautiful.'

Sarah laughed and placed a hand on her bulge, which was partially disguised by the cut of the gown. 'It must be because I am happy,' she said. 'I love Troy so much, Lucy. I was afraid it couldn't happen. Troy was so hurt, so vulnerable when I first saw him at the hospital. I wasn't sure he could bear to marry me.'

'But he loves you so dreadfully,' Lucy said. 'His eyes follow you all the time when you are in the room.'

'It is because he loves me that he feels it,' Sarah told her. 'He is much better now, but I know it still bothers him that he can't stand up to take his vows. He doesn't feel worthy of me, but of course he is.'

Lucy nodded, looking at her anxiously. 'It was a surprise when his brother turned up last evening, wasn't it?'

'None of us knew if he would get here,' Sarah said. 'Andrew was in France until the day before yesterday, but he was given compassionate leave to see his brother. He had no idea about the wedding until he got here.'

'Really?' Lucy laughed. 'How strange! He came home to see Troy thinking he was in hospital and found him at home and about to be married.'

'He just stared and stared, and then he kissed me and hugged Troy,' Sarah said, smiling. She broke off as someone knocked at her door. 'Please come in – Father!' She was surprised to see her father at the door. 'Do come in, sir.'

'May I have a word with you, please?'

'Yes, of course.'

Lucy looked at her. 'Shall I go or stay?'

'Go down and wait for me,' Sarah told her. 'It is all right. My father won't hurt me. I shall be down in a moment.'

Sir James looked at Sarah in silence as Lucy went out and closed the door. 'I wanted to give you something...' He handed her a box. Sarah opened it and saw a pearl choker-style necklace with a heavy diamond clasp. 'I always intended this for your wedding gift, Sarah. It belonged to my mother. I gave Marianne her diamonds, the pearls were always for you.'

'Thank you,' Sarah said. 'It is generous of you. I did not expect anything.'

'There will also be a gift of money for you and Troy. It is the settlement that would normally have been yours on marriage...'

'There is no need, Father. Lord Pelham has given us so much ... but thank you. I shall not refuse.'

'I cannot hide my disappointment over what has happened,' her father said, 'but I know my duty, Sarah, even if your mother and sister do not. I may not have been an affectionate father; it is not my nature. However, I will not have anyone say that I did not do what was right. You have the necklace and you have your portion. It only remains for me to wish you happiness in your future life.'

'That is extremely generous, Father,' Sarah said. He did not offer to kiss her and she did not attempt to kiss him. His gesture had been made because he considered it the honourable thing to do, and she would accept it in the same spirit. But she would wear the diamond and sapphire necklace that had been Troy's wedding gift to her.

'I shall wait for you downstairs,' her father said, and went out, closing the door behind him.

Sarah stood for a moment after he had gone. She closed her eyes feeling the sharp sting of tears but refusing to let them fall. Nothing had changed. Her father did not love her, but it did not matter. There were others who did...

* * *

Troy remained seated for most of the wedding ceremony, but he managed to stand with the aid of one crutch as they said their vows. Sarah saw the strain in his face and knew what the effort had cost him. He sat down afterwards, and when it was time for him to kiss her she bent down to kiss him on the lips.

Troy was wheeled into the long dining hall for the reception. Sarah stood by his side and received the congratulations of their guests. Troy was looking rather pale but he managed to smile and thank everyone for coming. He ate hardly anything and took no more than a sip of his wine when the toasts were made, but he hung on and stayed where he was until after the cake had been cut and the guests moved into the gallery. It had been cleared of furniture and music was playing. Some of the guests decided to dance.

Troy shook his head when Sarah asked if he wanted to watch.

'I shall let them put me to bed now,' he told her. 'I'm tired, Sarah. Please stay with your guests and dance if you wish. I shall be fine. It has been a long day and I shall be glad of a rest.'

'I'll come to say goodnight,' Sarah said. Her throat was tight because she could see that it had been a difficult day for him. He was still in pain from his thigh and he tired easily. 'I love you, Troy.'

'I love you,' he said. 'You look beautiful, Sarah. A lovely young bride who deserves a better deal than I can give her.'

'Please don't,' she whispered. It hurt to see him being wheeled away, to know that he felt too tired and too ill to stay and enjoy the reception. 'I love you so...'

Fighting the foolish tears, Sarah went to watch the dancing.

'Dance with me, Sarah,' a voice said behind her and she turned to see Lord Pelham. 'The bride should dance at least once – I'll stand in for Troy until he can stand up with you himself.'

'Yes, thank you,' she said, and accepted his hand.

The other dancers moved back to allow them to circle the floor and there was some clapping. Sarah put a smile on her face and kept it in place. She smothered the urge to run after Troy and be with him. She had always known that it was going to be like this, and he had made huge strides towards living as normal a life as possible. She would be a fool to long for more.

Sarah watched the dancers for a while but did not dance again. Tubby asked her but she refused with a smile, and everyone else accepted her decision. After an hour she left the reception and went to Troy's room. He had one small lamp burning by the side of the bed. She thought he might be asleep, but when she hesitated he asked her to come in.

'I thought you might be asleep,' she said, and walked towards the bed.

'No, just resting. You should be with your guests, Sarah.'

'I danced with your father,' Sarah told him, and sat on the edge of the bed. 'I did not wish to dance with anyone else. I can wait until you are well enough to dance with me.'

'It may be a long time,' he said. 'I am exhausted.'

'Yes, I know. I understand,' she said softly, and leaned forward, brushing her lips over his in a soft kiss. Troy put his left hand at the back of her head, as if wanting to hold her there. His kiss intensified, his tongue entering her mouth as it parted. His right hand moved to her breast, caressing her through the fine material of her gown. For a moment his fingers stroked but then he dropped his hand, letting her sit back. 'I love you, Troy. Do you want me to stay with you tonight?'

'No, not yet,' he said. 'I don't think I could bear it. I want this to be a proper wedding night, Sarah, but it can't be...'

'I know that, my darling. I knew it before we married. I can wait until—'

'It may be for ever,' he said, and there was a bleak look in his eyes. 'I am not sure it will ever happen. They tell me there is no physical reason why I can't ... but it isn't happening, Sarah.'

'It will,' she told him, and kissed him softly once more. 'One day. I shan't stop loving you if— but it will happen, Troy.'

'Perhaps,' he said. 'Damn it! I hate being half a man, Sarah! Go away before I say or do something I shall regret.'

'Troy...' Sarah faltered. 'I love you...'

'Love isn't enough,' Troy said. 'If I can't have you as I want you ... if I can't make love to you, be your husband ... love just isn't enough...'

'You are very tired,' Sarah said. The day had put an unbearable strain on him both physically and mentally. 'Things will look better tomorrow...'

Alone in her room after all the guests had either departed or said goodnight, Sarah undressed and sat on the edge of her bed. Only then did she allow the tears to trickle silently down her cheeks. It was so hard to accept this part of the bargain. The preparations for the wedding, the gifts, the excitement of greeting friends, had helped her to forget that her marriage was not a normal one. Only as she kissed Troy and felt the way his hand fumbled at her breast, his inability to touch her in the way he once had, had it come home to her how much they had lost. She knew how frustrated, how desperate he must feel because she was feeling some of that too, but for her the worst thing was knowing how hurt he was inside.

She hated to think of him lying alone in his bed on their wedding night. She wished that she could lie by his side, even if there was no more she could do to ease his hurt, but Troy hadn't wanted that; he would find it too difficult to accept her love when he could not hold her or touch her as he wanted.

Sarah got up and wandered to the window. At this moment she felt so alone, so restless that she ached with the hurt. Most of it was for

Troy, for his pain, his hurt, but some of it was for her alone.

She remembered how good she had felt in Troy's arms when they made love and she wanted that again. Needed it so much that she wanted to sob, shout and scream her grief aloud.

She brushed an angry hand across her eyes, banishing the tears of self-pity. She had known how things stood when she persuaded Troy to marry her and there was no point in complaining now.

She had to carry on as before and wait. She might have to wait for months, years, perhaps for ever...

Sarah's father left the next morning. He did not bother to see her again but took his leave of Lord Pelham. Sarah hardly noticed. For most of the morning she was saying goodbye to friends and relatives. Lucy and Tubby were to stay on for another week, but Barney said he had to get back to Marianne.

'I am sure she will want to visit when she is over her confinement,' he said. 'May I bring Marianne and the child to see you one day?'

'Yes, of course,' Sarah said, 'but only if she wishes to come. Please don't force her, Barney.'

'You and Troy are my friends,' he replied with dignity. 'Marianne must learn to think of others. I do not intend that there shall be a breach between us, Sarah.'

'I shall always be pleased to see both of you,'

Sarah replied.

Once the guests had gone, Sarah joined Tubby, Lucy and Andrew in Troy's room. They were discussing horses and the conversation seemed animated, lively. Troy seemed to have recovered from his exhaustion and held his hand out to her, smiling as she came forward to take it.

'Have they all gone?'

'Yes.' Sarah bent to kiss him. She pressed her lips to the scar on his cheek and felt him stiffen but he didn't draw away. 'Barney asked if he could come back with Marianne and the baby one day. I said they would always be welcome.'

'Yes, of course,' Troy said. 'If you wish it, Sarah.'

'She is my sister. I shall be happy to see her if she wishes to come, but I have told Barney he must not force her.' Lucy made a sound of disgust but said nothing. Tubby frowned at her and said he wanted to visit the stables. He asked her to walk down with him but Lucy refused. She said she had something she wanted to do and left. Andrew followed a few minutes later. Sarah sat down in the chair opposite Troy. 'Lucy is cross with Marianne, but I think she is having a bad time with the baby.'

'Barney says she may be having twins,' Troy said, and looked at her. 'You seem to glow more with each day that passes. You must tell me if you feel unwell. Father says that we should employ a doctor and midwife when the time comes.'

'Yes, he mentioned it, because of the house being some distance from the village. Father wants to have a midwife staying in the house in case I need her. I cannot refuse him, though at the moment I feel very well.'

'I am glad,' Troy said. 'But we want to take care of you, Sarah – I want to take care of you myself. Until I can, Father must stand in for me.'

'You will one day,' she told him. 'Yesterday was tiring for you, but you look better today.'

'I feel better,' he said. 'I was thinking that perhaps we should take advantage while Tubby is here. I should like to go out for a while on good days and he has offered to push me.'

'Yes, of course,' Sarah agreed. 'When you are feeling more yourself you may want to go down to the stables.'

'Tubby has suggested moving his brood mares here,' Troy said. 'It would mean that he might stay here more often – but you wouldn't mind that?'

'Why should I? I like Tubby.'

'Yes, he is a good sort. Even if I can't walk to the stables yet, I can still advise on the mares and the foals when they come.'

'I am sure Tubby would be grateful.'

'I think perhaps I should be grateful to him,' Troy said, and smiled oddly. 'It will be quite an upheaval for him. But he does respect my opinion and I may be able to help prevent some of the problems he has been experiencing. I may go into partnership with him on the breeding side if I can be of real value.'

'I am sure you will,' Sarah said. 'If you wanted to go outside any day I am sure I could push the chair.'

'And risk losing the child? No, we shall let Tubby help and when he isn't here Father or one of the men will help. We are fortunate that some of our men have been excused military service because they are needed on the land – and we have both younger and older servants who remain loyal to us.'

'They like working for your family,' Sarah said. 'I wish that Rose had been able to come down for the wedding but she could not get the time off. They are too busy at the hospital...'

'And you are busy too,' Troy said. 'Father told me that they were moving the first patients into the convalescent home today.'

'Yes, they are. I shall visit tomorrow and make sure they have all they need.'

'You will enjoy that,' Troy said. 'I shall have the horses and you have the convalescent home, and you will have the child – and Lucy seems to like staying here. You must ask her to come down often.' He was arranging a life that left no room for regrets, no room for the true marriage they both wanted and knew they could not have.

'When does Andrew have to leave?'

'Tomorrow,' Troy said. 'They are moving him to a training unit for a few months. He will be in Scotland helping to knock some of the raw recruits into shape. It means he may get down to see us more often.'

'Your father will be pleased to know he isn't

at risk.'

'Andrew wasn't too pleased about the change at first,' Troy said, 'but he seems to have accepted it now. I believe he rather likes Lucy...'

'Ah,' Sarah smiled. 'I see.'

'Lucy is a pretty girl,' Troy said. 'We shall wait and see what happens.'

Twelve

Sarah felt the warmth of the sun on her head and smiled. In some ways it had been a long winter, but in the past few days it had settled into the promise of a warm spring. She liked to walk in the gardens on fine days, though as the time of her confinement came nearer, she felt it safer not to stray too far from the house.

Shading her eyes, Sarah looked towards the shrubbery and saw Andrew and Lucy examining one of the rose bushes, which bore a single yellow bloom. She smiled because they seemed to get on so well, though as yet neither of them had shown any sign of feeling anything stronger, but perhaps that was because Andrew was aware that he could be called back to active service at any time, and Lucy was still very young. Andrew's sense of honour was if anything stronger than his brother's, and his manner towards Lucy showed a gentle care for her welfare. If he was courting her he was taking his time, going slowly so as not to rush her.

'Sarah...' Hearing her husband's voice, Sarah turned to see Troy walking towards her. He was still forced to use one crutch if he wished to walk more than a few yards, but of late he had become surer on his feet and she believed he walked as much as possible in his room, especially when no one was there to watch him. His right hand was almost normal, though sometimes his sense of feeling seemed to falter and he dropped things, which made him curse. However, his left hand was still stiff and awkward, though the fingers had healed at last. Troy was healing well in his body, but as yet he had said nothing about moving upstairs to the suite of rooms Sarah occupied in solitary state. Sometimes she lay alone in the darkness and wept, longing to go down to him even if only to snuggle into the warmth of his body, but she had respected his wishes, dropping into the easy companionship they had had before they became lovers. They had a comfortable life, but their marriage was still no more than it had been at the start. Now, she smiled and went to meet him, knowing that he had something to tell her. 'The foal is born, a female and beautiful...'

'That is good news,' Sarah said, because she knew that both Troy and Tubby had been worried that the mare might give birth prematurely. It had happened once before to this mare and she was valuable, a colt of hers having

307

shown promise at the racetrack. must be so pleased.'

'I am,' he said. 'I had been afraid she might not go full-term even though we've cosseted her as much as we could.'

'Tubby will be delighted when he hears,' Sarah said. 'He said he would be down this weekend. Andrew and Lucy are leaving tomorrow. Lucy has to go home, as you know, and Andrew says he will go with her – drive her there in the car on his way back to Scotland.'

'That may be just as well,' Troy said. 'Barney sent a telegram – he is bringing Marianne down for the weekend...'

'Do you think they will really come this time?' Sarah frowned, because once before Barney had promised to bring her sister and the twins. The visit had been cancelled at the last minute, with the excuse that the children were not well.

'His telegram said to expect them by luncheon tomorrow so we shall see.' Troy's gaze became anxious as he looked at her. 'Are you tired, Sarah? You haven't seemed as well this past week.'

'My back aches,' she admitted with a sigh. 'I feel well in myself but my ankles are swelling again and ... yes, I am tired.'

'Shall we go in and have some tea?'

'Yes, please.' She waved to her cousin as the couple came towards them. 'We're having tea in Troy's room. Will you join us?'

'Just coming,' Lucy said. 'You go on.'

'Do you think they will make a match of it?'

Troy asked as they went into the house. 'They are almost inseparable but neither of them says anything – at least to me.'

'Nor to me,' Sarah said. 'Rose wrote and said she might be able to come down for a few days this next week. I hope Marianne has gone by the time she comes. My sister would not be happy to see Rose as a guest here.'

'Marianne's likes and dislikes are really no concern of ours,' Troy said. 'I do not imagine she and Barney will stay for long.'

'No, perhaps not,' Sarah said. 'I am surprised she agreed to come at all.'

She smiled at him as they went into the house.

Sarah was sorry to see her cousin and Troy's brother leave the next morning, but she kissed them goodbye and told Lucy she hoped to see her again soon.

'I'll come and stay when the baby is due,' Lucy promised. 'Mama may come too if she can.'

'It isn't for some weeks yet,' Sarah told her. 'Three weeks I think, but the doctor said that babies can be late or early.'

'Well, I hope this one waits for me,' Lucy said, giving her a careful hug. 'I wouldn't go home but it is Father's birthday.'

'Of course you must go. Besides, Barney and Marianne are coming – and Rose may be here next week.'

Sarah went to sit in her favourite parlour after her guests had gone. She was working some smocking on a baby gown and felt pleased with the result, which was pretty and dainty.

Lord Pelham came to sit with her for a while. Troy had gone down to the stables and after an hour or so Lord Pelham went away to attend to a matter of business. Sarah shut her eyes, resting without really sleeping. It was perhaps twenty minutes later that she heard something outside her room and then the door opened and Marianne entered. Sarah struggled to her feet and went to greet her. She would have kissed her sister, but Marianne kept a distance between them.

'Where is Barney?'

'He stopped to speak to Lord Pelham in the hall,' Marianne said, and moved away to sit in the chair Sarah had been using, which was the most comfortable in the room. 'I am exhausted. Nothing would do for Barney except that we must arrive on time, which is ridiculous when I was tired and asked him to stop.'

'Barney likes to be punctual.'

'He is too polite,' Marianne said. 'What could it have mattered if we were half an hour late?'

'It would not have mattered to me.'

Marianne glared at her. 'You look very well. I was ill for months with the twins. Lucy told me that you have been well all the time.'

'I have been well enough, thank you.' Sarah had suffered recently with little things but was not in the habit of complaining to her friends.

'Well, it is typical,' Marianne said sourly. 'According to Lucy, everyone spoils you. She says that Lord Pelham cannot do enough for you.'

'Troy's father is very kind.'

'Well, I suppose he feels he has to make up to you for all the rest of it,' Marianne said. 'It cannot be much of a life for you, stuck here with a cripple, never going anywhere much.'

'Troy is not a cripple,' Sarah replied as calmly as she could. She dug her nails into her palms as she tried to hang on to her temper. 'He can walk a little way unaided now and he is getting stronger all the time.'

'Barney told me some of his fingers were bent over. He has a scar on his face and on other parts of his body for all I know. I do not know how you can bear to look at him. I certainly wouldn't wish to be married to a man like that.' Marianne gave a little shudder.

'I love Troy,' Sarah said quietly. 'I must ask you not to speak of things you do not understand, Marianne.'

'Mother says it serves you right for behaving so badly. She will not see you, Sarah. She disapproved of my coming, but Barney insisted. He wanted to bring the children and mend fences, but I do not see the point. We shall not meet often. You will hardly wish to mix in society.'

'I see no reason why we shouldn't in time.'

'With Troy the way he is? I should die of embarrassment if he were my husband.'

Sarah stared at her in disgust. 'You make me sick. Are you so eaten up with jealousy and spite that you must try to hurt others?' she

311

asked. 'Excuse me, I must see where my husband is.'

Sarah was so angry that she could not remain in the same room as Marianne. Her chest felt tight and it was all she could do not to scream at her sister. Marianne was a spiteful cat, just as Lucy had said. Sarah went out into the hall, her heart beating very fast, her head whirling as she tried to dismiss her sister's malicious words. It was very strange but she felt dizzy. As she put her foot on the bottom stair, intending to go up to her room and lie down, her head seemed to go round and round and then the floor came up to meet her and she fell.

Someone caught her, lowering her to the ground. She opened her eyes and saw Troy bending over her, his expression anxious, even frightened.

'It is all right,' Sarah said, and fainted.

She was hardly aware of being carried upstairs, but when she came to herself again she was lying on her bed, the covers turned back. Troy was bending over her, a cool cloth in his hand as he bathed her face.

'What happened?' Sarah asked.

'You fainted. I caught you but it was Barney who carried you here, Sarah. He was very concerned...'

'How very foolish of me,' Sarah said, and made to sit up, but as she did so the pain ripped through her and she gave a startled cry. 'Ahhh!'

'Are you hurt?' Troy asked, looking anxious. 'Did you hurt yourself as you fell?'

'I think it is the baby,' Sarah said, and gasped. She breathed deeply and clutched at his hand, feeling so much pain that it was all she could do not to scream. 'I believe it is coming early, Troy.'

Troy swore. The doctor and the midwife they had engaged were due to move in next week. No one had dreamed that the child would come this soon.

'I'll send word to the village,' Troy said. 'We shall have to ask the local doctor to come, and there must be someone who could help...' He turned to leave the room but Sarah caught his hand and he turned back to look at her. 'You don't want me to go? Barney is just outside the door, my love. He insisted on waiting to see if you needed anything.'

Sarah let go of his hand. The pain was receding. She could breathe again. She wondered if it were just a warning, and almost called out to stop Troy sending for the doctor but good sense told her it would be best to let the doctor examine her.

Troy was back with her in seconds. She noticed that he hardly limped at all. He sat on the edge of the bed and took her hand in his right hand. He lifted it to his cheek and then dropped a kiss in the palm.

'My poor darling,' he said. 'I am afraid the pain may be bad for you. I wish I could do this for you, Sarah.'

Sarah laughed. The idea was so strange and so funny that her fear slipped away. 'No, no, I can bear it,' she told him. 'Whatever happens, remember that I want this baby, Troy.'

'Yes, my love, of course,' he said, and bent down to kiss her on the mouth. He stroked her cheek with his fingers, an odd, needy expression in his eyes. 'I love you so much...'

Sarah could not answer because the pain had started again, just an ache in her back at first and then a ripping pain that seemed to flood through her until she arched in agony and gripped Troy's hand. As soon as the pain receded she let go and apologized.

'Your poor hand. I am sorry...'

'It doesn't hurt anymore,' Troy told her softly. 'I am well again, Sarah – as normal as I shall be. You do not have to worry about me. All we have to think about now is you.'

Troy looked at the doctor as they left Sarah's room. Lord Pelham's housekeeper was with her now, doing the things the midwife would have done had she been here. Mrs March had volunteered as soon as she learned Sarah was in labour, explaining that she had seen her daughter's three children into the world. It was not an ideal situation, but it was the best they could do until the midwife could get there, and that would not be until morning.

'How is she?' Troy asked. 'She has been so well, Doctor Wren. I cannot understand what brought this on.'

'She hasn't had a fall?'

'Well, a little one but I caught her before she hit the ground.'

'Sometimes a shock may do it – an upset,

anything of an emotional nature. However, babies have a way of deciding when they will come, sir. Early or late, it is a mystery we must all wonder at. I think Mrs Pelham will be in labour for quite some time yet. Mrs March is perfectly capable of caring for your wife at this early stage. I shall return later this afternoon, but it may be this evening or even tomorrow morning before the child finally arrives.'

'How can Sarah survive such a long ordeal?' Troy asked. 'Is there nothing you can do to help her?'

'I have seen a good many babes into the world in my time, sir. Most of the ladies manage very well without my assistance. However, I shall return. I must go. I have another patient to see but diverted here as your summons seemed urgent.'

'It is urgent! I want you to help Sarah. Can you not give her something for the pain?'

'If I did it might slow the birth and damage the child. No, sir, I am afraid you must be patient, hard as it is. May I suggest you leave your wife to the women and go for a long walk?'

Troy glared at him. He had to bite back the harsh words that hovered on his tongue. The man was a fool! It was the reason Lord Pelham had insisted on engaging a London doctor to come down for the confinement, but they had not reckoned on the child coming so soon. Since Doctor Wren was all they had they must make do with his services, and rudeness would not help Sarah's cause.

315

'Please return as soon as you can,' Troy said, retaining his temper. 'I am concerned for Sarah. She is young and this is her first child.'

'I am aware of that, sir. It is the reason I believe she will be in labour for many hours. However, at the moment there is little to concern you. She is healthy and strong and I am sure she will manage very well.'

Troy stared after the doctor as he left. For two pins he would have strangled the fool with his bare hands!

Tamping his anger down, Troy retraced his steps to the bedchamber. If Sarah must endure the pain for hours he would be with her. The suggestion that he should go and leave her to suffer alone made him angry. Damn the man for his casual attitude. It was his Sarah who was suffering and he loved her so!

'I've tied a knotted rope to the bedpost,' Mrs March said. 'When the pain comes hold on to it, and scream if you want. There's no point in trying to hold it in, Sarah my dear. We shan't think the less of you. We all scream at times like these.'

Sarah was panting hard. Her body seemed to be a mass of pain. How much longer could she endure it? Troy had been with her for hours. Mrs March had sent him to fetch a glass of porter. Sarah wasn't sure if it was for her or the housekeeper, who had hardly left her all day. It was night now and the pain was getting worse all the time, yet still her waters hadn't broken and she was beginning to feel so very tired. All she wanted to do was sleep, but Mrs March wouldn't let her. The pain was easing again. Sarah felt so weary. She wanted to go to sleep.

'Wake up, my love,' Mrs March said. 'Mr Troy has brought you this nice drink. You must swallow it because it will give you some strength.'

Sarah sipped the bitter drink and pulled a face, shaking her head. 'No ... please ... it makes me feel sick...'

'Come along now,' Mrs March coaxed. 'Drink it all. I know it doesn't taste nice but you need something to keep up your strength.'

'If she doesn't want it,' Troy said. 'Don't make her...'

'Perhaps a little honey might sweeten it. Would you mind, sir?'

Sarah heard him leave. She made a weak protest. She wanted Troy with her. Mrs March held the glass to her mouth again.

'Now swallow it all down, my love. Your husband is so worried about you. We don't want him upset after all the poor man has been through, do we? Just for a nasty taste ... think of all he had to endure...'

Sarah swallowed obediently. She didn't want to distress Troy. The drink was strong and made her gag, but it warmed her. She felt some of the lethargy melt away and smiled at Mrs March.

'That's better,' Mrs March said. She looked down at the bed. 'I think your waters are breaking, Sarah. Next time the pain comes I want you to start to push.'

★ ★ ★

Troy stood by the bed. He was stroking Sarah's forehead, wiping away the sweat from her brow. Her hair stuck to her skin as her body arched with the pain. He looked up as the door opened, expecting the return of Mrs March, who had gone off for a sit down and something to eat. Instead, he saw the doctor and he sent him a look of appeal.

'She is getting weaker,' Troy said. 'You must do something...'

'Mrs March told me the waters broke some hours ago. I should have thought we would be through the worst by now. Would you leave us for a while, sir? I want to examine your wife.'

Troy hesitated, then nodded tersely and went out. He stood just outside the door, listening as Sarah moaned and then screamed. His hand reached for the doorknob, stopped and fell to his side. He had never felt this helpless in his life, even when he was first lying in hospital and couldn't eat or drink without assistance. Sarah cried out again. He clenched his hands, wanting to rush back to her, knowing that if he did he might interrupt something. If that fool was hurting her! He gritted his teeth. He never wanted to go through this again. He would rather suffer a hundred shrapnel wounds than witness Sarah's agony!

The door opened and Doctor Wren smiled at him. 'If you want to see your child come into the world you had better come back. The head was turned – what we call a breech birth. A midwife would have known, but you can't blame Mrs March. I've managed to turn the baby and the head will be through shortly...'

Sarah's agonizing scream made the doctor hurry back to the bed. Troy followed swiftly and was in time to see the baby's head appear.

'You are doing very well, my dear,' Doctor Wren said. 'Now, you need to make another big effort and ... that's right ... good girl...'

In a slither of blood and mucus Sarah's baby slid out of her in a rush, almost as if making up for lost time. Troy felt tears well up in his eyes as he reached for Sarah's hand, holding it tightly. She lifted her head eagerly, looking down at the babe as Doctor Wren did all that was necessary.

'We have a son...' she said, and tears ran down her cheeks. 'Troy, we have a son...'

'Yes, my darling.' He bent and kissed the tip of her nose and then her forehead. 'You clever, brave girl.'

Doctor Wren wrapped the baby in a linen cloth and put him in Sarah's arms. She smiled down at him, kissing the tiny red face with a mop of dark hair, and then looked up at her husband.

'He looks just like you,' she said. 'He is so beautiful...'

'He is certainly beautiful,' Troy agreed, as the baby yawned and then opened his eyes. 'But he has your eyes, Sarah.'

Doctor Wren was washing his hands at the basin as Mrs March entered the room. She gave a cry of pleasure and came hurrying to look at the baby, who had started to wail.

319

'Well, I can leave the rest to you, Mrs March,' he said. 'We have done very well between us. I thought it might be hours yet. I must get off. I have an elderly patient who will not last the night. Goodbye for now. I shall call tomorrow to see how mother and baby go on, but I am sure there is nothing to worry about.'

'I will see you out,' Troy said. 'I will be back soon, Sarah.

He went out, closing the door as Mrs March began exclaiming over what a beautiful baby the new arrival was and how good Sarah had been.

In the hall downstairs the two men shook hands. 'I want to thank you, sir. I was afraid we were going to lose her.'

'A breech birth is always difficult. As I said, a midwife would have known and called me or turned the babe herself, but Mrs March has done well – and your wife is very strong. You are a very lucky man.'

'Yes, I am,' Troy said, and grinned as the relief burst through him. 'Very lucky indeed.'

He watched as the doctor went out to his pony and trap. As he turned towards the stairs Marianne came out into the hall. He hesitated, surprised to see that she was still there, because Barney had said they were leaving hours before.

'Marianne...' Her eyes were on him, on his face, and he saw the expression in her eyes, startled horror that turned eventually to pity. 'You may wish to know that Sarah has a son.'

'Is she all right?' Marianne asked. 'Will you

tell her I am sorry, please? I said some awful things to her when I arrived and I shouldn't have.'

'I wondered why she seemed upset.' Troy's expression was hard. 'Don't you think that you and Lady Trenwith have hurt her enough?'

'I was jealous and spiteful,' Marianne said. 'Barney said she might die and that ... I didn't want her to die. She is my sister and I do care, even if I haven't appeared to. Will you tell her I am sorry?'

'Yes, if you wish it,' Troy replied. 'For Sarah's sake.'

'Yes, of course – and I am sorry for what happened to you. It must be awful for you.'

'Actually, it doesn't matter anymore,' Troy said, and grinned at her. 'To be honest, I don't give a damn if the rest of the world thinks I am an ugly sod. Sarah loves me and I love her.'

'She is lucky,' Marianne said, and there was regret in her eyes. 'And so are you, Troy. She is a much better person than I am.'

'Yes, but you improve with age,' Troy said in a mood of forgiveness because everything was suddenly right with his world. 'Please come and stay again when Sarah is over this ... if you wish?'

'Yes, I shall,' Marianne replied. 'And I shall tell Mama that she should forgive Sarah too.'

'Thank you. I believe it would mean a lot to her,' Troy said, and smiled. 'Excuse me now. I must go back to her.'

'Yes, of course...'

Marianne was still staring after him as he ran

upstairs when Barney came into the hall.

'Have you apologized?'

Marianne turned to look at him. She gave him a half smile. Barney had put himself out over this visit and forced her to apologize in a masterful manner that had surprised her – and she quite liked it.

'Yes, I have,' she said. 'I am ready to leave when you are, Barney. We will visit again later in the year when Sarah is better.'

'Good.' Barney smiled at her. 'You know I love you, Marianne – but you can be a little tiresome at times.'

'Barney, for goodness' sake, stop complaining,' she said. 'I am sure we are not needed here for the moment. Please call for the automobile and let's go...'

Barney stared after her ruefully as she walked away. Marianne wouldn't change, even if she did have her softer moments. But that was all right because he loved her the way she was.

The sun was very warm that day. Sarah was sitting in the garden. Her chair had been set under the shade of an apple tree and she was reading when a shadow fell across her book. She looked up and smiled as Troy came up to her. He had completely abandoned his crutch and he sat down in a basket chair next to her, looking fit and slightly tanned by the sun.

'This is very pleasant, Sarah. Are you comfortable, my love? Is there anything you need?'

'Nothing at all,' Sarah said. Some weeks had passed since she gave birth to their son, whom

they had named George Andrew Tarquin Pelham. She was feeling perfectly well but the
doctor had prescribed a month of complete
rest and neither Troy nor her father-in-law
would hear of her doing anything other than
nurse her son. 'Do not look concerned, Troy. I
am perfectly well, I promise you.'

'We were afraid we might lose you,' he told
her, with a look that lavished love. 'You cannot
blame me if I still feel a little anxious.'

'Doctor Wren is a fusspot,' Sarah said, and
laughed. 'I walked around the park for an hour
this morning and it did me no harm at all. I
shall go down to the convalescent home tomorrow and see how everything is there. Father
told me that every bed is filled and I would like
to meet some of the new patients.'

'As long as you do not tire yourself, Sarah.'

'I had a baby, not a life-threatening opera-
tion,' Sarah said. Her eyes went over him,
noticing the way his body seemed alert and full
of energy, something she had not seen since
before his injuries. 'You seem well, Troy. I think
there is something different today.'

'I have been riding,' Troy told her. He held
his hands out for her to see, flexing the fingers.
His right hand was almost normal, two fingers
on his left still misshapen but clearly flexible
and capable of movement. 'It was wonderful to
be in the saddle again, Sarah. I waited until I
was certain I could manage the reins. It was so
easy that I wondered why I had put it off so
long.'

'That is wonderful, Troy,' Sarah said. 'I am so

pleased and I know how much it means to you.'

'I think I am almost as I was before it happened,' Troy told her. 'Obviously there are some things that will never be the same, but I feel like myself again.'

'That is wonderful,' Sarah said. She stood up and Troy rose to stand facing her. Sarah's heart raced as he looked at her. 'Shall we have tea?'

'Sarah...' Troy said, reaching out to put his arms about her. 'I've been feeling much better for some weeks, but I knew you needed time to let your body heal...' His head bent towards her. 'I've wanted to come to you, to be with you as you slept...'

'How I wish you had,' Sarah told him. She gazed up at him, her clear eyes shining with honesty and love. 'So many times I longed for you, wanted to come to you, but I was afraid of hurting you – of making you unhappy.'

'I am better at last,' he said softly, bending his head to touch his lips to hers in the lightest of kisses. 'I am ready to be your husband again if you will let me, my darling. Will you let me come to you tonight?'

'Why should we wait until tonight?' Sarah asked, and took his hand in hers. His fingers curled about hers, entwining with them. Some of the skin on the back of his hand was still discoloured, but the palms were soft and smooth. She knew that he had been diligent in using the creams he was given and in exercising his fingers to regain the flexibility. 'I want to be your wife, Troy. I have wanted it for such a long time...'

Later, as she lay in his arms, after their first fierce loving was done, Sarah stroked Troy's face and then leaned over to kiss the scarring, which was still pitted and discoloured and possibly always would be. She kissed his cheek, his eyelids, his nose and then his lips, letting her long hair fall over him as she pressed herself to his body. Her hands moved over him, discovering all the scars she had not previously seen, but had guessed were there. How much he had suffered! Her heart ached for all the nights of pain he had endured, nights when his pride had refused to let him seek comfort. She bent over his body, pressing her lips to each and every tender spot she found, exploring him, caressing and touching him as she claimed him for her own.

'Sarah my love,' he murmured, 'do you know what you are doing to me?'

'I want to know all of it,' she told him huskily. 'I want to know every part of you, to kiss it all better, as I longed to do when I knew it would hurt you too much to even touch you.'

Troy's hand smoothed down the silky arch of her back. He squeezed her buttocks as he pressed her against him and she felt the heat and throb of his desire as his manhood pressed against her thigh.

'What hurt most was that I couldn't let you come too close – couldn't touch you,' Troy told her. 'All the rest was as nothing. I was afraid I would never be able to make love to you again, never be the husband I wanted to be.'

Sarah straddled him, bending over him, the tantalizing perfume of her hair wafting into his nostrils as she let it swing loose about her shoulders and fall on to his face. He tangled his hands in it, burying his face in its softness, inhaling the scent of her. She leaned down to kiss him on the lips; their tongues tangled and danced as the desire became hot and strong once more.

'I love you...'

Sarah took the hard length of him into her hand, guiding him towards the heat and moistness of her entrance. He thrust up into her, arching his back as she came down to meet him and they both gasped with pleasure. She rocked back and forth, her breasts touching his face as she leaned over him. He nuzzled them with his mouth, and then sucked the dark rose nipples. His tongue laved her, its roughness sending little waves of pleasure shooting down to her core. And then he placed one hand each side of her waist, lifting her only to plunge her down so that he buried himself inside her right to the shaft.

Sarah shrieked with pleasure. Even when they had made love the first few times they had not been this much together. It seemed that their bodies were so well tuned that they instinctively knew what would please. They had become so close in the past few months that it was like coming home, a completion of the happiness they had already found in so many ways. When Troy rolled her over, pressing her down into the mattress, she felt his strength and gloried in it. He had come back to her, her wonderful lover, her confident man ... her husband. She gave herself to him completely, holding nothing back as they moved together in complete accord, reaching and achieving their release at the same moment.

Sarah's legs curled over Troy's back as she arched beneath him, her nails digging into his shoulders, her breath a sobbing gasp of pleasure as she cried his name aloud. Afterwards, they lay side by side, content, still entwined, still touching as if they could never have enough of each other. Sarah might have slept. Troy held her while he rested, and then they woke as the gong announced dinner.

Sarah looked into his eyes. 'I think we should go down, my love. Everyone will wonder where we are.'

'You must know that all the servants are perfectly aware of where we are,' Troy said. 'If you think you can keep something like this a secret you are mistaken. Be prepared for smiles all round when we do finally show ourselves.'

He got out of bed, reached for his clothes and began to dress but shook his head as Sarah threw back the covers. Her eyes questioned and he smiled.

'This is our honeymoon, Sarah. I am going to order a light supper to be served to us up here. Father may eat in solitary state for once. I do not think he will mind.'

Sarah blushed but lay back against the

pillows. 'Just as you wish, Troy. I am not terribly hungry anyway.'

'I am,' he replied, 'but not for food...'

Sarah giggled as she lay back against the pillows. She smoothed her hand over the pillows where Troy's head had been. How many nights she had longed for him to come to her, and now she would be alone no more.

Afterword

Sarah slit open the letter that had just been delivered to her. She had recognized the writing immediately as her mother's and she read the short paragraph with a frown.

'Is anything the matter?' Troy asked. He had just come in and was dressed in riding clothes since he now rode most mornings. They had been married for nearly eighteen months and he thought that his wife grew more lovely every day.

'This is from Mama,' Sarah said. 'She says that she has considered everything and decided that as we are settled and the scandal has blown over it is time to forgive me.'

'Ah...' He nodded his understanding of the glint in her eyes. 'You should not let her make you angry, Sarah. It must have taken considerable effort on her part to make her write that, you know.'

'Because she is stubborn and proud and does not like admitting she is wrong.'

'Yes, she is all of those things,' Troy said. 'But have you considered that you are also stubborn and proud, though you do admit when you are in the wrong – which is not often.'

'Am I ever wrong?' Sarah asked, but she was

laughing. 'Are you saying that I am like my mother, Troy?'

'In some ways, not in others,' Troy said, with a loving smile. 'You are more open-minded and forgiving – you forgave Marianne, and not every sister would have done that after the way she behaved, I know. Could you not forgive your mother since she has forgiven you?'

'I forgave my father for forbidding us to marry,' Sarah replied, and looked thoughtful. 'I cannot pretend that I love him, but he does not love me. However, he has done his duty by me and I am grateful for that. If you can forgive Mama, I shall.'

'I bear no grudges for what happened,' Troy said. 'I think it would please you if there was no longer a breach with Lady Trenwith – would it not?'

Sarah was silent for a moment and then she nodded. 'I suppose it would,' she admitted. 'I had made up my mind that it would never happen, but Mama has written and so I shall reply and ask her to come and stay.'

'Why not go further? We could visit your family, Sarah. Both Marianne and Luke have come here, but your mother may feel it easier to meet you on her own territory.'

'You are always so thoughtful,' Sarah replied, and lifted her face for him to kiss her. 'If you think it would be easier for her we shall go there.'

'You have won, Sarah,' Troy told her. 'She wants to see you and her grandchild. You can afford to be generous.'

'Yes, I can,' Sarah said, and smiled at him. 'I have so much more than Mama ever had. She was not a loving mother, but then she was married to my father and all he ever cared for was his honour. He is such a cold man and Mama has always done her duty as she sees it. I have you – and you care for me. I am so much luckier than Mama ever was.'

'We are lucky,' Troy said, and dropped a kiss on top of her head. 'Write and tell your mother that we shall come next weekend, Sarah. And then get ready to drive out with me.'

'Where are we going?' Sarah asked, rising to her feet.

'I think we should both order some new clothes,' Troy told her. 'If we are going up to town next month we shall need them...'

'To town?' Sarah arched her brows. 'Are you going to open the London house? Father hasn't been there for months and nor have we.'

'All the more reason why we should go,' Troy replied. 'It is too easy to stay here and enjoy ourselves. I think it is about time we gave a dinner and perhaps a dance in town. Our friends have been generous, coming to visit, giving us their time and their company when I was unable to go anywhere. Besides, you deserve to be spoiled, my love. We shall go shopping and entertain our friends, visit the theatre – all the things we have not done together.'

'Troy, could we?' Sarah asked. 'The news from the war is so gloomy...'

'All the more reason to help our friends

forget it for a while,' Troy replied. 'We both do our share to help those less fortunate than ourselves, Sarah. I see nothing wrong in indulging ourselves for once. Besides, I have an idea that Andrew is planning to ask Lucy to become engaged and it would be the very thing if they were to announce it at our dance. I daresay we may invite thirty couples, just a small affair – but we ought to do something. People have been generous to us and it is about time we repaid some hospitality.'

'Yes, it is,' Sarah said. She moved closer, put her arms about his waist and kissed him. 'You are very right, Troy. I shall go and write the letter to Mama now...'